"Elwood's ⋯ ⋯ and comes
mere stale ⋯ ⋯ ⋯
through cl⋯ ⋯ nonetheless,
ELWOOD ⋯ ⋯ ND HE SUC-
CEEDS."

"*The Christening* is SCARY AND IMAGIN⋯ ⋯ the time we
finish this book, we have no illusions left; Satan indeed is ⋯ r enemy; he is
powerful; and he is devoted to destroying us.

"And yet Satan is far from being invincible. He can be resisted. There is
victory over him.

"*The Christening* does not tread an easy path in its disturbing clarity
about the nature of our archenemy.... BE ASSURED OF A STORY THAT
IS BOTH FRIGHTENING AND COMPELLING."

—Harold Lindsell

"THANK GOD, THERE IS AN ANSWER TO THE PROBLEM OF SIN
AND ITS FURIES, AND ELWOOD REVEALS IT. But not until he has
stood you on your head, raised the hair on your neck, and shaken you real
hard!"

—Joe D. Davis, Vice President & Director
Joni and Friends

"Roger Elwood, a MASTER STORYTELLER, has achieved the unachievable
in a BRILLIANT TREATMENT OF THE PARADOX in *The Christening*.
In bone-chilling defiance of mere reason, he describes the indescribable, he
gives credence to the unbelievable, and in the end as if by sleight of the
mind HE TRANSFORMS THE IRREDEEMABLE INTO HOPE."

—Dwight Hooten, Editor
The Christian Reader

The Christening

The Christening

ROGER ELWOOD

HARVEST HOUSE PUBLISHERS
Eugene, Oregon 97402

Verses marked NKJV are taken from the New King James Version, Copyright © 1979, 1980, 1982 by Thomas Nelson, Inc., Publishers. Used by permission.

No book is a solo effort.
It may originate with the author,
but a number of stages are involved
in getting into the marketplace.
For Harvest House's support and insights
during much of that process,
I express my gratitude.
I would also like to express
my personal gratitude to John Long,
who was the Lord's instrument
in bringing Harvest House and myself together
on *The Christening*,
one of the more challenging books
of my life.

NOTE FROM THE PUBLISHER

Scripture is clear that in the last days there will be an increase in occult practices and spiritual phenomena. It behooves every person to be aware of the dangers and adequately equipped for spiritual warfare.

The reader should bear in mind, however, that this novel, while portraying events similar to certain ones that have actually occurred, is nevertheless a fictional story and includes some element of fantasy.

THE CHRISTENING

Copyright © 1989 by Roger Elwood
Published by Harvest House Publishers
Eugene, Oregon 97402

Library of Congress Cataloging-in-Publication Data

Elwood, Roger
    The Christening / Roger Elwood.
    ISBN 0-89081-736-7
    I. Title

Printed in the United States of America.

To Walter Martin,
dear friend, brother in Christ,
and one of those with whom reunion in Heaven
is eagerly awaited.

We see Satan making a determined effort to corrupt the whole of the [human] race...by [an] irruption of demon forces into the earth.

—Dr. Donald Grey Barnhouse

1

VALLEY FALLS
A New Kind of Community
Devoted to the Values in God's Word
Population: 5500

As Paul DeKorte stopped his car beside the sign on the edge of Valley Falls, ghostly images surfaced in his mind, sending laser-thin chills up and down his spine.

The creature confronting them was a personification of all the centuries-old depictions of demonic evil, huge leathery wings flapping with unbridled rage, cloven feet stamping the ground, taloned hands reaching down toward the children, a face with fanglike teeth protruding from the mouth, pronounced cheekbones, eyes that were blood-red and maniacal.

More than five years had passed since he left this place....

Valley Falls. Devoted to the values in God's Word.

Ironically, the signpost for the old Valley Falls had proclaimed nothing about the faith of its citizens. Yet in the town itself there had been much apparent manifestation of Christianity. Only one church served the community, but it had been well-packed for both Sunday morning and evening services, not to mention Wednesday night prayer meeting. A city council mandate had prohibited the sale of pornographic materials in the town, and the weekly newspaper ran regular editorials denouncing such evils as abortion and those who would legislate against a Christian influence in the country.

Until ...

The holocaust....

Right here, DeKorte said to himself. *It happened right here....*

A large crowd had gathered about the square. Some of the towns-people were dancing. Being led into their midst was a group of young children, while several men hauled slabs of concrete toward a pile of bricks in the center....

He drove the short remaining distance into the center of town and parked his car on the north side of the town square. Stepping

7

out slowly, he felt a strange apprehension. It was the first time he had seen the new town that had risen phoenixlike from the ashes of the old. Gone was the turn-of-the-century look of the Valley Falls he had known.

Sixty-five months, three weeks, and five days, and now I am back....

Tender sounds nudged him, and he listened for the source.

> *Rock of Ages, cleft for me,*
> *Let me hide myself in Thee;*
> *Let the water and the blood,*
> *From Thy wounded side which flowed,*
> *Be of sin the double cure,*
> *Save from wrath, and make me pure.*

Familiar words in a now unfamiliar place....

The notes of the hymn drifted past church doors that opened onto the west side of the square. As DeKorte walked across the neatly mowed grass, he spotted a granite monument in the center of the square. Pausing in front of it, he fought back tears as he read the chiseled inscription.

> *1980*
> *The Year a New Town Was Started*
> *From the Ashes of the Old*
> *With the Hope....*

There was more, but he could not continue reading. Despite the passage of years, the memories were as fresh as they had been a scant month after those final moments....

Every few feet blasphemous shapes hung in the air, their spectral presence just barely visible. Great surging masses of them, wave after wave, like a monstrous army of misshapen....

"Lord, You are my Deliverer," he said aloud. "Thank You, Lord."

As he reached the steps leading up to the church entrance, he hesitated. The building was new, a redwood structure with modern lines and simple design; there was nothing familiar about it.

Nothing would have been salvageable from the old, he thought. *But on this very spot...*

He looked up over the entrance, saw the plain wooden cross, and smiled knowingly. Then he entered the sanctuary and quietly found a place in the back corner of the last pew.

The pastor had begun his sermon.

"Cheap grace is the vogue these days," he was saying. "We turn on our televisions and hear it preached to the accompaniment of orchestrally perfect musical numbers. You'll never detect any musical notes out of tune, but, beloved, you'll hear plenty of false spiritual notes."

He walked back and forth behind the plain wooden pulpit as he spoke.

"Cheap grace is fashionable because it requires little or no sacrifice, a trend somehow appropriate to this age that is ruled by the tyranny of the immediate and the superficial. It is based upon emotional gratification rather than adherence to the often hard realities that are apparent when we turn to Scripture.

"The apostles never heard of cheap grace. They paid for their faith—often with their lives. They suffered hunger, thirst, loneliness, and death. Yes, they paid dearly. And doubtless they would be appalled at the trends today and with those who equate God's blessings with smiles and laughter and recreational vehicles and VCRs.

"I remember visiting the Mamertine Prison in Rome, just across the way from the Forum, and within walking distance of the Coliseum. I stood there where Paul must have stood centuries ago, surrounded by the same rough-hewn rock walls and ceiling, feeling the same dampness he must have felt, smelling the same odor of mustiness, my eyes trying to adjust to the same oppressive darkness.

"Beloved, I started to cry. Not just the tears that welled in my eyes, but a cry that racked my entire being as I realized what Paul had written as he was confined in that awful, gloomy dungeon—words that would be out of place in today's environment of cheap grace. We've all heard them so often that they may have lost their significance. But let me tell you, when I stood in that place, tears streaming down my cheeks, those words were more alive than ever.

" *I have learned in whatsoever state I am, therewith to be content.* "

"Simple words, until you realize where they were written—until you understand that, not very far from that place, Paul would soon be put to death."

The pastor closed his Bible and surveyed the worshipers before him.

"The way we act as stewards of God's gifts, spiritual as well as material, sends a message to the unsaved world. If they see us wallowing in emotional excess, preaching about God as though He is some kind of generous heavenly treasurer, if they look at our attitudes toward the poor and find them lacking in compassion, if they look at ministries building extravagant monuments not to Almighty God but to the egos of those whose names are engraved in 14-carat lettering, if they see all this, they will surely turn away in disgust, and rightly so.

"Salvation should lead to emancipation, a breaking of the shackles of sin. If we continue to be slaves to sin, then the unbelieving world has every right to look with scorn at those of us who claim the name of the Savior."

* * *

As the people filed out after the service, DeKorte remained in his seat, reading through the bulletin someone had handed him when he first sat down. Before long, an usher who was straightening hymnbooks noticed him.

"Can I help you, sir?" the man asked.

DeKorte looked up.

"I would like to speak with your pastor if he has time."

"I'm sure he'll be glad to see you. It may be a few minutes, but I'll tell him you're here."

"Thank you very much," said DeKorte. "I'd appreciate it."

DeKorte waited, not impatiently, feeling a gathering sense of familiarity even though the building was different. Fragments from that earlier period of his life rose to the surface of his mind.

He looked up at the ceiling, his cheeks now moist. Lord, what have I done? Suddenly he reached out and turned the table over, spilling the contents in a dozen directions. Oh, God, what a fool I have been!

He shook his head, driving the recollection momentarily away but aware that it would return, as it always did, not with the mocking tone it once held but as a reminder that that day was behind him, that he no longer had to be defeated in his daily walk by its once virulent residue of shame and guilt and suffocating regret; he had gotten his life back together, including his ministry, though in a different place.

Again he murmured, "Thank You, Lord."

"How can I help you, sir?"

The pastor's voice cut through his thoughts.

DeKorte smiled, held out his hand, and introduced himself, "Thank you for seeing me."

"I'm Philip Marsden," the young man said, shaking the visitor's hand with a firm grip. "DeKorte...DeKorte...that sounds so familiar."

And then he realized who the tall, sandy-haired man was.

"You've come back!" he exclaimed.

"Yes. Just for a brief visit."

"It's wonderful to have you here but—"

"But why?" DeKorte finished the question. "To see what Valley Falls is like today. And to lay it to rest some old phantoms. I suspect that some members of my present congregation were wondering why I *hadn't* returned. And I began to hear talk that perhaps, despite my brave and outspoken sermons, I didn't have the spiritual fortitude to face the demons of the past, in a sense. I guess now that my own scars are healed I needed to see if there were any scars here."

"Not any visible ones," said Marsden. "About the only obvious reminder is the monument on the town square. Did you see it?"

When DeKorte nodded, he continued, "As for the residents, only one remains from the original Valley Falls."

"There *is* one?" DeKorte asked in surprise.

"Yes. Would you like to see her?"

"By all means."

Marsden spoke briefly with one of the ushers who was closing up the building, asking him to lock his study door, and then joined DeKorte. Outside, the autumn air had a comfortably cool edge, and as they walked, DeKorte noticed that the leaves had begun to change color.

"Your doctrinal approach seems quite conservative," he said to Marsden.

"Oh, it is. We learned some hard lessons from—from—"

"Don't be ashamed of your honesty," DeKorte assured him.

"Thank you. It is true that we have tried our best, with the Lord's help, to offer a dissimilar message."

"Stripped of the name-it-claim-it cloak, I see. That ever-popular 'gospel' that equates prosperity with piety and implies that material blessings are somehow proof of salvation."

"Indeed. We acknowledge the Lord's blessings, the validity of all His gifts. And we have our petitions, of course. But never do we pave with dollar bills the road that Christ would have us travel."

DeKorte winced a bit, knowing at the same time that this young pastor, probably not more than thirty years old, showed a spiritual wisdom that was just what the new Valley Falls needed—a wisdom that had come too late for the old.

"How would you summarize what really happened here, sir?" Marsden asked him gently.

DeKorte had been handed that question many times since leaving Valley Falls. Most who asked were seeking sensation, not truth. Not so the man who walked beside him now.

"We became victims of our prosperity," said DeKorte. "The insulated existence we led seemed to be shielding us from the thorns, and we set our eyes only on the roses, their physical beauty as well as their aroma. But then the thorns rose up and tore us to bits."

"Satan?"

"Yes. He saw an opening, and he moved in with devastating effect."

"But you preached against Satan, didn't you?" Marsden asked.

"Oh, I did," DeKorte assured him. "But it is one thing to talk theology, and quite another to face something in one's own life that is, shall we say, theology living and breathing right before your eyes."

"You actually confronted demonic possession?"

"In ways you could hardly believe and I hope you never have to see."

DeKorte paused, pulled a clipping out of his coat pocket, and handed it to Marsden. He glanced at the newspaper headline:

Satan Worship among Teenagers Growing at an Alarming Rate

"The battle goes on, doesn't it?"

"Everywhere. That's why I've taken a leave of absence from my church and have been speaking at churches and other gatherings all across the country. I've held seminars, workshops, and addressed conventions."

"Do they listen?"

"Everyone listens. The question is how much do they act upon what they hear?"

Marsden had stopped beside a picket fence that bordered the tiny yard of a neat white cottage.

"This is the place."

"You still haven't told me who it is."

"I think when you see her you'll understand why I would prefer to surprise you."

As they approached the front door, Marsden said, "She's very frail. But you'll notice another change immediately."

He rang the bell, and a few seconds later, the door was opened.

Edith Van Halen!

Standing with only a cane for support!

"Indeed, Paul DeKorte," she said, smiling broadly, "not everything was delusion back then."

He greeted her after the service as he had done for years, and she reached up from her wheelchair and smiled cheerfully.

"Mrs. Van Halen, how are you feeling today?" he asked her.

"Pretty good. Still praying for a miracle, though."

She hesitated, then, "Reverend DeKorte, will you have some time to join me at the house for tea and some of my little cakes?"

And he nodded appreciatively and assured her he would be happy to come over. . . .

Nearly six years ago, and now . . .

"Edith," DeKorte held out his hand, then moved to embrace her.

"Dear, dear friend," she said warmly. "For that is how I think of you now, Paul DeKorte. I really do, you know."

She invited them into her cozy living room, clean but cluttered with the accumulation of years.

Marsden was right, he thought. She is frail. Part of the toll . . . the earthly results that cannot be retracted.

Her hair was completely white, her face deeply lined, and her voiced trembled a bit. But her blue eyes were clear and serene. She seemed to sense what he was thinking.

"Older but wiser, my friend," she said. Then her expression became intent. "Please, let me see your hand."

He held out his right hand, and she examined it closely.

"Thank God it healed well," she said, sighing with relief.

She sank into an easy chair that was obviously her accustomed place, situated beside the front window and surrounded by books and magazines.

"It is fine," DeKorte told her as he and Marsden sat down on the sofa.

There were only a barely visible scar on the back of his hand and in the middle of the palm, very slight considering the size of the blade that had caused it.

"That was the deepest pit of all," she said. "To do that to a man of God!"

She shuddered visibly and leaned forward.

"Can you guess what I went through, Paul?" she asked.

"I can only imagine. But I know anything I conjectured would fall far short of the reality."

She took out a handkerchief and wiped her eyes. "How we survived—how I survived—it's only by the grace of our heavenly Father. I should have perished like—like—" She began sobbing.

Quickly DeKorte knelt beside her, taking her hands gently in his own.

"Take the victory," he told her. "Don't let Satan cause you to wallow in what was once defeat. Believe me, I know how he can use an emotion that should have been banished long ago."

"I'm the only one left, did you realize that?" she said. "The others ran, you know. They feared that God had cursed this place forever, like Sodom and Gomorrah."

"They viewed the Lord through their own limitations, then," said DeKorte. "I suppose I could be accused of that too, or of spiritual cowardice. But that's not really true."

"Why did you go, may I ask?" said Marsden, speaking for the first time since they had entered the house.

"At first, of course, it was a matter of survival. The holocaust—for that's what it was—shook the foundations of everything I was, ripped my life to pieces," DeKorte said, reaching for words to adequately describe what had happened. "Later, when I was able to face the future and what God would have me do with it, I knew I had to reach the world with the message. All you have to do is read the headlines and you know there are other Valley Falls out there. This time I don't want my message to come too late."

"That is the way I feel about my presence here," Edith Van Halen said. "I feel so clean now. I am helping the people here. I teach a Sunday school class for young parents. We talk about Satan and the importance of safeguarding their children and how it can be done. I hold Bible studies in their homes. Praise the Lord . . . He has made me part of the solution."

She stood and asked to be excused for a moment. When she returned, she was carrying a large scrapbook. She sat down between the two men on the sofa and opened the cover. The book was filled with clippings and letters.

"This is my extended ministry," she explained as she pointed to a headline.

Mother of Four
Slaughters Entire Family—
Says "Satan Made Me Do It!"

"I have been corresponding with that woman," she said, and showed them several of the letters—pages filled with intense anguish, with obscene language that conveyed the depths to which the woman's soul had sunk, plus other occasional flashes of defiance rooted in a belief that her master Satan was going to triumph in the end.

"I have tried to direct her to those portions of the Bible that show the prophesied defeat of Satan and all the fallen angels and every single one of their human followers," she said.

"But if she rejects the Bible, those verses have no impact," Marsden added.

"And yet the Holy Spirit can plant the seeds through them."

Each clipping the elderly woman pointed to seemed more appalling than the last, until she came to one that read

TV Evangelist Declares,
"We Become Christ
The Moment We Are Saved!"

"Oh, the injury that is done to the cause of Christ," Marsden said sadly.

"And the wider we open the door to Satan," added DeKorte.

"I don't know if that man is a demon posing as an angel of light," said Edith Van Halen, "but if he suddenly developed wings and cloven feet and horns, I wouldn't be surprised!"

She held up another clipping.

"I know you need to be going," she said, "but here is just one more I wanted to show you."

Huge Numbers of Satanists
Functioning in the
U.S. Government
The Total Could Be
In the Hundreds

The three were silent for several moments, soaking in the implications.

Finally Marsden asked, "How many evangelicals are sticking their heads in the sand and ignoring all this?"

"Too many," DeKorte replied. "And in the meantime the demonic activity goes on; the infiltration of Satan at every level of society continues."

"Even now, as this old brain thinks about what happened here, my nerves rebel," Edith Van Halen said, turning to Marsden. "It was awful beyond imagining. The enemy doesn't take defeat gracefully. He fights back with a viciousness only he possesses. He knows his end is the lake of fire, but until then he will not give up."

They spent nearly an hour looking through the scrapbook, and both men expressed admiration for the thoroughness with which she had gathered this impressive support with its prophetic implications.

"You know, most of this has happened since Valley Falls went through what it did," she said quietly. "Which may be just a coincidence. But I don't think so. There's a place in Missouri where three teenage boys clubbed another one to death with a baseball bat. Up in Oregon more than one area has been affected in the same way. And down in Mexico—"

She stopped, pressing her hand to her lips as she shook her head sadly. "It's spreading. Do you think it's the end times?" she asked, looking from one man to the other.

"The end times," said DeKorte, half in question, half in confirmation. "When the powers of darkness will wage their final battle."

"A period of demons," said Marsden. "Of the spreading power of the occult, with sorcerers and astrologers and false preachers spitting out doctrines from hell itself. And later, the appearance of the Antichrist."

Edith Van Halen leaned forward, looking at DeKorte intently. "What do you think, my friend?"

*   *   *

It was obvious that the elderly woman was growing weary, and the two men got up to leave.

"Where will you go now?" she asked DeKorte.

"Wherever the Lord wants to send me."

"I wish I could join you."

"You are needed here, Edith. Gather the facts. Write the letters. Be what you are right here," DeKorte said.

"And tell everyone about what I was!" she affirmed. "And you do the same, dear friend. Valley Falls can serve as a warning. Nobody who learns what really happened will ever find Satan mesmerizing them the way he did here. Help others to see what depths even someone of my age can sink to if they allow Satan to enter their lives. And follow the dream the Lord has given you."

DeKorte was nearly overwhelmed with emotion at these last words. The moment was a blessing beyond anything he had expected in this place.

As the two of them were turning toward the front door, Mrs. Van Halen asked them if they could wait just a minute longer.

"There is something I very much want to give to you," she said to DeKorte.

He nodded.

She soon returned with a small leather-bound book.

"It's my diary," she explained. "I kept entries in it for a year or so, up to the time for those final moments in the town square. I would like to give it to you."

"No, no," DeKorte protested. "Surely you—,"

"Too many of the wrong kinds of memories. But it can serve as a warning. It can help others to see what the depths are that even someone of my age can sink to if they allow Satan to enter their lives. Use it as you wish."

"I don't know what to say," DeKorte said, fumbling for the right words.

She smiled, briefly, then added, "Follow the dream the Lord has given you."

DeKorte reacted with ill-concealed surprise.

"I wish I could stay longer," he admitted.

"Please don't think in that manner," she said. "The Lord has a road map laid out before you, and a timetable. Seek out His guidance, and His only. Listen to no other voice, not even your own."

After they had reached the pavement Marsden asked, "Do you mind if I ask why you seemed so startled when she mentioned the dream?"

"Not at all," said DeKorte, "but I've taken so much of your time already. Won't your family be waiting dinner for you?"

Marsden shook his head. "Don't worry about that. In fact, why don't you come and eat with us?"

"Thank you, but I'd rather not. I've some other things I need to do, and this is a rather emotional time for me. I think I need to be alone."

"I understand," said Marsden. He pointed toward a bench on the square near DeKorte's car. "Let's just sit here for a few minutes then. I'd really like to hear the rest of your story."

The seat of the bench was warm from the midday sun, and DeKorte welcomed its comfort as he began.

"After I left here, I didn't have a place to go immediately," he recalled, fighting back tears. "So I stayed with friends, moving from one to another and feeling very embarrassed about taking advantage of their hospitality. It was really troubling me, to the point where one night I had difficulty going to sleep. Eventually though I drifted off. I thought I was still awake, but I wasn't, and I found myself in the most vivid and profound dream I've ever had."

He cleared his throat. "I've described that dream to no one before now," he admitted. "But I guess it's the Lord's own timing." He paused, hesitantly, then began. "In my dream..."

I had returned to Valley Falls just after the fires had burned down to glowing embers. Everyone had left and the town was deserted. I stood in the middle of the square where thin swirls of smoke were still rising from the mounds of ash and burnt corpses.

Everywhere I walked, I came across those awful remains, like a scene out of Dachau or Hiroshima or...Hell itself. The odors in the air were nearly overwhelming.

Then I heard a sound. A strange weeping. A wailing. It was the saddest utterance I had ever heard.

I couldn't detect where it was coming from at first. And then I saw, at the very edge of the square, something I will never forget, at least not in this life.

It was demonic, no question about that. Its wings hung by its sides, its fearsome head was bowed, and the sound escaped from its twisted lips. As I approached, the thing looked up, and I could see tears streaking its parchment-like skin.

"Paul DeKorte!" it shrieked.

"You know me?" I asked.

"Oh, yes. We know you. We—"

Then it lapsed into language that made me step back in horror.

"Paul, you're shaking," Marsden said softly.

"Forgive me," DeKorte said. "But no one will ever know how that creature spoke to me."

"Was that the end?" asked Marsden.

"No...."

Finally the demon stopped its shrieking and stood upright, spreading its wings.

"You have nothing to fear from me," it said. "But my kind and I have everything to fear from you."

My expression must have been one of utter puzzlement, for it immediately replied, "Because God has anointed you in a special way. Because you will be a special instrument of His will."

"Why are you telling me this?" I asked.

The demon's next words were mumbled, as though it didn't want to speak them.

"I was once unfallen, you know. I could have stayed by God's side. But I chose Lucifer instead."

Then the creature threw back its head and let out a cry of such anguish that I thought it would explode from the sheer intensity.

"And then what?" Marsden asked.

"That was the end, that final, awful cry."

"And that is what compels you now?" asked Marsden.

"That and all my memories of what happened in this place. How can I do otherwise? How could I ever again just settle into a comfortable pastorate after what I have seen...knowing what I know? God holds me responsible to use that for His sake."

DeKorte stood and shook his head, as though ridding himself of mental cobwebs.

"Where will you go now?" asked Marsden.

"To visit the cemetery," DeKorte replied.

"The cemetery?"

"Yes, my wife is buried there, you know. I want to spend a little time at her grave."

"Paul, you won't have heard, but—"

"What is it?" DeKorte asked with a sudden sense of terrible foreboding.

"The cemetery...it doesn't exist any longer."

"Doesn't exist? What do you mean?"

"Well, I came long after it happened, of course, but from what I've gathered, something horrible occurred during that final cataclysm. The townspeople dug up the graves and took the bodies and—and—"

"And what? What did they do?"

When Marsden told him, DeKorte's face went white.

"Lord help us!" he exclaimed.

"That is our only hope."

* * *

In a short while, Paul DeKorte left Valley Falls for the second time in his life, maybe the last. Perhaps he would return again someday, perhaps not. Too much had happened here....

As Philip Marsden watched DeKorte's car pass from sight, tears came to his eyes. He turned and looked around at the new houses, the new church, the repaved street, and the monument in the square. And as he tried to imagine what it had once been like there in Valley Falls, he felt a sudden chill....

How many of you are well-to-do? You have a good job, you have an automobile, you have a television set, you have a nice home to go to, you have three square meals a day, you're pretty rich. You have a certain amount of security, but if these things are more important than Christ, you have the worst kind of poverty—spiritual poverty. You're very, very, very poor. You have no riches toward God.

—Dr. Billy Graham

"How you are fallen from heaven, O Lucifer, son of the morning! How you are cut down to the ground, you who weakened the nations!

For you have said in your heart: "I will ascend into heaven, I will exalt my throne above the stars of God; I will also sit on the mount of the congregation on the farthest sides of the north; I will ascend above the heights of the clouds. I will be like the Most High." Yet you shall be brought down to Sheol, to the lowest depths of the Pit."

—Isaiah 14:12-15

* * *

From everywhere they descended upon the ancient graveyard, these pathetic yet terrifying creatures of darkness and decay. The conference was an important one, and their leader had demanded they all attend. Most greeted the gathering with enthusiasm, thinking it was long overdue.

Perched on vine-draped mausoleums, clustered about lichen-covered gravestones, thousands waited for the Master. Tree branches rustled eerily against a backdrop of dark sky above this scene straight out of the pit of damnation.

These were the devil gods who satiated their fiendish desires by spreading child abuse and pornography, who enjoyed driving their hosts to perverse acts of bestiality, who took special glee in seeing bits and pieces of babies ripped from protective wombs, who reveled as they watched unfortunate souls destroy themselves with drugs— a living death that killed them slowly from the inside.

"Quiet!" The hissing chorus swept over the crowd.

The Master was about to make his entrance, to tell them what he had planned for the residents of Valley Falls.

* * *

2

Paul DeKorte sat on the steps of the church he had shepherded for nearly ten years. Spread out before him in the large town square was the current fund-raising bazaar. Clusters of balloons bobbed around in the air. Several children were holding cherry-colored puffs of cotton candy. Scents mixed together from popcorn and roasted peanuts wafted past his nostrils, and he breathed these in, enjoying their familiarity.

A score of booths were in operation, including the traditional shooting gallery and a perky-looking teenage girl selling kisses, for which there was no paucity of buyers, with streamers whipped by moderate breezes and, as always, the sounds of people, cheerful, talkative.

"Mary," he found himself saying out loud. "My beloved . . . I miss you so."

Just six months before she had sat with him on these same steps. How readily their conversation came back to him.

"God has been good to us, hasn't He, sweetheart?"

"Oh, He has, Paul. This is the best pastorate you've ever had."

"The people are just great." He noticed her nibbling on her lower lip then and asked, *"Anything wrong, Mary?"*

She turned and looked at him. "Don't you worry sometimes?"

"About what?"

"The foundation."

"I don't know what you mean, Mary."

"They come, they worship, and then they leave to enjoy the fruits of their faith."

"What in the world is wrong with that?"

"I worry about their faith, Paul. Are they putting it on a convenient little shelf throughout the week, until the next Sunday when they take it off for public display?"

He had been tolerant with her then, but made it clear, in the gentlest terms, that she really had nothing to worry about.

"But what happens when there is pain, when there is financial need, when—"

"*Mary, Mary, God will provide. Don't try to second-guess Him, please. It'll all work out.*"

He knew she hadn't been satisfied by that, for occasionally she would voice similar thoughts. He vividly recalled one night, when they were resting in one another's arms.

"*Scott Pennio came to see me today, Paul.*"

"*What did he want?*"

"*He seemed really troubled. Said he couldn't talk to his parents anymore.*"

"*That's pretty typical of most teenagers at some point.*"

"*True. But he was really upset . . . almost bitter. He said he had tried to talk to his parents about some spiritual matters and they told him they didn't have time just then. He said they were more interested in talking about their latest stock market investments than in him.*"

As he ran his fingers through Mary's soft dark hair, Paul had promised to talk with Scott within the next few days.

He never fulfilled that promise, for less than a week later, Mary was dead.

* * *

It was a windy Tuesday morning in March. Paul had just started working on his Sunday morning sermon when Ben Connelly, the church custodian, burst into his study.

"Pastor, pastor!" Heavy-set Ben was wild-eyed and gasping for breath.

"I was working out at the side, and your wife ran out of the church basement all cut and bleeding. Looked like she'd been attacked or something."

He paused, trying to catch his breath. "I tried to go after her to help her, but she got into your car and drove off. Headed south out of town."

Connelly held out a set of keys. "We can take my car."

A few miles out of Valley Falls, they caught up with her. Blind with terror and pain, Mary had run the stop sign at the highway intersection, and an oncoming car had broadsided her. They managed to drag her out of the wreckage.

She was not yet dead.

He held her in his arms.

"Mary, Mary—"

She managed to say something, her voice raspy with pain.

"Please, Paul, I'm so ashamed...please believe me, I didn't know—I didn't want him to—begged him—"

"Don't talk, my love, don't—"

For one final moment, then, her voice was strong, almost vibrant.

"I love you so much, my darling. Don't hate him, please. Dear, dear Paul. Our Lord taught us to forgive. You must believe that He knows what—"

And then she was gone, her head dropping backward, her long hair touching the asphalt.

The subsequent investigation turned up no real clues, at least none that could be classified as helpful. What the authorities did discover, in fact, only added to the mystery. Mary's dress had been nearly shredded, and her body was covered with claw-like cuts. In the church basement one room showed signs of a struggle, and they found traces of Mary's blood on the floor and on the doorknob. Since the room was used for Sunday school classes and other purposes, getting fingerprints as a lead proved impossible—there were just too many of them.

At first, of course, Mary's violent death attracted much attention. Yet within a few weeks it seemed to have faded, as though everyone had lost interest.

To be fair, Paul had to admit that the perplexing lack of evidence presented a blind alley. And the local authorities had consulted the FBI, who also were unable to produce anything that suggested the identity of Mary's assailant.

"It looks as though an animal attacked her," one FBI agent told him. "But an animal as powerful as that could not have entered the church and left without being seen. It would have been just too big—of monstrous size."

Whoever did this to you, my beloved, is out there free, unharmed, unpunished.

He found that singular fact one of the hardest to accept.

A familiar voice intruded upon his memories.

"A silver dollar for your thoughts, my friend."

He looked up into the thin, bony face of Dr. Douglas Rogers, the only physician Valley Falls had known for more than a quarter of a century.

"You were thinking about Mary, weren't you?"

DeKorte nodded, and the doctor settled his long, lean frame on the step.

"I know how you're feeling, Paul. I've been a widower for twenty years now," Rogers said. "I loved Ellen as much as any man could love a woman. When she died, I felt as though a team of surgeons had performed open heart surgery on me without anaesthesia."

Somehow the kind expression on the craggy face and the sympathy in the brown eyes warmed DeKorte.

"As you know, I don't believe in the God you preach about, Paul, but I can believe in the resiliency of human beings if they give themselves the slightest chance. And there is no way in the world Mary would ever want the love you two shared to be anything other than the sweetest blessing, my friend. Don't make it a curse."

As the two men talked, DeKorte found himself marveling at his friendship with this man who had been a confirmed atheist for years, yet who had never once ridiculed his own religious beliefs, though he expressed honest disagreement with them.

"Paul, what do you think of this?" Rogers was saying now. He held out a piece of wood about three inches long. It was a carving of a figure faintly Aztec in appearance. DeKorte reached into his pocket and pulled out an identical carving and handed it to his friend.

"You found one, too!" the doctor exclaimed.

"Tied to the steering wheel of my car."

"I found this one in my waiting room yesterday. What are they? Any idea?"

"Probably just some kid's idea of a joke."

Rogers nodded. "Here, you want this one too?"

"Sure. I'll stick them in my miscellaneous file. The strangest things come in handy for a minister!" DeKorte chuckled.

Rogers stretched expansively.

"It's great, all this old-fashioned, small-town atmosphere," he said, sweeping his arm toward the square.

"Absolutely. The big cities have nothing like this."

"It's great for our kids especially. I wonder if they ever realize how thankful they should be for what they have here?"

"Well, most of them are good kids, Doug."

"I know. I've delivered most of them!"

"On that note, let's go have an ice cream cone," said DeKorte.

As the men stood up, Rogers glanced at the cross above the church entrance.

"I must admit it's impressive," he said.

The cross was an exceptional piece of work, made of wood gathered from the same trees used for those instruments of torture and death at the time of Christ. Even the nails holding up the hanging form were painstakingly fine reproductions. And the figure of

Christ was sculpted with extraordinary attention to detail, as life-like as human hands could make it. The body hung in an anatomically correct manner, veins pronounced, head tilted slightly forward, eyelids partially closed, fingers curling outward, the soles of the feet pressed on top of one another, a single nail through both, a gash in the side where a Roman spear had been thrust, and a crown of thorns on top of the head.

"So you finally agree!" DeKorte laughed, reminding his friend of their old disagreement.

"But still too expensive, Paul. How many of the poor could have been helped with just part of the cost?"

"But we're already doing that. This is a tribute to our Lord."

"Your Lord, not mine." Then, realizing he had spoken harshly, he said, "Forgive me for that, my friend."

"That's the point, Doug. Christ's death 2000 years ago—"

"Enough! Enough! Let's enjoy ourselves."

As they walked across the square, DeKorte said, "I dislike legends, Doug. They're too often mythological, and pagan to boot, with plenty of wild fantasy thrown in. But a few are tolerable."

"Is there one about that cross?" Rogers asked.

"Not that one specifically, but about crosses in general. Supposedly, just before the reign of the Antichrist in the end times, all the figures of Jesus will disappear from all the churches everywhere in the world, leaving only bare crosses. But it won't happen all at once: first at a church in, say, England, then Italy, then—"

"Some sort of sign?"

"It would seem so. But it will be gradual, virtually unnoticed at first, starting in small towns in Europe and then spreading. And then the Antichrist will come upon the scene in his full frightening impact, deceiving entire nations."

"Why so slowly?"

"I suppose because the Christian influence is slowly dissipating. What began as a Christian nation here, for example, has been accelerating in terms of its degradation. The Pilgrims and Puritans would be shocked. Perhaps the greater the incidence of these disappearances, the nearer we come to the Rapture," DeKorte sighed. "Well, it's only a legend."

"This analytical mind of mine suggests something else, Paul."

"What's that?"

"The Rapture, as you call it, is supposed to happen all at once, right?"

"Right."

"Well, perhaps the legend is wrong in saying that the disappearances won't happen all at once. Maybe it's a matter of the news getting out in spurts, bits and pieces being heard, and then a surge. When a disaster happens, for example, like the earthquake in Armenia, the early reports are always sketchy. Same thing could be true here, only it would take much longer. Communications in out-of-the-way villages aren't always the best, you know."

"And also, no one wants to be accused of religious hysteria or some kind of hoax in this scientific age of ours," added DeKorte.

"Exactly."

"Very good, Doug! But I really must stress that this is all speculative. Still, the significance is certainly Christ-honoring because the Bible does tell us that, even as bad as the world is today, Satan's full rampaging is being restrained by the presence of believing Christians who are acting as the salt to preserve Planet Earth for the moment."

DeKorte couldn't seem to shake the concept, though.

"The idea of Christ figures vanishing all over the world carries with it a graphic visual statement, if nothing else. When they're all gone, especially from those congregations in which such figures have become the central focus of a kind of Christianized idolworship, and, in fact, the Rapture has occurred, then the world system will be fully given over to the control of evil and reprobate minds."

"But aren't there other interpretations?" Rogers pointed out. "I mean, one that even an aging unbeliever like myself has heard over the years is that Christians will actually endure part of the reign of the Antichrist rather than escape it, as you imply."

DeKorte was about to respond when he noticed a gray-haired woman in a wheelchair approaching them.

"Good evening, Pastor DeKorte, Doctor Rogers," she said, reaching up to shake hands with each of them.

"Hello, Edith," said DeKorte.

"Good to see you out and about," added Rogers.

Paul DeKorte never ceased to marvel at Edith Van Halen. Injured in a riding accident on her honeymoon over forty years before, she had been in a wheelchair ever since. Though widowed now, and handicapped, she never seemed bitter or depressed.

"I never give up praying for healing," she had said more than once when someone marveled at her spirit.

As the two men chatted with her about the beautiful evening and other mundane matters, something slipped off her lap.

DeKorte bent down to pick it up and saw that it was a small wood carving like the ones he and Rogers had found.

"You found one too," he said.

"Yes," she said. Her smile faded for an instant, and a strange, almost sly look clouded her blue eyes. Then she smiled once more, held out her hand to take the carving, and told them she had to be going.

"Curious, isn't it?" Rogers said as they watched her wheelchair move away from them down the sidewalk.

"Very," DeKorte agreed. "A new fad?"

"Must be. But Edith Van Halen?" They exchanged glances and shrugged their shoulders almost simultaneously.

"Come on," said Rogers. "I'll buy you a double-dip."

As the two men walked out of Sue's Parlor a few minutes later, enjoying their ice cream in easy silence, DeKorte noticed Rose Pennio coming toward them. He saw her husband across the street, sitting on a bench in the square, finishing up a dish of ice cream.

"Pastor, I'm sorry to bother you, but I need to talk to you about Scott."

Rogers courteously stepped away to look at a nearby window display.

"What's the problem, Rose?" asked DeKorte, thinking about the coincidence of this encounter following his earlier memory of Mary's concern.

"I found Scott trying to hide his sheets," she told him.

"Yes?" DeKorte said, puzzled.

"They were all bloody. Not just a drop here and there, but big splotches of it."

"What did he tell you?"

"Nothing. I'm almost afraid to ask."

"What does your husband say?"

"We're both very worried. Scott's been—"

The sound of someone shouting interrupted her.

The main street of Valley Falls formed the entrance to the square, with storefronts and the church grouped around it in cul-de-sac fashion.

"Help me! In God's name, help me!"

Running down the street was a blond-haired teenage boy named Patrick McCloskey.

The activity in the square came to an immediate halt.

Patrick was shirtless, his chest riddled with cuts and scratches. His dungarees were nearly shredded.

He stopped only a few feet from DeKorte.

"It's got to end. Now! It's got to end before—before—we all—we—"

DeKorte rushed up to him. The teenager collapsed in his arms. A crowd circled the two of them.

Patrick's eyes darted from side to side.

"It's not drugs, you know. I—I bet that's what you're thinking. Much worse, much worse than—"

He started to double up in pain, and then choked, gagging, and vomited over himself and DeKorte.

"Precious Jesus, precious Jesus, precious Jesus," he said, his voice trembling.

He looked up at DeKorte.

"I'm dying, pastor. I'm dying."

The teenager's expression changed, and he smiled weakly as greenish fluids seeped out of the sides of his mouth.

"Surround yourself with the Word, sir," he said. "That's what I did. They could claim only my body."

He died as convulsions ripped through his body, shaking him as though he were undergoing epileptic seizures.

Something fell from his left hand as it opened once, then closed again in death.

Another of the wood carvings, this one smeared with Patrick McCloskey's blood.

3

Patrick's death weakened Paul DeKorte's fragile recovery from the tragedy he himself had so recently faced. He had no idea how he could stand before Patrick's parents and the rest of the townspeople and deliver the funeral message.

I'm supposed to be a symbol of stability, he thought. They look to me for guidance. He had dozed off that night, and awoke trying to wipe off Patrick's blood that had been washed away hours earlier. As he sank back on the mattress, memories of Mary and Patrick competed for his attention.

First you, Mary, and now the boy you loved almost as your own.

Patrick had been one of Mary's favorite Sunday school students, an intelligent, personable youngster who had spoken of becoming a missionary in China. *What a burden that boy had for the lost! Surely some will question why this was allowed to happen, even as they had with Mary.*

Patrick's social life had sometimes suffered a bit because of his dedication to the cause of Christ. DeKorte himself, who was all for personal sacrifice, remembered approaching the boy and raising the subject with him.

"Pastor, didn't the rich young ruler fail the test Christ presented to him?" Patrick had replied.

"That's true, son, but—"

"I don't intend to fail. If it's a choice between friends and fun or my Lord, I must choose Him."

Patrick had been the nearest thing to the child he and Mary had never had, a relationship the boy's own parents had encouraged.

Patrick, oh, Patrick, what happened?

The dream from which DeKorte had awakened was a twisted replay of those horrible last moments with Patrick in his arms. But in the nightmarish episode there had been oppressive presences that at first remained out of sight, and then became visible: grotesque faces laughing, pointing to the dying boy, and making blasphemous statements about faith and love and the divinity of Jesus Christ. Only by holding Patrick tightly against him could he prevent the demonic entities from grabbing the boy and taking him with them.

Suddenly he saw that the creatures were not apparitions at all, but his friends and neighbors in Valley Falls.

That was when reality returned, pulling him from sleep. When he awoke, his body felt like it was encased in solid ice.

It was the middle of the night, and he did what he could for himself by reading the Bible and praying, but even that wasn't enough. After an hour or more of this, he dialed Douglas Rogers's number.

"Hello." Rogers's voice was croaky with sleep.

"It's Paul."

"In the middle of the night? Call me—"

"No, please, I've got to talk."

"Talk to another Christian. I'm an atheist, remember?"

"Doug, I really need you."

Rogers hesitated.

"You do sound awful," he acknowledged.

"Will you meet me at the church?"

"Only if you'll promise to take one of my calls after midnight someday when my atheism wears thin. I do admit that possibility, you know."

"You've got it. Listen, come as soon as you can."

Doug isn't saved, Lord, DeKorte mused to himself. *Why do I find myself turning to him in such moments as this?*

Especially after Mary's death, too.

Isn't there anyone in my own congregation I could talk with?

Even as he completed the thought, he realized that there wasn't. It was the age-old problem of clergymen.

We are looked upon as comforters, as spiritual problem-solvers. People turn to us again and again, expecting strength and wisdom. But where do we, who are only human, find the same?

In his case, the problem was compounded by the unfailing doctrine of cheer he had expounded for the better part of a decade. Every problem was a possibility in disguise; every negative thought was a dart from Satan. Look to the future, he had exhorted again and again, a future filled with vibrant potential.

But not Douglas, thought DeKorte as he walked across the parking lot to the church. He would have none of that.

"I have a *realistic* view of life," the doctor had once commented, "not one steeped in some kind of encapsulated Pollyanna nonsense, to be swallowed once a week as a seven-day, time-release vitamin."

* * *

It was 2:30 in the morning when the two of them sat in the church auditorium, no lights on, only the glow from a full moon filtering in through the stained glass windows.

"One after the other," DeKorte said. "First Mary ... then Patrick, who was like a son to us."

"I don't have your frame of reference, Paul," Rogers admitted, "but the way I reacted to my own wife's death proved something to me. I almost took my own life when she died. I felt I had nothing to live for without her. She was a strong believer in Christ, and yet I disputed everything she held dear. It was no comfort to me that she believed she was going to heaven, because I don't believe in heaven. But where do you find comfort when your beloved wife is now simply a pile of dust?"

Tears welled in his eyes, and he wiped them with the back of his hand.

"I kept going, in the end, because I knew that the only way she could survive in any form was as memories up here." He tapped his forehead. "If I ended my life prematurely, those memories would cease as well, and then it would be as though neither of us had ever existed."

The doctor put one hand on DeKorte's shoulder.

"What you have is something I crave but can't believe for myself. Just as I am certain that everything ends at death, you are as certain that we go on. In that sense, my friend, no matter how I feel about it, you have the advantage. For you at least have hope. Though right now you recoil from the tragedies, the suddenness of having those you love ripped from your life, most of what you feel in your sorrow is the awful reality of living the next thirty years without Mary beside you—to talk to, to laugh with, to touch and hold. Eventually, though, you believe there is the promise of re-union for eternity. For me, my good and dear friend, there is nothing of the kind."

By this time, both men were crying.

We have seen God's glory ... we have heard the brokenhearted sing.

The words came back to DeKorte, and he spoke them out loud.

"If I could accept what you say, if I could believe that we would one day walk those golden streets you've talked about, Paul, it would be wonderful. But I cannot. And yet you *do* believe. You *can* claim the victory that comes with such faith and give that wonderful boy the eulogy he deserves."

They went back to their homes a little while later. DeKorte stayed up for a few minutes in prayer and then closed his eyes and never opened them again until morning.

* * *

The sky was overcast the day of Patrick's funeral. DeKorte stood by the rosewood coffin at the graveside service, surveying the crowd. Patrick's classmates and many of the townspeople were in attendance.

"You are here because of the sort of young man Patrick McCloskey was," he began. "He proved himself to be quite remarkable during his brief lifetime. My wife Mary always believed he was going to be a great lawyer or doctor or whatever he chose to be. He had intelligence and decency and real faith."

He cleared his throat.

"We go on without—"

Something caught his attention. Three teenage boys dressed in black leather, standing to one side.

"—Patrick, yes, somehow we can indeed manage that, for it is the nature of things here on Planet Earth. But we will be poorer—"

They were walking slowly forward.

"—all of us who knew him, because he will no longer be here to enrich our lives."

He took out a handkerchief and wiped his eyes.

"Good-bye, Mary's friend, my friend, the friend of so many here. Our Lord—"

The three teenagers stood near the front of the crowd.

"—has taken whatever your burdens were at last upon Himself, and that will be, as His Word promises, for all eternity."

One of the boys stepped forward, and several of the girls present turned and eyed him.

"Yes, Scott, did you want to say something?" DeKorte asked.

The teenager turned and faced the other mourners.

"Patrick was my friend," he said. "I loved him, you know, I mean I really did."

He took something out of his pocket and rested it on top of the casket, then rejoined his two friends.

In a few minutes, everyone had drifted away except DeKorte and the three boys. Then they too started to leave. As his two friends walked ahead, Scott paused and glanced at the minister for a few seconds.

"Scott?" DeKorte said as their eyes met, thinking the boy wanted to say something.

But he shook his head and joined his friends.

DeKorte bent down and picked up the object Scott Pennio had placed on the casket. Somehow he wasn't surprised when he saw what it was.

* * *

DeKorte didn't leave the cemetery immediately, but walked the short distance to Mary's grave and stood there, his head bowed.

Oh, Mary, I miss you so....

He fell to his knees, not caring if anyone saw him.

If only—

That unfinished thought was as grievous as his loss. Not knowing what had happened to Mary or who had been responsible for her death ate at him. And yet he knew he had to leave it with the Lord with whom Mary was now walking.

But I miss her so, Lord....

Finally he stood and turned away from that place.

* * *

It was working beautifully, they all admitted.

Yes, step by step the screws were being tightened, fear was being planted, and since that was the opposite of faith, the demonic midwives were delighted.

"Especially that Scott kid," one demon whispered to another. "So good-looking, my oh my!"

"You may be the spirit of perversion," the one next to him remarked proudly, "but that's not what I'm responsible for, I assure you. I prefer simpler evils, like lying and cheating."

"I prefer playing with Scott."

"I'm sure you do."

* * *

4

Scott Pennio sat up in bed, images from Patrick's funeral staying with him, no matter how hard he tried to drown them out with the music piped through his stereo earphones.

It seemed like such a great idea. We would push him as far as he could go, and then stop, like a frat prank.

He abruptly pulled off the earphones and threw them on the floor.

My hands are shaking. Why?

He stood and walked over to the bathroom door, leaning against the frame.

Across from him was the mirror on the medicine cabinet.

I look lousy. I—

He held up his hands, looked at them.

I didn't do it alone. Wayne and Mark were there, helping me. They must share the guilt, they—

Suddenly he became sick to his stomach and rushed to the toilet, bending down over it, heaving once, twice, again.

We were actually responsible for someone dying. After awhile, nothing could stop us. We had to finish up. We had to go all the way.

He stopped vomiting. Very weak, he stumbled to his bed and flopped down on it. Tears were next as he realized how much had happened in six short months—from laughing at astrology and tarot cards and Ouija boards, to trying them out, to needing them day after day.

And now Patrick's gone. It's not a game we can decide to end, and then life is back to normal again.

He reached up under the headboard, pulled off a thin plastic packet of white powder. Tapping out a small pile on his thumbnail, he raised it to his nose and inhaled the tiny, tiny crystals.

And then he grabbed the earphones, put them on, started playing another cassette.

Where has all the fun gone?

He smiled, his lips curling up in a cynical, smirking—

—all the fun gone?

The music filled his mind, yeah, like always, as he rubbed some of the powder on his gums and closed his eyes.

That voice, as before, part of the lyrics maybe, maybe not, but present somehow, a slight echo to it, the words coming to life as the cocaine lifted him up, up, up.

* * *

It all began for Scott Pennio when he and Wayne Mulrooney and Mark Jacobson noticed a Ouija board on sale at the local toy store. It seemed like a kicky thing to try.

Almost immediately Scott became fascinated. He borrowed a book from the library and studied the history of the "game."

> OUIJA BOARD (from the French *oui* and the German *ja),* a wooden tripod on rollers which, under the hand of the medium, moves over a polished board and spells out messages by pointing at letters. As an invention, it is very old. It was in use in the days of Pythagoras, about 540 B.C. ...
>
> It remains, through the centuries, an excellent device for use in breaking through the material world of substance and making contact with the world of the supernatural, preferably the demonic.

When Scott and his friends started using the board, it seemed harmless enough, and they laughed at the results. After all, even the county's daily newspaper carried a column called "Star Gazing Guide to Health and Happiness," as did most of the popular magazines. What was the harm?

However, Scott kept thinking back to that one phrase in the book ... *preferably the demonic.* He felt chills all over his body when he thought about it.

After school the next day, he returned the book to the library, and that evening he had his first nightmare.

* * *

Lots of mist ... walking through thick clouds of it. And then clearing suddenly.

A church.

Directly in front of him.

People in the auditorium, their eyes closed, their hands raised. He sat down and joined them.

And he saw something, there in his mind, though he had not tried to visualize it, coming as an intruder.

He saw—

Scott screamed himself awake. When his parents rushed in, he muttered an embarrassed assurance that he was all right. It was just a bad dream. After they left, he lay there crying to himself from his encounter with the awfulness of that . . . thing.

In the morning he awoke drenched with perspiration, his body trembling. He was exhausted, for he had feared to let himself slip too deeply into sleep. Feared that the same scene would haunt him again.

Later at school, during lunch period, he took Wayne and Mark aside and told them what he had dreamed.

"In church?" Mark said, astonished. "Man, that's—"

"Heavy duty?" Scott interrupted. "I know."

"Scott, you're not going to do it, are you?" Wayne asked.

Scott didn't answer.

Two weeks later, at the Sunday morning visualization group, he tried what he had dreamed.

And made contact.

From then on, the descent was quite rapid. Day by day, week by week, Scott and his friends got ever deeper. Each bought a crystal pyramid, a pack of tarot cards, and each studied a daily astrology chart. But these were toys compared to that night in the old cemetery when it all came together. . . .

*　*　*

Scott's parents were out for the evening, so the boys had the house to themselves. They were sitting on the floor in Scott's bedroom, shirtless, their chests glistening with perspiration. Spread out before them on an oval-shaped mirror was the white powder Scott had just finished cutting with a razor, dividing it into several thin lines.

"Good stuff," he told Wayne and Mark. "Just a little baby laxative this time. Not quite pure magic but close."

He bent down and, using a rolled dollar bill, inhaled one line of the powder. Immediately he felt a burst of satisfaction, sexual in its intensity.

"Great!" he said, as he handed the bill to Wayne.

The drug killed the pain, at least temporarily. Not a physical pain, since all three boys were athletic and healthy, but the pain of reaching out with questions and finding no answers from those who were supposed to love them.

"Dad will tell me about stock market margins," Scott had told his two friends earlier, "but try talking to him about sex, and he clams up, like he's embarrassed."

"I know what you mean," Wayne said. "When I first started having wet dreams I really didn't know what was happening. I tried to talk to Dad about it, but he pretended he was too busy and would talk to me later. But he never did."

Mark laughed.

"They hate the idea of us learning about sex in school, but they sure aren't about to help us."

"What did you guys ever find out from your folks?" Scott asked.

"Nothing," Mark said simply. "I had to do on-the-spot research." And the three of them laughed.

"They've got time for everything in their lives but us," Scott said. He closed his eyes. "Another hit?" he asked.

"You bet!" Mark replied.

They each did another line, and then another.

"The best!" Wayne exclaimed.

"The best ever!" Scott's heart pounded. He had so much energy; he wanted to go outside and shout. Or maybe he could climb out on the roof and jump off and suddenly be able to fly!

He looked about the room, feeling caged. "Outside," he said. "Let's go outside, do something."

He got to his feet and stood at the window, where the cool evening breeze gently touched his face.

"Take the tarot cards and the Ouija board," Mark suggested.

"Yeah!" Scott said, his eyes widening. "We'll do it in that weird old cemetery out on Route 12." He swung around, his interest crystallized.

"That's pretty extreme, isn't it?" Wayne said hesitantly. "Maybe we shouldn't be messing around with—"

"The devil?" Scott interrupted. "DeKorte would say we started down that road when we snorted white magic the first time."

Wayne relented.

"Okay," he said. "Count me in."

*　*　*

The old cemetery was not the same place where Patrick McCloskey and Mary DeKorte had been buried. This one was some miles in the opposite direction and had not been used since the turn of the century. It was preserved as an historical site, since some of the headstones dated back before the American Revolution.

"Is it midnight yet?" Scott asked.

Mark looked at his watch. "Yeah," he said.

Scott put his hands on the Ouija board, stretching his fingers straight out as he rested them on the little triangular object with the rounded pinnacles. Wayne and Mark sat on the ground on either side of him, anxious for the message they knew would come.

They didn't have to wait long.

W E L C O M E

"Wow!" Mark exclaimed. "That was quicker than ever."

"Yeah.," said Wayne with notable lack of enthusiasm. "Yeah it was."

Several seconds passed.

T O N I G H T

What about tonight? Scott thought. *Tell me, please!*
Nothing.
Why are we here? he tried again.

B E C A U S E

"Stop playing games!" Scott said aloud. .

Just then a mournful sound filled the air.

"What the—?" Mark said, looking around fearfully.

T H I S   N I G H T
E V I L   G R O W S

Evil? Scott thought. *Sounds like DeKorte, not—*

I N   Y O U

"Scott, this is really crazy," Wayne protested. "It—"

M U C H   M O R E
T H A N   T H A T

Scott's eyes were closed. Suddenly he felt a hand on his shoulder and he screamed. Wayne and Mark did the same.

A hand. Attached to an arm. But the arm wasn't attached to anything....

The three ran to the car and broke all speed limits in leaving the cemetery behind them.

5

The boys tried to ignore what had happened. They threw away their tarot cards and the Ouija board. But they still used cocaine each weekend, convincing themselves that the drug was helping them forget that encounter in the old cemetery.

"I never want to go near that place again," Wayne said, wiping the white powder from around the edges of his nostrils.

"I'm with you there, man," Mark agreed. "That was uncool."

They were in Scott's bedroom as usual, heavy metal music playing in the background.

Scott thought back to the church service they had attended that morning, where Reverend DeKorte had delivered a sermon about financial prosperity as a blessing from the Lord.

Money from heaven, he told himself. *That's mostly what he talks about these days.* He shivered briefly. *So empty, so phony....*

They have all the answers, Scott thought, the cocaine sending his mind on psychic tracks that stretched before him as far as he could see. He was trapped on them, much like a train out of control, the brakes gone, threatening to derail.

All the answers, all the answers, everything so neat, so neat, so neat, neat, neat, all wrapped up and, and, and, and predigested, and fed intravenously so, so, so, that, that when, when I wake, I wake, I wake up, I'll, yeah, yeah, I'll, yeah, I'll be just like them.

His eyes widened.

Like them! Like a freak show of phonies and I'm next, next, next....

Scott had returned home from church only to hear his parents talking about getting a new car, analyzing the different offers made to them by the dealers they had seen thus far. He wanted to go to the stairs and shout down to them to shut up, to listen to themselves, to open their eyes.

They don't know what it's all about. They just don't know. In frustration he turned on the television in his room and saw someone in the midst of a heavy emotional crisis heading toward the liquor cabinet. He changed the channel and found a movie featuring a child killer with a fetish for dolls that looked like his victims.

Thoughts of snow-white powder filled his mind.

* * *

Toward dusk, he went outside for a walk and ended up in the middle of the town square. For a moment he thought he heard voices and the crackling of flames, then realized it was his imagination. Or perhaps the creaking of limbs on the trees surrounding the square.

Directly ahead was the church he had attended every Sunday of his life. Scott remembered a time when being there meant something to him, when he still felt a sense of fulfillment by singing the hymns and listening to the sermons and meeting with the youth group.

He tried to pinpoint just when it had all changed. Had it started with Reverend DeKorte's prosperity kick? Or when the people at church began invoking the name of Christ as they claimed everything from healing of warts and gallstones to help in paying their mortgages to winning the local basketball championship?

Or had it started with Ellie Sumner? He'd had a crush on her from the moment they first met in sophomore English. They dated for months, spending more and more time together, their affection becoming more and more physical.

Then Ellie began to change. She became moody, unpredictable. Soon she refused to see him anymore. She hung up on him when he called.

Scott couldn't understand why. *I hadn't done anything. We never went to bed or anything like that. I told her I loved her.*

Finally he managed to corner her alone near her locker one day.

"What's wrong, Ellie?" he begged.

And she told him.

Her mother was terribly ill and didn't seem to be getting better. One night Ellie and her father went to a healing service at a church in a nearby town. They went to pray for Ellie's mother, who was too ill to attend herself. There they were told that the problem was unconfessed sin. God didn't want anyone to be as ill as her mother had become. Ellie or her father or her mother, or maybe all of them, had done something to offend God.

Ellie walked away then and never spoke to Scott again. A short while later her mother died, and Ellie and her father left Valley Falls.

She blamed herself and maybe me. She thought we shouldn't have behaved the way we did sometimes, even though we never went all the way.

Two days later, Scott lost his virginity....

He shook those thoughts out of his head as he approached the church. He glanced at the large cross over the entrance, mesmerized by the figure on it.

The nails were turning, turning, becoming loose and then—

Suddenly there was pain in his forehead and his neck and his chest; he doubled over with it. It lasted only seconds, then was gone.

What's wrong with me?

The front door of the church was never locked, and he went inside. Seeking comfort? Safety? Perhaps Reverend DeKorte could help him.

He handled the pamphlets on the table directly in front of him. One was shaped like a bank passbook, another like a check. He stood at the back of the sanctuary, looking at the stained glass windows, the pulpit.

Then the pain struck again, doubling him over and sending him sprawling onto the floor. He realized, with growing terror, that his arms were outstretched, his legs spread apart.

He stumbled to his feet, dizzy, then steadied himself and ran from the church. Back home in his room he wrapped himself in a blanket, trying to get warm. But the chill came from inside somewhere...somewhere he could not reach.

In the background he could hear the television downstairs and recognized the theme music. His parents were watching a racy prime time soap. From the Bible on Sunday to Dallas on Friday!

He did a couple lines of powder and lost himself once more in his music. And he knew then, with a terrible certainty, what he would do.

That familiar high, a sense of rising exaltation, like he was in a dark tunnel, stumbling. Abruptly a light was turned on, and he reached out to embrace it only to find that the light was himself.

6

Paul DeKorte was shocked by the town's reaction to Patrick's death. Within a few days after the funeral, no one even mentioned the boy's name anymore, let alone the strange circumstances surrounding his death. It was as though he had never existed, never mattered. Like Mary.

"No one even seems to be investigating it," he told Doug Rogers one Tuesday morning at the Cozy Coffee Clatch, where the two friends had met twice a week for the past couple years.

"It's crazy to think that a probe isn't in progress, Paul," Rogers said.

"But they seem to be ignoring the whole thing."

"That may be the impression you get, but I'm sure something is being done." Rogers paused. "As to whether it is a matter of high priority, well, that's another story, my friend."

"But that's my point, Doug! Patrick was only seventeen. One of the brightest, most popular kids in town. And it's like a rock was thrown into a lake, with ripples for a second or two, and then nothing!"

"Maybe that's because the negative aftermath of a tragedy like this doesn't compute in this town. After all, it violates all the principles of positive thinking."

It violates all the principles of positive thinking.

His friend's words stayed with DeKorte long after they left the coffee shop. They stung his subconscious later that week at the banquet given in his honor at a Spanish-style restaurant several miles north of Valley Falls, rented for the occasion. Several hundred members of his congregation were on hand.

"And we toast the man who has been our shepherd for more than a decade!"

The words broke through his reverie. He blinked his eyes several times and managed to smile at the speaker who stood beside him, Sheriff Daniel Wilburn.

"We want you to know how much we appreciate you. You have been our pastor for ten years, and they have been wonderful years indeed."

Wonderful? With Mary gone? Patrick gone? Doesn't that—?

"As a token of our affection and esteem, we wanted to give you something special."

Wilburn stepped back from the podium, reached into his vest pocket and took out a small square package wrapped in gold paper. With a flourish, he handed it to DeKorte.

DeKorte tore off the paper, and opened the box. Keys. Car keys.

"It's out back," Wilburn said proudly.

Everyone followed him out to the parking lot. There, with a ribbon tied to the hood ornament, sat a new luxury sedan.

"I don't know what to say," DeKorte told them.

"It's because of the way you taught us to worship that all of us here are prospering," Wilburn said. "This car is a small enough percentage, I can tell you that."

"I don't know what to say," he repeated.

"We're the ones who should be making the speeches," Wilburn said.

A strange litany sounded in DeKorte's mind.

The missions fund had been cut less than a year earlier.

"Keep more of the money here among us," someone had said. "Concentrate on the flock here, instead of strangers thousands of miles away." Oh, Lord, he had asked himself more than once since then, did I try hard enough to stop it? Did I want to? Mary and I were going to go shopping for a new car, he remembered. But nothing this luxurious....

He hesitated a moment, then climbed in and turned on the ignition. There was a burst of applause from the crowd surrounding the sedan.

"That's power!" Wilburn exclaimed. "Have fun with it!"

Have fun?

He put his foot on the accelerator. The car responded instantly.

Power, he mused. *We measure power these days by the horses under our car hoods. What about the power and glory of Jesus Christ?*

He drove off, waving to the group. The smell of leather was strong. He examined the dashboard...a stereo cassette unit, six speaker premium sound system, cruise control, electric windows. Ordinarily he would have been exultant, and touched, and—

Patrick's pain-filled eyes stared up at him, life quickly flowing from them. They remained open after death. The boy's grip froze on his wrist; the fingers had to be pried off.

Gone!

The word rang with awful finality. Patrick somehow submerged beneath and washed away on the currents of positive thinking.

But there was another image competing with that one, an image of a middle-aged couple waving farewell to a sad-eyed group gathered before a thatch-roofed hut in a remote mountain village. A couple called home due to lack of funds.

In that moment the leather and the stereo and all the rest seemed more a collective accusation than a gift. He shivered then, gripped by a chill no earthly warmth could reach.

* * *

The demons had taken a break and would gather together later for another phase of the attack.

One of them, a witch from the Santaria district of a major American city, noticed that another witch, from Mexico City, was huddled in a corner, shivering.

"What ails you, my sister in evil?" the Santarian inquired.

"I know we should rejoice as we serve the Master," the other told her, "but I've seen it happen elsewhere, especially in Europe during the Dark Ages, and I know what is coming."

"And how is that so?"

"It starts with hooking them in a form of religion that seems to fulfill all the requirements of that which is being counterfeited, but which leads them only to destruction."

"Yes?"

"But what is happening in that little town is a special stroke of planning. They have become lovers of materialism rather than of God, and they don't even realize what has taken place."

"Wonderful, isn't it!"

"Oh, yes, I agree, but sad in a way. Sad to think that the man in whom they placed so much trust is actually a blind man himself and of no use to them in their own blindness. What if we are ultimately like they and—"

"Such a terrible thought! Why are you acting like this? You should be thrilled, and not allow yourself to harbor these defeatist thoughts."

"Yes, but I know what is going to happen because I've seen it before. And in the end we are the ones who will—"

"Will what?"

"Nothing . . . nothing at all."

* * *

7

A standing-room-only crowd jammed the auditorium at Valley Falls High School. The sign over the stage proclaimed "12th Annual Valley Falls Teen Songfest."

Young people came from all over the county for this popular annual event, some to compete, others just to watch and listen. Many adults enjoyed the entertainment also, among them Paul DeKorte and Doug Rogers. Both had attended most of the songfests through the years.

"I wonder, after all these years, if anybody has gone on from here to the big time," said DeKorte.

"You're forgetting Elvis!" Rogers said with astonishment.

"Elvis? Are you serious? I never heard that."

"You didn't? Why Elvis Molinari did a hit record a few years ago!"

DeKorte realized that he had just been fooled again by his old friend. This wasn't the first time; he had lost count over the years.

"How many do I owe you, Doug?" he asked.

"Sorry. I left my pocket calculator back at the office!"

"Yeah, yeah," grunted DeKorte and returned his attention to the stage.

The next scheduled act was due, now that a brief intermission was over. DeKorte wasn't a fan of rock music, though he didn't hold the view that all of it was satanic by design. But he was in total agreement with the critics of heavy metal and punk rock, not just because of the overtly erotic beat but because of the lyrics, with their incitations to lust, violence, and devil worship.

Jami Arlen was the next performer. She was a senior who had appeared at previous songfests and had played the lead in several of the high school musicals.

A couple moments into the song, however, it became evident that something was wrong.

"She must be out of practice," Rogers said.

"Well," DeKorte said, leaning close to his friend's ear, "there is some mention in the Bible about making a joyful noise!"

Rogers wasn't smiling. "Look at her left hand, Paul," he whispered.

The girl was holding the microphone in her right hand; the fingers of her left were clenched into a fist. And sticking up just over the edge of her thumb was the tiny head of a wood carving.

Someone behind DeKorte whispered, "What the dickens is wrong with that girl? She's better than that!"

Finally she finished, and the audience clapped politely, without enthusiasm. Jami hesitated a moment and then, knowing she hadn't done well, made an obscene gesture with her finger. A murmur swept through the adults and teenagers as she turned and walked off the stage.

"Another of those carvings," said Rogers. The two men looked into each other's eyes with puzzlement and concern.

Scott, Wayne, and Mark, dressed in the black leather garb they seemed to wear constantly now, came on stage next and began a dirge-like rock number. Though difficult to understand at times, it soon became evident that the lyrics were all about satanic seduction and masturbation.

"And when he comes on the wings of night," Scott sang, "and you fall before him, his blood-stained hands move over every inch of—"

Abruptly the sound system went dead, and in a second or two the school principal, Clement Albertson, hurried out from backstage.

"Ladies and gentlemen, I'm sorry," he announced, "but we seem to be having some electrical problems."

"You lying creep!" Scott threw his guitar to one side and yelled at the principal. Even minus amplification, Scott's voice could be heard by everyone in the auditorium. "You did that on purpose, and you know it!"

Albertson tried to ignore the boy, but Scott grabbed his shoulder. "Man, I'm talkin' to you!"

Albertson, a huge man who could handle himself in any situation, whirled around and grabbed Scott under the armpits and hoisted him several inches off the ground.

"You got that right," he said, his nose touching Scott's. "I'm a man, a married man. And I know a lot more about honest, healthy God-ordained sex than you could ever imagine. And I don't want my kids or anybody else's listening to your sick, perverted garbage."

Suddenly Albertson let go and the teenager fell flat on the stage. He got to his feet, but didn't approach the man again. Though Scott was exceptionally muscular, even he would have found the 6'4" ex-football hero a rough opponent.

The three boys gathered up their equipment and stalked off the stage. As Scott swung a side door open, he smashed his fist through the glass insert, sending shards flying out in several directions.

Albertson faced the audience once more.

"Sadly, these boys are like so many young people today," he said, "and that is why those among us who believe in the efficacious nature of prayer must come before God daily and ask for His guidance. Believe me when I say that otherwise there will be Hell to pay—and that is not a figure of speech!"

Rogers leaned over to DeKorte.

"I bet the ACLU gets on the horn about this," he whispered, chuckling.

Lance Setterman came on next, the high school's handsome, dark-haired, 6′7″ basketball star. The mood changed abruptly as he sang a moving rendition of "My Tribute: To God Be the Glory."

Later, as the crowd filed out, Clement Albertson motioned DeKorte to one side. "Can you come to my office, pastor?" he asked. "I mean, do you have the time?"

"Sure."

"I'll walk home, Paul," Rogers said. "These old legs need the exercise."

"Thanks," DeKorte told him. "I'll call you later."

"God bless you for showing some guts," Rogers said to Albertson, then grinned sheepishly as he realized what he had said. It had been a long, long time since he had invoked the Lord's name in that way.

8

"It chills my blood," Albertson said. "This generation is being raised on a diet that will destroy it." He held up a loose-leaf notebook. "I keep in contact with some other principals from around the country; we FAX these reports to one another. And what I'm hearing is monstrous."

DeKorte shifted uncomfortably in his chair. "Tied in with Scott's behavior tonight?" he asked, already suspecting the answer.

"Precisely."

"Any real connection you can validate?"

"In a word?" said Albertson. "Yes. Violence."

He was pacing the floor in agitation. "If it's not gangs, it's sexual violence. Frequently a combination of the two. And there is what we might call implied violence that comes in verbal outbursts, like delighting in obscene words thrown in the faces of teachers and parents—or the nearest authority figure. And then there is that music."

"Like we heard tonight?"

"Indeed. But as much as I hated their lyrics, I must admit that those were fairly mild—"

"Mild?"

"Mild compared to heavy metal weirdos like Iron Maiden and others. The problem is that the boys may well graduate, if I can use that word, to the more violent manifestations of this syndrome."

"Is it true that rape is sometimes glorified in those rock lyrics?" DeKorte asked.

"Absolutely," Albertson confirmed. "And more than occasionally, I should add. The world of heavy metal music and videos is rampant with conflicting signals. One suggests that the way to prove your masculinity is to overpower a girl by raping her. Another says there is nothing wrong with homosexual or bisexual behavior. But that's not all. Sadomasochism is extolled, along with bestiality and other depraved acts. It's a whole catalogue of antisocial behavior or, to use your terminology, sin."

"You're a Christian. It should be your terminology as well."

51

"It is. But right now I'm speaking as a high school principal. For us, it's antisocial behavior!" Albertson was visibly shaking with anger now.

"I'm concerned too, Clement. I don't like what I saw here tonight—with Jami or with Scott. Something's terribly wrong in Valley Falls."

"Something's terribly wrong all over," said Albertson, who had gotten his anger under control and was speaking more calmly. "Believe it or not, the public school system is one of the channels for the destructive patterns emerging. When our forefathers established schools in this country, the teachers considered their calling to be a sacred trust for them to guide the minds of the young. They realized that those formative years would dictate the overall direction of a lifetime. But today we are so concerned with the civil rights of our young people that we forget it is better to trample on a few of those rights from time to time in order to preserve another right: their right of survival with as few psychological and spiritual scars as possible."

Albertson paused again.

"You know, pastor, when prayer was thrown out of public schools, Satan moved right in to fill the void, not only with the students but the teachers. You'd be surprised at how many practicing members of the Church of Satan are in key positions in our educational system in this country.

"Furthermore, and not unrelated, if a gay teacher wanted to apply here, and he was qualified, I might be forced to accept that individual. While he might not do anything overtly to campaign for homosexuality, his very presence would be de facto tolerance of that lifestyle. If that weren't the case, then he would never be hired."

"The signals we send to the young!" DeKorte said.

"And the price we have to pay!" said Albertson. "You know, the people we put on pedestals today frequently have the morals of alley cats. And what does that say to our young people, who look to them as role models? The rock stars, the Brat Pack of actors and actresses, and others I could mention—such individuals are what young people are confronted with these days due to the media hype. Which amounts to feeding them spiritual, ethical, and moral junk food! It is little wonder that their sin natures give in to whatever Satan throws their way."

"You're suggesting that the near-beatification, I almost said, deification, of such people is encouraged by Satan?"

"I believe it absolutely. More and more, I suspect that sort of thing is part of a secret agenda. I—" The principal stopped himself.

"Forgive me for spouting off like this, but it's hard to react otherwise in the midst of the rising sea of corruption I see at every level of society. I remember studying a book written by the late Peter Marshall's son in which he spoke of the Pilgrim and Puritan dream of a new Israel here in America."

"Now we have something that resembles Sodom and Gomorrah instead," DeKorte added, with equal conviction.

"We do, we do, even though Valley Falls has been more fortunate than most." Albertson looked straight at DeKorte. "Until recently."

"What do you mean?"

The principal reached into a desk drawer.

"Look at this," he said, handing DeKorte snapshots of the mutilated bodies of cats and dogs.

"Where did you get these?" DeKorte asked.

"I found them on the floor in one of the classrooms. One of the students apparently dropped them."

"Do you have any idea which student?"

"Taken with certain other evidence, I suspect it was Scott Pennio."

DeKorte was stunned.

"You think Scott committed this—this carnage?"

"I have no way of knowing. But it fits."

"Fits?"

"Yes. It fits the profile of a kid getting heavily into Satan worship."

"But Scott is a member of my congregation, as you are. How—?"

"How could he have failed to listen to you?"

"Yes."

Albertson hesitated.

"Tell me what you're thinking," DeKorte urged him. "Don't be afraid of hurting my feelings, if that's what's making you hold back."

"Paul, listen to me. When was the last time you preached anything about Satan? Your typical sermon is about gifts from heaven, not about our enemy from Hell. That's why I've been attending a Bible study and prayer meeting for the past few weeks at Elk's Crossing."

DeKorte was startled. He hadn't even noticed that Albertson had been missing from the midweek service. "Elk's Crossing? That's a half hour away."

"It is. But I needed the spiritual food. You've been starving us."

For a second or two, DeKorte was on the verge of an angry

outburst. Then he sank back in his chair. Clement Albertson would never say these things if he wasn't seriously concerned. And there could be no doubt that he was expressing his true feelings only with the greatest reluctance.

"Think back, Paul. Open your eyes... your ears... before it's too late."

Before it's too late. DeKorte felt a flash of something almost palpable at the base of his spine, cold and—

"Clement, are you implying that Scott is not the only one?"

"Yes. I believe Mark Jacobson and Wayne Mulrooney are involved, too, and I strongly suspect that they are trying to proselytize other kids... and that they are proving to.be more than a little successful."

"But what leads you to believe this? You must have some evidence—other than just that song today, which, let's face it, could have been done for kicks—to make you feel this strongly about it."

"Bits and pieces of conversation that I overhear as I pass through the corridors. Talk about meetings at midnight... the need for more pets—"

"All that could be quite innocent," DeKorte interrupted.

"Plus talk of tarot cards, Ouija boards, and seances calling up certain spirits."

"But you can't condemn kids for idle conversation. You and I both know that their words are often exaggerated for effect, usually to impress each other."

It was apparent that Albertson was becoming more and more aggravated.

"Paul, Paul, you still don't see what could be happening, do you?"

"Nothing you've picked up is conclusive, Clement. Nothing—"

"Perhaps not," Albertson interrupted this time, "but what does it say about the psychological health of kids when you overhear them spouting off about actually having brought back the spirit of—" He stopped himself again.

"What?" DeKorte said.

"Maybe I shouldn't get into it now," said the principal.

"Tell me, Clement. If it's something I should be aware—"

"All right, all right. It's Mary. Scott claimed to have brought back an apparition that identified itself as your wife's spirit!"

DeKorte sat back, speechless, as though someone had punched him in the stomach. Finally he said, "But Mary was a believer. She's in heaven now. Not all the powers of all the demons can call her back from there."

"I quite agree, Paul. So there can be only two explanations. Either Scott's boast is a cruel but careless lie, or Satan is capable of ordering his demons to impersonate someone and using that guise to entrap the unwary."

"Clement, your knowledge seems to surpass my own," DeKorte said, his face reddening with embarrassment. "Yet I should be the one wise on such matters."

"I was a teacher before I was a principal. I've been in other school systems. You learn a lot, Paul. It's like a cop pounding a beat. After a decade, there isn't much you haven't seen. And I've seen this sort of thing creeping up on our young people for a long time. It hasn't been overnight. There were problems along these lines in the 1970s. I remember a book called *Strange Things Are Happening*. The title tells the story. Satan has always been involved here on Planet Earth—you know that. The difference, today, is the pervasiveness of what is going on."

"Well, I must admit I have been concerned about some of the things I've observed lately, especially after Mary's death and Patrick's, both violent and unexplained. But I certainly never even considered something as dreadful as this."

"There's one more thing, Paul," said Albertson, while taking a sheet of paper from the center drawer of his desk. "Read this."

As DeKorte read the paper, his free hand clenched into a fist so tight that his nails cut into the palm.

"Where did you find this?"

"A student gave it to me. He said he got it from Scott right after Patrick died."

"Scott's mother came to me, concerned because she had found some bloody sheets in his room," DeKorte told the principal. "But almost immediately after that Patrick died, and in all that's happened I never did follow through. Clement, I don't know what to say. I just never dreamed...."

Albertson came over and laid his hand on DeKorte's forearm.

"It's not too late. Sometimes we get so close to everything that we miss the real truth going on around us."

DeKorte nodded almost absentmindedly, then turned toward the door. Albertson held it for him as he said, "My brother in Christ, is it possible that you need a time of separation, time to examine yourself and those who look to you for guidance?"

Once again DeKorte nodded, but his mind seemed miles away. In truth he was remembering the words he had read on that sheet of paper. They were lodged in his mind, no matter how much he wished they weren't there at all.

In nomine dei Satanas, Lucifer excelsi! In the name of our great God, Satan, Lucifer, the ruler of the mystic pits. I command thee, O Prince of Darkness, to come forth out of the black realms, with your hordes at your side. Come forth, in the name of all that is unholy. Open the doors of hell! Now!

9

Mark was quiet as he got into the car with Scott and Wayne. Scott had insisted that tonight was the night to try a seance. "That's all," he said. Just a seance, with their spirits joined as one as they reached out to the beyond.

Mark didn't like to admit it to himself, but he knew deep down that Scott was becoming more and more the center of his world and the dictator of his actions. Anything that Scott wanted, Scott got. *Anything....*

He shuddered as he remembered the first time they had killed an animal and dedicated it to Satan... *the awful cries, the blood... and the rest....* At first all three recoiled as they realized what they had done. None of them could sleep soundly for days afterward.

Later it was sex. *But that's only normal,* Mark consoled himself. *Losing your virginity is a rite of passage in this day and age.* After all, his hormones were as active as any teenager's, and he couldn't do much about that biological reality. And yet, over the last few months, it had been different, he recalled, the last tattered pieces of shame gripping him. Different from anything anybody else at school could possibly have imagined, going beyond the purely biological and entering another realm altogether.

And now tonight, somehow, it's going to be the ultimate.

Mark rubbed his arm, shivering.

Not a woman this time.

* * *

At the cemetery, the three sat down in the oldest part of the burial ground and joined hands.

It began almost immediately. The sensation of evil. Like before but more intense. A cold breeze wove through the ancient headstones, rustling leaves on nearby trees. They could hear movement. Movement under the ground.

"Scott!" Wayne spoke up. "I don't think we—"

And then the hands started to appear, reaching up from the

earth. Grotesque skeleton hands. Dry white bones reaching up all around them.

They closed their eyes, thinking that when they looked again it would all be an hallucination.

Then they heard something in the air. Fluttering, buzzing noises.

They opened their eyes.

The hands had opened, releasing dozens of winged creatures into the air.

"Let's run," Wayne begged. "Let's—"

Suddenly they were surrounded, as though they had stepped into the midst of a nest of hornets. Claws tore at their clothes, ripping them to shreds.

"I can't breathe!" Mark screamed. The creatures seemed to be ramming up into his nose, through his sinuses and into his brain.

Scott jumped to his feet, trying to break free. He stumbled forward to what looked like an open grave. Saw the creature resting there, its torso draped in shimmering mist, its barely visible head a demonic monstrosity with a long beak and pointed teeth poking out from behind blood-red lips. The eyelids, edged with black lashes, shot open.

Those awful lips moved. A serpentine tongue darted out, then back in, then out.

Scott, I will have you, you know, as I have had all the damned over the ages. Every part of you . . . your mind, your body, your immortal spirit. But for now it is your body I want.

Abruptly the dark shapes flew to nearby branches and sat there, as though obeying some master command, ready to witness what was about to take place.

Clothes shredded, skin torn and bleeding, the three boys stood immobilized as the creature from hell seduced them.

10

The day after his meeting with Clement Albertson, DeKorte called Scott's mother and asked her how the boy was doing.

"His behavior seems to be changing more and more rapidly." Mrs. Pennio's voice sounded strained, almost hoarse. "And his vocabulary . . . strange words seem to be creeping into it."

"Can you give me any examples?" he asked, the memory of the songfest and the paper Albertson had showed him vivid in his mind.

"Yes. I wrote them down. Words like *incubus* and *rakshasa and ankh*." She spelled each out for him.

"Strange indeed," he mused.

"There's more, pastor. *Mandragoras* and *harmaxobii* and *azael*. He's spoken some, written the others down on little scraps of paper. I may have some of the spellings wrong. What does it all mean?"

"I don't know, Rose. But this, coupled with some other things I've come across, makes me very concerned for Scott. Can I stop by this afternoon after school and talk with him?"

"Oh, please, I wish you would. Joe and I are really worried."

DeKorte had recognized only one of the words, incubus. He turned first to the dictionary. *Incubus: a spirit that has intercourse with women while they are sleeping*.

He searched through the books in his study for clues to the other terms, but found nothing. Finally he decided to leaf through a Bible encyclopedia. One particular paragraph stopped him.

Lucifer is a well-known name for Satan as he existed in Heaven before he was cast out, along with such fallen angels—referred to in legend—as Buriel, Itzah, Azael and—

Azael!

* * *

Walking up the pathway to the front door of the Pennio home, DeKorte pulled his overcoat more closely about him. *Curious*, he thought as he rang the doorbell. *It's quite warm today. Why am I suddenly so cold?*

He could hear footsteps inside, and Scott opened the door.

"Reverend DeKorte!" he said, seeming surprised. "Did you want to see my mother?"

"No, Scott," he said. "Actually, I wondered if I could talk with you for a few minutes."

"Sure. I guess. Come on in," the boy said and led him into the living room. He looked up, not quite meeting the minister's eyes. "I guess you were at the songfest, huh?"

DeKorte nodded.

"I guess you were shocked?"

"That's one word for it. Shocked. Surprised. Saddened. Those lyrics were pretty strong, Scott."

"They don't seem strange to us. We listen to that stuff all the time. It's just our music of today. You had yours. We have ours."

"It's a little more than that, isn't it? I mean there is rock music that doesn't go to that extreme."

Scott frowned. "Bubble gum rock...kid's stuff! Besides, this music is honest. It expresses the way I feel sometimes. Isn't that what you're always preaching about?"

"About feelings?"

"Yeah. About being honest, just letting go...pouring our souls out."

"In prayer, yes, Scott. Not in the sorts of things you were glorifying."

Scott stood and started pacing. "Oh, you mean feelings are okay as long as you approve them, is that it?"

"What I approve really has nothing to do with it. It's what God thinks that matters."

"God gave us those desires in the first place, didn't He?"

"You mean sexual desires?"

"Yes. Sex!"

"He gave us those desires to be used in marriage."

"Nobody buys that anymore." Scott, who had his back turned to DeKorte, spun around and faced him now. "We're tired!" he said.

"Tired of what?" DeKorte asked, desperately trying to fathom the teenager's motives.

"Being forced to live according to someone else's standards."

"But they're God's standards, Scott."

"By whose definition? You call it sinful for a guy and a girl to have sex even if both of them are in love—and yet it's okay if you appeal to people to fatten their bank accounts by beating a trail to the banks of Heaven!"

DeKorte was taken aback. "But, Scott, even were that the case—and I don't grant that it is—you were singing about something quite different...perverted—"

"Like mass orgies you mean, right under the sanctified noses of our parents? I bet that really grossed you out. God didn't mind much apparently. I'm still here. So are Wayne and Mark. He didn't strike us dead."

"Scott, what's happened to you? Where is the boy I taught in Sunday school—"

"Chill out, man. Like I said before, that's kid's stuff. Besides, you're all a bunch of hypocrites. Week after week you preach Christianity by cash register...and yet let me suggest some good old sex and you're all offended." Scott threw his head back. DeKorte couldn't tell if he was fighting off anger or tears. "Besides, you never really listen to us. You've all got your canned, stale answers from a book written 2000 years ago."

A slight smile curled his lips. "Not to worry, though," he said. "We've found someone who really does listen to us, someone who cares a lot!"

"Scott, you're not naive. Surely you realize that drug dealers pretend to—"

Scott burst into hysterical laughter. "True to form," he said. "Stupid as ever."

He walked to the front door, opened it, and stood there, the laughter replaced by a frown.

"Which of us offends God more, preacher? Could it be you, with your prosperity mumbo jumbo, your appeals to greed? Because that's what it is, you know. You make greed sound good, like it's another of those gifts from God you keep talking about. Did you ever think that maybe God hates what you're doing?"

DeKorte left without further comment. He desperately needed to get through to Scott, but at the moment he was at a loss. Outside, he sat quietly in his car, not turning the ignition.

Which of us offends God more? It was a devastating moment for him, further eroding the image he had of himself as a caring individual who was pleasing the Lord as much as he possibly could, someone who was not reluctant to expose sin when he saw it.

Which of us offends God more?

As he started the car and drove home, he wondered if God was already giving him an answer that would make it very hard for him to ever view himself in quite the same way again.

11

Scott wished he had never let the minister in the house.

I could have blurted out everything to him. I could have told him what happened at the cemetery. I—

So sore.

He took off his clothes and stood before the full-length mirror in his bedroom.

Bruises.

On his chest. His thighs.

Scratches down his back and on his buttocks.

It got up out of the cold earth and violated us.

He turned away and quickly put his clothes back on.

Hours later, long after he had gone to bed and fallen asleep, the nightmare came. So stark and detailed he could almost believe it was real and not some nighttime fantasy—real and vivid and ready to claim him forever.

The walls of his room fell away, and he tumbled down the center of a tornado-like maelstrom of flame. He could feel the heat, intense enough to blister his flesh but somehow there was only discomfort, not outright pain. He heard voices shouting obscenities, taunting him. Faces among the flames wavered in and out of sight, distorted, tormented.

Suddenly all that ceased.

He was sitting in the middle of a vast plain of white sand beneath a blood-red sky. Objects in the distance caught his eye, and he started to walk toward them. The sand kicked up a bit as he went, and he noticed, within the pinpoint grains, larger pieces.

He picked up a handful and let it drift through his fingers.

Pieces of bone?

He grabbed another handful. Looked closely.

Tiny hands . . . feet . . . skulls no larger than the nail on his little finger. The "sand" was made up of tiny bodies ground to powder, a few pieces still partially intact.

In the distance the objects beckoned to him. They were crying now, the sound carried along by vagrant breezes from nowhere.

Mother, help me!

The words were clear.

It hurts. It hurts. Stop it, please!

Separate piles of stones stretched out in every direction, each with a large, flat, altar-like stone on top. A shape lying on each one. Some quite still. Others squirming, crying....

He was only yards away now. He could identify the forms.

Babies! So many he could never count them all. And beside each a long curved knife.

Get closer. What is this?

Yes, it was a baby, tiny and trusting. Her eyes met his, and he saw the hint of a smile. Huge blue eyes, rosy cheeks, clear skin, and—

A giant shadow swept across the plain toward him, its outline terrifying, with the suggestion of wings. Like the thing in the cemetery. He felt the same chill radiate through his body, causing his nerve ends to tremble.

"You won't have me!" he screamed. "And you won't take any of these helpless ones."

Suddenly a booming voice drowned out his own. "From their mothers' wombs they have joined my grisly parade."

The shadow seemed to darken all of that place.

"Do the deed!"

"I will not kill a baby!" he cried. "There is no way you can make me do it."

"Yes, my rebellious one, yes, I can. And many more besides. Look around you. If I were to command you to do so, you would rip the heart out of each and every one."

Scott spun around.

Many more altars appeared from nowhere, with squirming shapes on top ... thousands now ... surrounding him as he stood in their midst ... the sounds of their cries filling the air.

"You will take that knife in front of you," the voice ordered, "and you will cut out one or a thousand hearts at my command."

Scott grabbed the knife and threw it on the sand at his feet, a defiant expression on his face. "I've done some wrong things lately," he said, "but I won't add this to the list."

"In the end," the voice continued, "you will do what I say because you want what only I can give."

... you want what only I can give.

Scott wanted to fling the words back at the shadow, wanted to run from that place and never again unlock the door to it. But suddenly his head started pounding, like the worst migraine imaginable but more intense.

He closed his eyes briefly. When he opened them again, the babies and the altars had disappeared. In their place he saw his parents, standing directly ahead of him.

"You want power over them," said the voice. "You never again want them to dominate you. You want freedom!"

And then a blond-haired teenage boy materialized in front of him, tall, quite handsome, a look of innocence on his face.

"You want someone like him by your side. The girls you've known aren't what you really desire deep down inside you, Scott."

"No!" Scott screamed as the boy beckoned for him to come closer.

"Perhaps he's too virginal, Scott. Perhaps you want someone more experienced, more—"

Scott turned away, refusing to look any longer. Turned away just as the innocent one became a young man dressed in black leather, with chains for a belt, and a look of anticipation.

"You can't make me think such things. You—"

The voice cut through coldly.

"I didn't take them from my mind, but yours, Scott. They are born out of your frustrations, ripped from your dreams of longing— that part of you that cries out for their embrace."

Another apparition appeared. Jesus at Calvary, hanging from the cross.

"You want to be the one plunging the sword into His side, to be free from the bondage of His laws and His morality."

The words cut through the facade Scott had erected over the years: the good churchgoing youngster, eager to obey the adults in his life, eager to assimilate as his own their preconceptions about how to conduct himself, what career to choose, what church to attend, all the rest. They choked him, stifled him. He felt an accelerating restlessness, a need to get away, to throw everything overboard.

Scott heard laughter.

"I hit close to home that time, didn't I?"

The boy found no words of protest, only a growing sense of transparency. It was almost as if the shadow knew what he was thinking.

"The sword, it is at your feet. Pick it up. Take it there to the cross. Wound this man called Jesus."

Scott shook his fist at the shadow. "I will not! I believe—"

"Yes, you do believe. In the cocoon-like security of an opportunistic faith. But you have little time for the Giver."

"Oh, God, help me, it's not true, it's—" Scott fell to his knees, tears pouring from his eyes and down his cheeks.

"Does God respond? Does God help you? Does He come at your bidding?"

Scott looked up, his eyes wide with anger. "You cannot do this. God will protect me."

That laughter again, so powerful that it shook the ground beneath him. "How quickly you invoke the Almighty's name when it suits the moment. But just as easily you shove Him to some back compartment of your life when any immediate crisis passes."

The ground shook once more.

"I shall be *more* demanding, Scott Pennio, you can be assured of that. Besides, there is no reason to grovel in the dust for His mercy. You see, that mercy has stopped, my young slave. I already have you, Scott Pennio. You are mine. You became mine that night in the cemetery. You were ripe fruit, and I plucked you with the greatest ease."

His mother and his father were running toward him now, their chests drenched in blood. Just a few yards from him, they fell to the sand, dragging themselves toward him, inch by inch, their words reverberating inside his head.

"Why have you done this to us?" they cried. "Why have you—?" And then they fell forward on their faces, their blood slowly seeping into the sand around them.

"Your first human sacrifices, Scott!"

"N—o—!" Scott scrambled to his feet. "Patrick was the first," he screamed.

Then realizing what he had just admitted, he started running.

The voice pursued him. "How right you are! You know the truth. There is already blood on your hands. Next time it will be so much easier!"

A leathery fluttering of giant wings hovered above him. There was no escape from his pursuer.

And suddenly he saw what had caused that shadow, saw the source of that voice with its demanding tone, saw a face so ghastly that his sanity exploded like shrapnel, saw the hypnotic eyes peering into his own; invading every aspect of his being.

There was no longer anything he could do, his resistance worn down, his determination lying in waste before him.

And so he fell to his knees, muttering a single word,

"Master."

12

Paul DeKorte was in his study at church when a single knock at the door interrupted his thoughts. He had been planning a sermon on the subject of the family, realizing with some irony that he had never been able to raise one of his own. He counseled with many parents, but Mary's death had removed that dimension from his life, at least for the foreseeable future. He wondered if he would ever find someone who could take her place; the way she had died, nearly as much as her life itself, had seared her image in his mind in such a way that—

"Come in," he said, shaking his head slightly in order to clear it.

"Hello, Reverend DeKorte."

He looked up.

Scott.

I don't want to be here. I wish I could just drop it all now. And I don't want to go on afterward and do the rest of what the Master has demanded. If only I can break through his control and tell Pastor DeKorte, surely he could help me, surely—

"Are you feeling better now?" DeKorte said, trying to be cheerful, but wary at the same time.

A smile crossed the teenager's face then.

"Yes," he replied, "a lot better, thank you."

Don't be flippant. Try to—

DeKorte sensed something about Scott—something about the way he stood, the slight tilt of his head—which somehow bordered on arrogance.

"Sit down, please," DeKorte said. "I'm sorry I lost my temper earlier. Let's talk it out now."

"I want to stand right where I am, *capeice?*" Scott told him, a sneer replacing the smile, the words spit out in a contemptuous manner.

DeKorte studied the boy he had watched grow from rough-and-tumble youngster to handsome teenager. What was going on behind that too-handsome face? He was uneasy. Today there was something different about him—almost . . . evil?

66

"Something's troubling you, Scott. I don't know what it is, but I want to help you. I know you're at a difficult age . . . I've been there myself—"

"Cut the crap, preacher." Scott spat on the floor. "That's what I think of you and all you stand for!"

Dear God, I'm doing it all . . . following the Master as though I am a puppet tied to his strings and have no will of my own. . . .

"Scott! What's gotten into you? I've never seen you like this before."

"What's gotten into me?"

A note of hysteria crept into the boy's laughter.

"You'd be surprised," he added.

Then Scott put his palms on DeKorte's desk and leaned across it.

"You've never seen me like this, you say. That's the problem . . . you've never seen me . . . period. Just like my folks and the other stupid adults in this town. Well, you're all gonna see me now. This town's gonna realize how important this kid is."

I can't break loose. Why didn't anyone really notice what was happening to me, to the others, and do something about it? They must have seen some clues! And now, beyond just this town, in so many other places, it will be repeated a hundred—

DeKorte noticed a red splotch on the teenager's left hand.

"Scott, what happened to your hand? That looks like—"

"Blood? You bet it is. Would you like to know whose?"

Perspiration started to form on DeKorte's back and beneath his arms, causing his shirt to stick to his skin. What should he do? Call the boy's parents? Something was terribly wrong here.

Scott had turned his attention to the bookcase on his right.

"Let's see now, you have a lot of stuff here about miracles and junk like that."

"Yes, I—"

"Reverend-sir, what do you think about people being raised from the dead?" Scott interrupted. "I mean, right out of their caskets?"

"Well, certainly in Scripture there were some miracles like that. Lazarus, for instance, and—"

"Well, that's just great to hear, sir, because it's going to happen real soon, right here in this stupid town."

Scott took a book off the shelf.

"What do we have here? *The Psychology of Being a Minister.* Sounds real hot!"

He picked out another one.

"*Freud and the Human Spirit.* How great!"

He turned to a third book.

"*Possibility Thinking—The Road to Personal Enrichment.*"

Without warning he tossed that book across the study, knocking some framed diplomas off the wall.

"None of this crap is going to help, you know. It's all useless motivational mumbo jumbo."

He spun around, facing DeKorte.

"What kind of diet have you been forcing down our throats, Reverend-sir?" he said, spitting out the words. "You should have been giving us what we craved, something for our souls, and yet you filled us with spiritual junk food."

He reached into the inner pocket of the leather jacket he was wearing.

If he only knew what I am hiding in here. She was already dead when I—

"And now look at what you've made us become!"

A knife. He jammed it down through the wood top of DeKorte's desk.

"If you'll look at the blade, you'll see that it's got splotches of red on it, the red blood of my parents, you sanctimonious hypocrite."

I slaughtered them both. I didn't really want to but the Master demanded it.

DeKorte jumped to his feet.

"Scott, if I had known you were—"

"If you had known I would become a murderer, you would have gotten in there sooner and tried to help me solve my problems, is that it?"

In a motion so swift that DeKorte was unprepared, Scott leaned across the desk and grabbed him by the neck with one hand while, with the other, he got the knife loose and held the blade against the minister's neck.

I'm supposed to kill this misguided but decent man. I'm supposed to let the life dribble away while I watch and laugh!

"We were shriveling up inside, you blind idiot! Yet all you seemed concerned with was convincing everyone they could have a fat bank account if they followed some sort of divine plan for material riches."

"Please, Scott, I beg you . . . whatever's wrong, it's not too late."

No! With any strength, any will I have left, I will NOT do this awful thing. I—

Scott contemptuously pushed DeKorte back into his chair.

"You haven't been listening, fool! Mom and Dad are lying in a puddle of blood, and yet you cling to the positive thinking garbage that has been strangling us for a long time."

He's so blind, overwhelmed by his own false doctrine!

"Is it drugs, Scott?" DeKorte said, his voice hoarse.

"Isn't that the standard accusation? Can't you think of something a little more original to say?"

Scott's eyes widened, saliva dripping out of the corners of his mouth.

"What I'm into is much more, ah, meaningful, yeah, that's the word. My fantasies run circles around anything you've had to say for a long time. And I'm going to make every one of them come true!"

He turned and walked toward the door, then stopped and smiled at DeKorte.

"I almost forgot to tell you. That wife of yours was nothing more than a tramp, yeah, a sexy tramp. Believe me, I'm talking firsthand experience here!"

DeKorte got to his feet and ran after Scott, but the teenager was much faster, heading down one of the sanctuary's aisles and out through a side exit.

Please, sir, please, please, please, forgive me. I have turned over control to someone else, someone so terrible—

For an instant Scott, his face a mask of torment, turned and glanced at the minister, and then was gone.

By the time DeKorte made it outside, the boy had jumped into a waiting car and was yelling an obscenity at him as he threw something out into the gutter.

Oh, Mom, dear, dear Mom, sweet and loving....

DeKorte saw what it was and blanched.

The wedding ring Dad scrimped and saved for so long to be able to afford because he loved her so much ... look at that ... on Mom's finger as always.

To enlist the help of Satan and demons, a pact is often made with the powers of evil, which is a Satanic counterpart of dedication to God's Will. The subject consciously and willingly gives himself over to Satan and the various demonic agencies who will help him perform . . . supernatural feats. Ordinarily the body is cut and the compact with the devil is . . . [confirmed] . . . in one's own blood.

—Merrill F. Unger

13

It was an isolated spot, a spot that at times became a beacon for teenage lovers and an occasional drug transaction as well as, however incongruously, those of devout religious conviction who wanted to get away from the outside world into a haven that seemed perhaps like a low-rent Eden.

It was attractive, this place of a small waterfall that had been spilling over into the lake below for longer than there had been a town nearby named Valley Falls. The early settlers had stumbled upon its beguiling, understated beauty, set up camp, and, as it turned out, never left.

"Quiet here, isn't it?" Scott remarked, standing on the lakeshore.

"Yeah, real quiet," agreed Mark.

"Like a tomb," Wayne added.

"But that's the point," Scott shot back. "Isn't it?"

"I guess," said Wayne, his voice trailing off.

The point? No matter how much he tried to pretend otherwise, Wayne knew Scott was right. *Like a tomb. . . . He could imagine the odor of death already.*

"We're lucky there's no one else here," Mark said self-consciously.

Scott glanced up at the clear night sky.

"Look at the moon," he told them. "Full and beautiful and—"

And that it was, casting its silvery glow over the plunging waters and the jutting rocks and the night-blackened evergreens.

But also quite cold, a light devoid of life cast from a dead planet, romantic lyrics from old-fashioned songs notwithstanding.

"Like a movie scene," Scott whispered, getting high on the self-proscribed "perfection" of that moment.

Wayne walked a few feet to one side and sat down on a flat-topped rock. His hands were shaking. He hoped Scott didn't notice.

Scott did. "You're not going to turn chicken on us, are you?" he asked.

"Scott, we're taking the final step tonight. Do you expect me to treat it like a joke of some sort?"

"Not a joke, no, but it *is* supposed to be fun!"

Fun? They had ripped out the dog's heart while it was still alive, a blow to its head stunning it so that it could offer no defense. And they put that organ onto an altar and—

Wayne jumped up suddenly, agitated.

"You'll be dead by the time it's over, and you call that fun? Man, there's something wrong with you."

"Not dead, Wayne, you know that. Maybe this hunk of flesh called a body, yeah, but I'll still be very much alive afterward. Even Christ had to die in order to be resurrected."

Wayne looked at his friend with amazement.

"But you're no Christ, Scott. Is that what this is all about? Trying to imitate Him?"

Wayne's mind vibrated with something he recalled from a Sunday school lesson, about how Satan would attempt to counterfeit virtually everything that God did, even to a kind of unholy trinity involving himself, the Antichrist, and the fearsome Beast foretold in the Book of Revelation.

An unholy trinity. The truth ricocheted through his brain like a bullet. *There are three of us here. A trinity!*

"Is that so bad?" Scott responded sarcastically. "Aren't we supposed to be Christ-like?"

"You're crazy, man! Christ didn't murder himself!"

"But He allowed others to do it, didn't He?"

"That was part of God's plan, you know that."

Scott grabbed Wayne and shook him. "But now we have another plan, don't we? Besides, where is Christ now? I don't see Him. Do you?"

Scott pushed Wayne away and stomped about the area, mockingly conducting a search behind boulders and trees, savoring every second of his blasphemy.

"Where are You, Jesus?" he shouted. "I want You to show Yourself. Stop hiding behind the Bible, will You? You arose from Your tomb 2000 years ago. I need some pointers before I play that scene myself. What's it like, Jesus?"

He came back to his two friends. "See?" he said, smiling. "He doesn't really care. He lets us alone to do whatever we want."

I need some pointers before I play that scene myself. Chills grabbed Wayne's spine and held on. He wanted to run as far and as fast as he could. He—

Scott walked back to the edge of the water, stood quietly for a few seconds, his head bowed. Finally he swung around and faced them.

"It is time...now!" he declared. With that he took off his shirt and waded out into the lake.

"Follow me," he demanded.

Mark was unbuttoning his own shirt, ready to join Scott.

"You can't do it!" Wayne begged.

"You knew what we were going to do," Mark said. "Are you trying to back out?"

"I know, I know. When it was just talk, I guess it seemed easy, maybe even safe. Talk couldn't hurt us. But this—"

Just then the sound of Scott's voice interrupted them both. The lake was shallow for quite some distance, and he was standing as far out as he could, the water hitting just above his waist. He had taken out a knife from his jeans pocket.

"Come unto me and drink!" he demanded.

And with that he sliced the knife across his chest. There was no emotion on his face, not even the slightest hint of pain.

Wayne and Mark looked at Scott, then at one another.

"Don't you see?" Wayne said. "It's a perversion of—"

Mark hesitated only briefly.

"That doesn't matter, Wayne. I'm fed up with the whole scene back there in town. And it's not any better in other places, you know that! The politicians lie to us. The media twist things around. Our parents lecture us about drugs while they're guzzling their booze and tranquilizers. We have nothing and no one to trust anymore."

He placed a hand on Wayne's shoulders.

"Listen up, buddy," he said. "Kids like us have no one."

The words were coming in a torrent now.

"Maybe we've been betting on the wrong horse all this time, did that ever occur to you? This is a chance to turn it all around, do something different. Think of what we can link in with beginning right now!"

He jumped into the lake and started to wade toward Scott.

"Don't!" Wayne shouted. "Mark, don't!"

Too late.

In horror Wayne watched the rite taking place. After it was over, Mark turned and called, "Join us. He has more to go around."

With that, Wayne turned and ran as fast as he could, tripped, fell, and started to get up.

"Wayne! Help me! You gotta help me!" It was Mark's voice, terrified, breaking through the dark silence.

He hesitated. It could be a trick to get him back there. It—

A shrieking sound! Tearing through the night air like a thousand banshees from Hell itself.

Wayne ran back to the lake. His two friends were struggling furiously, and it was apparent that Scott was trying to drown Mark. Wayne waded frantically into the water.

Scott looked up as he approached, his face twisted, his mouth encrusted with blood, his eyes...

"Scott!" Wayne cried. "What are you doing? Stop!"

Wayne rushed him and caught him off guard, hitting him hard enough to make Scott stagger back and release his hold on Mark.

"He was...trying to...kill...me," Mark said, coughing up water.

"He's gone crazy!" Wayne yelled. "Let's get out—"

Suddenly Scott shot up from under the water in back of them. He knocked Mark to one side and grabbed Wayne's neck with both hands.

"No one stands in the way of the Master!" he screamed. "No one!"

Wayne was strong, but Scott was gripped by something stronger. His strength was overpowering.

"Your knife!" Wayne managed to choke out. "Use your knife!"

Mark reached into his pocket for his own knife, and once he had it hesitated for only a split second before plunging the blade into Scott's back. Again and again he stabbed, his hand slashing through the air even after Scott had fallen forward and sunk under the water.

"Enough, man!" Wayne grabbed his arm. "He must be dead. I mean, really dead."

Mark looked at him with an uncomprehending expression, then with overwhelming fear.

"We murdered him!"

"It was self-defense. He would have killed both of us."

"No one will believe that."

Scott's body floated to the surface just inches away from them, his head turned in their direction. There seemed to be something like a smile on his face.

"Let's get him out of here onto the shore."

"No!" Mark said. "Let's get ourselves out of here. Move!"

They hurried back to shore and ran to the car they had left parked on the dirt road leading to the spot. Soaking wet, bloody and shaking, they drove off, looking fearfully behind them from time to time, as though somehow Scott would rise from the water to pursue them....

Crickets chirped a steady chorus. An owl hooted mournfully. The birds were asleep for the night.

Everything was normal again at Hidden Lake. Quiet... peaceful....

Except for the laughter. Dead laughter. Colder than the moon's glow.

14

DeKorte called Sheriff Wilburn and told him what had happened. Wilburn arrived at the parsonage a few minutes later.

DeKorte leaned against the front entrance of the church, watching him. After putting a plastic bag with its grisly contents on the backseat of the patrol car, Wilburn approached the minister and the two of them stood on the steps, trying to deal with what had happened.

"A terrible year, this one," Wilburn said.

"The worst in memory," DeKorte agreed.

They looked out over the town square.

"Happy times there," Wilburn said.

"Yes, Mary and I used to sit on one of the benches and look up at the clear sky."

"And be thankful for clean air!"

"Yes. Not every place in this country can say that anymore."

Wilburn shook his head slowly and sadly a couple of times.

"What's wrong?" DeKorte asked.

"Dunno. Headaches lately."

"Been to Rogers?"

"Yeah, I have."

"What did he say?"

"Couldn't find a thing. Called it nerves or something."

"What do you think?"

Wilburn was silent.

"Is there something you're not telling me?" DeKorte asked.

There was a slight smile on the sheriff's face.

"Perceptive as always," he replied. "Paul, I've been hearing things lately."

"Things?"

"Yeah. People talking and yet no one else around. And my dreams...awful, awful dreams."

"Any ideas?"

"No. And my wife's been experiencing the same thing."

In a nervous gesture he started rubbing the pocket of his shirt, which had a small bulge in it.

"Something else. She tells me I've been changing... you know, when the two of us, uh, get together."

"When you have relations?"

"Yes. She says I've been a lot more aggressive."

"Anything wrong with that between a man and his wife?"

"No. But, Paul, this is different."

"How do you mean?"

"It was almost like—like—"

DeKorte put his hand on Wilburn's shoulder.

"I know what you're trying to say. Can I help? Do you and Helen want to talk it out sometime?"

Wilburn nodded, looking somewhat relieved.

Just then a call came over the patrol car's radio, and Wilburn hurried to answer it.

After he had finished listening and then muttering a response, he got out of the car and walked up to DeKorte.

"Paul?" he said, his face sheet-white.

"What's wrong?"

"They found—"

The radio again!

"I gotta go, Paul."

DeKorte nodded.

Wilburn usually operated on a pretty even emotional keel, one of the qualities he had that inspired confidence. But not this time.

After the squad car had pulled away from the curb, DeKorte went back to his study.

On top of his desk was a pile of notes. He hadn't paid undue attention to them before, but now...

He started leafing through, looking at a sentence here, a paragraph there.

All different but the same.

Intimate comments about matters between husbands and wives, told to him in confidence with real concern.

Each one involved changes in behavior, some quite insignificant perhaps, but changes nevertheless; others more extreme. Ordinary people in a small town, people whose sexual appetites were being altered.

He repeated that last thought aloud.

"Being altered," he said, stressing the first word.

Had the Lord put precisely that word in his mind? If so, for what reason?

He bowed his head.

What are You trying to tell me? he prayed. *Have I blocked the channels between us with barriers of piled dollars?*

The ringing of the phone intruded.

"Paul!"

It was Rogers.

"What's happening around here, Doug?" DeKorte asked. "Wilburn just picked up—"

DeKorte's demeanor cracked a bit as he told Rogers what had happened.

"That's why I'm calling, as it turns out," the doctor said. "Paul, be ready to join me at a moment's notice."

"What—?"

"I can't tell you now," Rogers interrupted. "I'm leaving right after I hang up."

"For where?"

"The Pennio residence."

DeKorte gulped a couple of times.

"I'll be ready whenever you call," he said.

"Paul—"

"Yes?"

A second of silence.

"Later."

DeKorte hung up.

He was suddenly very tired, and found himself dozing off as he idly glanced at the rest of the notes.

The dream he had then was unexpected . . . and unwelcome.

He was walking down a long series of corridors, like a maze. On either side were doors. He was responding to a woman's voice calling him, like a mythical siren.

"Paul, Paul! Here! Please hurry . . . Paul . . . hurry!"

He called back to her.

"Mary, my love! I don't know where you are. Tell me! Show me!"

More corridors.

He was dizzy now, starting to fall, leaning against one of the doors for support.

It opened abruptly, and he fell into a dark place, pitch dark, except for the floor.

The floor was transparent.

Below him was a garishly lit bedroom. He saw Mary on the bed. She was looking up at him, reaching out her arms toward him, her eyes beckoning.

"We can be together again. Paul. I need you now. . . ."

Suddenly, a muscular figure with a leather mask covering its entire head entered the scene. It stood menacingly beside the bed.

"Don't touch her!" he screamed. "Don't—"

In an instant the floor disappeared, just after Mary shouted something else at him. He was plunging, slow motion, toward the bed below. The masked figure stepped aside—and it was no longer a living Mary holding out her arms toward him. The arms were still outstretched, yes, but this time she was a long-dead corpse, and he fell right on top of her, screaming. What was left of her splattered on impact.

And in his brain, echoing through the netherworld that exists between the conscious and the subconscious, words screamed their awful accusation with ghastly clarity.

At the edge of his vision he could see that muscular figure. . . .

DeKorte shot up in his chair, awakened by someone slapping him.

Rogers.

"Thank God!" he said. "I thought you might be having a heart attack."

"Doug, I think it was Scott who attacked Mary that day, I—"

"I'm not surprised."

"You're not?"

"I tried calling you, as I promised. When you didn't answer, I hurried on over."

"The Pennios?"

Rogers nodded.

"Your nightmare must have been awful, Paul," he said. "But get prepared for something worse."

DeKorte's heart started pounding faster at that revelation. And he began to wonder, in a deep pit within himself, how much more of the nightmare was left to play itself out, and what role the Lord had in it for him from that moment on.

15

Douglas Rogers had seen plenty of death over the years, resulting from auto accidents and heart attacks and drownings and much more, but somehow nothing was as startling as the sight of someone who had been murdered.

"You don't have to see this," he told DeKorte, who had waited outside while the doctor went in as the official medical examiner. "Back out any time and nobody will think less of you."

"It's okay, Doug. I can handle it. I think I've been running away from the tough things for too long."

Inside the Pennio residence, uniformed police officials were everywhere, along with plainclothes detectives. Daniel Wilburn was standing in the living room.

"It's the worst I've ever seen, Paul," he said. "Like a slaughterhouse!"

Joseph Pennio stared up at them from the dining room floor, his eyes frozen open. There was blood everywhere. Carpet. Walls. DeKorte turned away from what was left of the man's bare chest.

"Rose?" he was able to say, but the words came out in a hoarse whisper.

"In the kitchen," said Wilburn.

"Paul—" Rogers tried to stop him.

DeKorte ignored his friend and walked into the kitchen.

Rose Pennio appeared to be sitting, her upper torso propped against one of the lower kitchen cabinets, her arms tied behind her back. Obviously the killer had spent more time with her.

Mom was no trouble at all. I had time with her. I could do a better, slower job. Dad came in suddenly and surprised me—it was over with quick as far as he was concerned. But Mom, yeah, we had a good old time.

Her chest...the same as her husband's...but not only that.

Wait until they look in the freezer....

Outside, the air was cool and refreshing. DeKorte and Rogers stood together on the sidewalk in front of the house, breathing deeply, as though returning from an alien atmosphere. Sheriff Wilburn came out to them, holding a flame-seared sheet of ruled paper.

"We found this in a wastebasket in Scott's bedroom."

Only a few phrases were legible.

... so much pain ... only one way ... eager for this life to end ... no choice ... must die ... new Master....

"A suicide note?" DeKorte asked.

"If it was, why did he burn it?" said the sheriff.

"Could it have been burned by whoever committed the murders?" Rogers asked.

DeKorte told him about Scott's visit to his study, and Wilburn showed him the plastic bag with its grisly contents.

"Scott threw that at me as he was leaving," said DeKorte. "When I saw what it was, I called Dan. And you know the rest."

"And now there's another wrinkle," said Wilburn.

"What's that?"

"I just got a call that Scott's two friends, Wayne and Mark, turned themselves in down at the station."

"For what?"

"They claim they murdered Scott."

"What!" DeKorte and Rogers said at the same time.

"That's not all," said the sheriff. "According to them, Scott *bragged* about murdering his parents."

* * *

Paul DeKorte wanted to see Wayne and Mark. Perhaps he could help them, and also try to make some sense from all this madness. But the sheriff said he would have to wait until the following day at least; their interrogation would go long into the night.

After Rogers dropped him off at the parsonage, DeKorte walked the short distance to the church. Once inside, he fell to his knees at the altar.

Mary ... Patrick ... now Joe and Rose.... Dear God, what is happening? Tonight I stepped into a house where evil held sway. Help me, Lord.

He looked up at the stained glass window behind the pulpit where Christ, the Good Shepherd, held a lamb in His arms.

"Whatever is happening here in Valley Falls must be stopped."

Knowing that, saying it in the familiar confines of a church building where he had held services for more than a decade was one thing, and a surge of spiritual adrenaline briefly fired up his very being. But getting beyond the conducive physical trappings and the fleeting nature of that moment and somehow finding the spiritual stability and energy to be the Lord's instrument, he knew ... he knew, he knew ... was something else altogether.

* * *

"We're winning!" said one of the demons, gargoyle-like in appearance as he perched triumphantly on an obelisk monument in the old graveyard.

"It appears so," the Master agreed.

"You sound unconvinced," observed the same malevolent creature.

"I have learned, over the years, not to underestimate Him."

"But surely the signs are good this time."

"It would seem so." And the Master turned away, as though to forestall any further questioning.

"The Master seemed impatient with you," said another grotesque demon who had recently arrived.

"That he was."

"But why?" asked the newcomer. "Are things going badly?"

"No, our escapades in Valley Falls are proving very successful. Yet it's almost like the Master seems less than certain that in winning we have won . . . where have you been, by the way?"

"I'm late, but not without reason. I was able to get some terrorists to destroy another planeload of innocent travelers."

"Wonderful!" the first demon exclaimed.

"Oh, it was really something. And as frosting on the cake, I was able to get some looters to steal rings and money from the dead."

"Great!"

"But tell me about Valley Falls. I've heard rumors, of course, so fill me in."

The gargoyle told him all that had happened.

"Teenagers prove very fertile ground these days," he concluded.

"I agree. The world we've created around them helps."

"They don't know how to cope, and we can move right in."

"So tell me more about our latest victim," the newcomer said gleefully.

"This kid was ripe for the plucking. He had looks, intelligence, and enough money to afford anything he wanted. As you know, it's an entrapment that seldom fails. A mirage promising much and offering nothing."

"Enhanced by a dose of heavy metal music and a dash of pornography perhaps?"

"Right. He fell for every trick in the book, even the old Sodom and Gomorrah gambit."

"Fantastic!"

The two gloated for several minutes over this record of current infamy.

"*What's next?*" *the newcomer finally asked.*

"*You'll be able to see for yourself,*" *the gargoyle reminded him.*

"*Something spectacular?*"

"*That's what the Master has promised. Lots of suffering. And plenty of damnation.*"

"*I can hardly wait.*"

* * *

16

Valley Falls garnered more media attention in the course of a few days than it had in decades previously. Three television networks sent news crews, as did a number of cable stations. The town made headlines in major urban dailies, weekly tabloids, and national news magazines.

The ACLU indicated that they were concerned that the civil rights of the two teenagers were being violated.

And a popular TV host named Hector Ramirez trucked in his crew to start taping a syndicated prime-time special.

DeKorte could see part of the town square from his study. It had become a media center, with photographers and reporters and others setting up tents and other facilities.

He sighed.

And the heathen rage....

He smiled sardonically as that verse came to mind.

Later, after his morning coffee with Doug Rogers, he walked through the square. Within just a few moments he heard a crescendo of the worst profanity, saw more than one individual smoking a marijuana cigarette, and overheard snatches of conversation that indicated those involved were motivated by TV ratings and not at all by the basic ingredients of the story that had attracted them to Valley Falls.

As he turned and started to head back to his study, he was approached by a man in his mid-fifties with a thick head of snow-white hair and a tiny moustache; he was wearing an expensive English tweed suit.

"Sir, may I speak with you a moment?" the man asked, his baritone voice clear and commanding.

Ordinarily DeKorte would have tried to duck any dialogue with anyone connected with the media, but this man's manner was different enough to make him hesitate.

DeKorte nodded and extended his hand.

"I'm the president of the ICB-TV news division. My name is Phillips Lafferty."

"What can I do for you?" DeKorte asked.

"You are the clergyman who was the spiritual counselor for the three boys, aren't you?"

"I still am, Mr. Lafferty. Scott Pennio's body hasn't been found, which means his death hasn't been confirmed. And Wayne Mulrooney and Mark Jacobson haven't been executed as yet, at least as far as I can tell."

He tried to say what he did without sarcasm, but found a measure of it creeping into his voice.

"Forgive me for that, Mr. Lafferty. All this has been an ordeal for everyone involved."

"I can imagine. Would you be interested in joining me for lunch? It's about that time, I see."

DeKorte considered turning down the invitation, but the man's professional manner persuaded him to keep a reasonably open mind.

"I discovered a little place about ten miles from here," Lafferty said. "Would it put a severe burden on your schedule if we went there?"

"You find our luncheonette unappealing?" DeKorte laughed.

"Would you rather eat there, sir?"

DeKorte laughed again.

"I like your first idea better."

* * *

The restaurant was faintly Continental in its decor but otherwise without distinction in its appearance. The food, however, was exceptional, as were the high prices.

"We all get used to a certain lifestyle, Reverend DeKorte," Lafferty was saying.

"Please call me Paul," DeKorte told him.

"Fine. Well, Paul, it's true, you know. When you've had money for a while, you get used to it. When you're very poor, you wonder if you will ever be anything else, and you subconsciously prepare yourself for lifelong poverty. A factory worker thinks he will always be a factory worker because his father was and so was his grandfather.

"I couldn't picture ever not being in charge. And I wonder if you could see yourself in any profession other than the ministry?"

"Probably not," said DeKorte. "But for me it's not the profession as such but the mission that God has given me. That is why I am where I am."

"Very noble. For the rest of us, though, it may not be as lofty as reaching the souls of men. The truth may be a little closer to the pocketbook, I'm afraid."

After they had finished the main course and were having coffee, Lafferty surprised DeKorte with a question.

"Paul, isn't it true that you have been teaching that prosperity is one evidence Christians use in ascertaining whether they are in God's will or not?"

DeKorte put his cup down and looked at the other man.

"Your point?" he asked.

"Let me first tell you that I came upon that knowledge from talking with some of the members of your congregation, which I should say is the bulk of those who live in Valley Falls. They all seem to feel that having material blessings is a proof of their salvation."

DeKorte said nothing, feeling a growing sense of discomfort.

"Let me offer you this," Lafferty said, reaching into his jacket and taking out a plain white envelope.

"What's that?"

"Open it."

Inside was money, a great deal of money—a thick pile of hundred dollar bills.

"That, Paul, is the first installment."

"Installment for what?"

"Getting exclusive coverage that the other networks would like but won't be able to get if you help us."

"And you think this money is what will do it?"

"That money is part of it, Paul. There will be more, as I said. And a focus of attention on your town and an influx of business beyond anything you can imagine. I can guarantee—"

DeKorte waved the envelope away.

"Not interested," he said.

"But you're the logical person to tell the story. From what I understand, the kids are pointing the finger, at least in part, at you."

DeKorte's anger showed as he replied, "I have no idea what you're talking about. How could you possibly know—"

"I have sources. Money can buy a great deal, as you know."

"I may know that, but I can't be bought by any stack of bills you might wave in front of me."

"But isn't that what you've been doing with your own congregation?"

"I've simply taught them what the Bible says."

"You've bribed them with your own interpretation of the Bible. The Bible says that the poor are blessed, and it condemns the rich young ruler. The Bible—"

"But—"

"But nothing, Paul. My father was a preacher, you know. He never worried about money. He taught what he called the plan of salvation plus nothing—not fat wallets and emotional ecstasy. He died almost penniless. I don't intend to do the same."

"And so you buy whatever ensures your continuing success?"

"And *you* offer whatever brings those supporters of yours back Sunday after Sunday. Otherwise you wouldn't have a car to drive, a roof over your head, and—"

"We should go now," DeKorte interrupted. "No more discussion, please."

"I'll take you back, sure, but let me ask you one question: If God somehow told you that your message from now on should be the opposite of what you've been telling everyone . . . I mean, that they should deny themselves and give their riches to the poor, accumulating very little for themselves . . . would you obey Him? Even if it meant the specter of poverty for yourself? That is, in the event that the idea of sacrifice proved unacceptable to that group of well-heeled Christians you call the members of your congregation?"

That group of well-heeled Christians . . .

Those words lodged in DeKorte's consciousness, stuck there like something caught in his throat, and no matter how much he tried to get them loose, nothing would help.

They were only a couple miles away from Valley Falls when DeKorte asked Lafferty to pull the car over to the side of the road.

"Aren't you feeling well?" the other man asked, genuinely concerned, since the expression on the minister's face was hardly reassuring.

DeKorte got out and walked up the road a few yards. Lafferty followed him.

"In there is an old cemetery," DeKorte said finally, pointing at the trees to his left. "It has been unused for nearly a hundred years."

He turned and faced Lafferty.

"You could be worth ten million dollars and end up there. You could be worth fifty cents. The grave is the bottom line, no matter what the circumstances of our lives."

"But having money makes the life that we do enjoy so much happier."

DeKorte smiled a bit and said, "Years ago there was a man who built and sold entire housing developments. In his personal dealings he paid cash for everything, never used a credit card, hated what he called plastic money, and bragged about saving 18 to 24 percent interest that way.

"One day when he was away from home he became ill. He pulled his car over to the side of the road and blacked out. When he came to an hour or so later, in addition to everything else—the nausea, the dizziness—he had a touch of amnesia for some reason. He wandered away from the car, leaving his wallet behind in his attaché case, where he usually kept it.

"He finally entered a little country town. No one there knew him, of course, and no one would give him credit—not the local pharmacy, nor the local restaurant, not a single merchant. The reason? He had never established a credit rating. The local bank could find nothing about him when they checked out his TRW rating."

"But he was obviously ill, wasn't he? And you said he had amnesia."

"Oh, no, that spell passed. But he was still very confused. The problem was that the townspeople mistook his strange, erratic manner for the fact that he just wasn't a very good liar.

"Realizing that he was getting nowhere, he started to walk back to his car. But, still confused, he went in the opposite direction. He walked for a long time, never finding the car, of course. Later that day, his body was found in the ditch beside the road; he had had a massive heart attack and died."

After a minute or two, Lafferty said with unexpected gentleness, "Valley Falls was that town, wasn't it?

DeKorte nodded.

"And my wife and I were the ones who found him. We pieced together the story, learning a great deal about him in the process. You know, there was 2000 dollars in his attaché case when his car was discovered the next morning. He had money, more than enough to get medicine or treatment or whatever he needed. But in the final analysis, it did him no good."

"But it was the greed of the townspeople that caused his death."

DeKorte muttered a yes.

"Well, then, Paul, what did you do about it?"

"Nothing."

"No sermons against avarice?"

DeKorte shook his head.

"Why not?"

"Mary and I rationalized the whole thing away, decided that this man had acted so suspiciously that the reaction of our fellow citizens seemed reasonable enough."

Surprisingly, Lafferty's tone, when he spoke next, was neither gloating nor condemning.

"Then you and I are both prisoners of what I suppose you would call the deception that we've chosen to accept as truth."

"Yes, I guess...."

As they were walking back toward the car, Lafferty said, "I know it's getting late, but I wonder if you would let me take a very brief side trip."

DeKorte had no trouble with that.

"It'll mean a delay of about an hour."

"Fine."

* * *

Instead of going straight ahead at the next intersection, Lafferty turned left. As the minutes passed, DeKorte realized that they were heading into a poor section of the county.

In a few minutes ramshackle houses were in evidence. The automobiles were old or rusty or both. The people, principally black, had managed to avoid wearing rags as such, but that was about it.

"I've always wondered what my father saw in reaching out to people like this," Lafferty said as he braked the car in front of an old church building.

He got out and walked up to a fence that surrounded the church grounds where an elderly black man was tending to the shrubbery in front.

"Sir," Lafferty called to him, "are you the minister here?"

"I am, sir. Can I help you?" he asked as he placed the hoe he had been using on the ground and walked over to the gate.

"I have something for you," Lafferty told him.

"And what might that be, my brother?"

Lafferty took out the envelope and handed it to the old preacher.

"My, oh my, what is this?"

"Let's just say it's a gift from my father."

"And who is he, brother?"

"You don't know him."

The old man's eyes widened as he saw what was inside the envelope.

"Can I meet your father and thank him? This—this is a wonderful gift."

Lafferty's eyes were filling with tears.

"I suspect you will someday."

"Then I look forward to shaking your father's hand, son."

Lafferty started to turn away.

"Won't you let me get you something to eat?" the preacher asked. "Don't you want to meet some of the folks this will be helping? My wife's been needin' an operation on her eyes. I—I think she can have it now, and there will be plenty left over."

"No, no, I have to go now. Spend it as you see fit."

An old, black, wrinkled hand reached out and grabbed his own.

"Take this, please," he said, and placed a tiny New Testament in Lafferty's palm.

"Thank you," he said, barely able to speak.

"And God bless you, my brother."

DeKorte was leaning against the car when Lafferty approached.

"Do you want me to drive?" DeKorte asked him.

Lafferty nodded.

They didn't speak on the way back to Valley Falls, but anger had nothing to do with it this time.

17

After saying good-bye to Phillips Lafferty, DeKorte started toward the church. He glanced back once and saw Lafferty, sitting on a folding chair beside one of the media tents, still reading the New Testament the old preacher had given him.

Just outside the front door of the church, he was approached by a member of his congregation, a young man with an unruly head of hair.

"Reverend DeKorte," he said breathlessly, "God is so good."

"Yes, He is," DeKorte agreed somewhat warily.

"I just sold the rights to my story."

"What story?"

"About my friendship with the Pennios. Isn't that just great? What an opportunity for Christian witness. Praise God!"

There was a time when DeKorte's immediate reaction would have been to let this pass without saying anything. But not anymore.

"No, it isn't great," he told the man. "In fact, it's plainly offensive."

"Offensive? I don't understand."

"To commercialize a tragedy and make money from others' grief."

"Now wait a minute, pastor!"

"No, you wait," DeKorte said, his anger fueled by a surge of adrenaline. "That is what you are doing. And you're rationalizing it all under the guise of 'giving your testimony.' You are selling suffering for thirty pieces of silver. Don't you realize that?"

"I got a lot more than that!" the man declared.

"May God forgive you," DeKorte said, more in pity than in anger.

"Why are you looking at me like that?" the man asked, puzzled and annoyed. "I got five thousand dollars! Here's the first check, for half the amount. And the church will benefit from my tithe!"

DeKorte slammed the front door behind him and walked into the auditorium, intending to spend some time there alone, praying.

But Laura Jacobson, Mark's mother, was in the front pew, her head bowed. She looked up when she heard his steps and motioned for him to join her. They sat there together in silence for several minutes.

"You know what the hardest part of all this is?" she said finally, her expression heavy—not with bits and pieces of regret that could somehow be discarded, but with suffocating waves that threatened to drag her down in a kind of emotional undertow.

"Tell me, Laura," he said softly, grateful for being able to concentrate on someone's else feelings just then.

"Trying to understand how totally I let my son slip through my fingers, as though I couldn't have done anything but watch...just watch it happen." She started trembling.

"To have been so blind!" she said. "It was all there, right before our eyes. Why didn't we see it?."

"But I share in that, too," he told her. "I'm supposed to be the spiritual expert, a discerning shepherd leading the flock. Why didn't I see the danger signals? Why wasn't I more concerned?"

"Scott came to see me today, Paul...said he couldn't talk to his parents anymore"...Scott and Mark and Wayne at Patrick's funeral...at the concert..."Scott's behavior seems to be changing...his vocabulary...incubus...azael...."

The images crept into the conscious part of his mind, and he felt a compulsion to stand up and scream in frustration...and fear. But he couldn't. He was denied that freedom just then, he whom others looked to for comfort and strength. Somehow he had to draw together the pieces of himself that were threatening to scatter in a hundred different directions and keep them tightly bound.

"Now my son may be a murderer," Laura Jacobson's voice broke through his thoughts. "And those...those vultures out there...I wouldn't be surprised if they started selling reserved seats for the execution."

"Laura, Laura," he said, putting his hands on her shoulders, "don't jump to conclusions."

"But Mark told me they did it."

"Yes, but the claim is self-defense, isn't it?"

She turned and looked at him as tears streamed down her cheeks.

"He was there, wasn't he? My son and the Mulrooney boy went to the falls to murder Scott. He admits that. And now Scott is dead."

"But no body has been found, Laura."

"What about the Pennios? We have their bodies. And the boys knew about that!"

In his effort to comfort her, he had once more tripped into the old positive-thinking trap. And given the circumstances, that not only was comfortless, but spiritually unsound.

"I'm sorry, Laura. You're right. The only answer is the Lord. We've got to trust Him to see us through this, whatever the outcome."

She pulled a handkerchief from a pocket in her dress and wiped her eyes.

"I know what you've taught us about seeing through a glass darkly, pastor. You've delivered more than one sermon on the subject. But it doesn't help when you realize that you're the worst sort of failure at what should have mattered the most—parenthood," she said. "Ted and I have failed as parents. Sure, we thought we were instilling the right values in Mark, but now that's proved an illusion."

"These are tough times to be a parent, Laura. These are tough times to be a kid. With readily available drugs, violence so common that it's almost glorified on TV and movie screens, every conceivable kind of pornography, and now AIDS...well the list goes on and on."

"But, pastor, this is so different," she said, "I mean, this involvement in the occult and all. I feel so utterly helpless. It's not just that my son has done something horribly, horribly wrong, but that he may be—"

She couldn't bring herself to say the word. It had always been something she read about or saw portrayed in a sensationalized motion picture, with swiveling heads and green vomit and blasphemous dialogue. Mark had loved that kind of movie.

"I found this in Mark's room last night," she said, handing DeKorte a tiny carved wood figure.

"These have been cropping up all over town, you know," he said.

"What is it? It looks so strange...so evil. What does it mean? Why did my son have that thing? Where did he get it?"

He shook his head. "I don't know, but I'm certainly going to try to find out."

Suddenly Laura Jacobson rubbed her hands up and down her upper arms, trying to warm herself.

"Did you feel that, pastor?"

"Feel what?"

"So cold all of a sudden." She stood up. "I've got to go. Ted's probably worried about me. Pray for us, please."

"I think we should pray right now," he said.

She nodded, and they got down on their knees in the center aisle.

"Lord, there has been tragedy . . . tragedy unexpected . . . tragedy which we have so little strength on our own to face, to cope with, to understand the reason for it," DeKorte prayed.

"It is clear that the enemy of our souls is on the rampage. But it is also clear that we cannot allow him any victory. We cannot allow him to go unchallenged.

"What he would want us to do is wallow in our sorrow, drowning in it as though we had been thrown into a lake of tears and forgotten how to swim. But You offer a life raft, Lord, a life raft of Your Word, Your promises. And You have guaranteed that You will take our burdens upon Yourself, that You will lift our yoke and make it Your own.

"Please, Lord, we need the reality of what You have offered, for the burdens are many and the yoke weighs us down. Take this mother from this place, Lord, and be her Comforter."

DeKorte walked with her to the door and waved to her husband, who was waiting outside in the car.

As he turned to go back through the sanctuary to his office, he noticed the pamphlets piled on the table in the foyer. One in particular caught his eye: *MONEY FROM HEAVEN: Visualize Yourself Out of Debt and into Riches.* He looked up at the ceiling, his cheeks moist with tears.

Lord, what I have done!

Suddenly he reached out and turned the table over, spilling the contents in a dozen directions.

Oh, God, what a fool I've been!

Then he sank to his knees as waves of shame and regret swept over him.

Forgive me, Lord. Forgive me.

18

In such moments of voluntary isolation when he was able to take stock of himself and his relationship with Christ, Paul DeKorte had to admit that he had been blessedly free of wrenching traumas until he had lost Mary.

Perhaps that was what made me so effective when I preached positive thinking, he chided himself later that day. After his visit with Mark's mother and the disturbing insights sparked by the pamphlet, he had returned to the parsonage to make himself some supper. But the food seemed strangely unappealing and he couldn't finish. Too restless to read or watch television, he had walked back to the church and locked himself in his study.

Today my positivity finally collapsed in the face of reality.

Years before, he had been privileged to meet a noted Christian speaker, a woman who had survived the Holocaust. Guilty of sheltering Jews in her hometown in Holland during World War II, she and her family had been sent to a Nazi concentration camp. Only she and her brother survived. Her father, mother, and sister had perished there.

He had met the woman when she spoke at a church in a city about two hours from his pastorate. The pastor, a friend of his, arranged for the two of them to spend a little time together in his study after the service.

"I am familiar with you," she said after they were introduced. "You have written many articles."

He was pleased, until he heard her next words.

"But I am worried about you and about your message. Carried to an extreme, what you have been teaching can plant seeds that bring forth dangerous fruit."

Then she told of the cold January day when her sister had died in her arms.

"I did not think positively then," she said. "How could I? God didn't make us superhuman."

He respected her, but he had been in his own glory days then, pastoring a growing congregation in a thriving farming community in the Midwest.

"I have confidence that the gift of healing is still very much a part of God's plan for this age of ours," she said. "Nor have prophecies ceased. You see, I do embrace all the gifts, and would fight any who say that all such were part of the New Testament period but that the Lord has withheld them ever since."

She paused as though she sensed that he wasn't really listening, that his interested expression was only a polite facade for boredom or unconcern.

"Be very careful. Any of the gifts magnified to such an extent that they are sought for themselves, rather than the Lord who bestows them, can become distorted and destructive." She concluded simply, "Do not be overwhelmed by your own words, my dear brother."

Do not be overwhelmed by your own words.

Although he had ignored her admonition, he had never forgotten it.

You have written many articles.

How many articles had he written? How many people had taken his advice and let it rule their lives?

He stood before the bookshelves where Scott had read off some of the titles just days earlier. On the top shelf were binders holding copies of the magazines in which his material had appeared. One publication had 125,000 readers; another 80,000; others ranged from 35,000 on up to 250,000. How many seeds had been planted? How much wayward fruit would spring up all across the country?

As he sat down at his desk, stark thoughts of demonic activity slipped into his mind, and he was astonished to realize how rarely he had spent time studying the subject of Satan and the activities of his realm. Sermons concerned with the Devil and sin and Hell could hardly be called positive. At what point had he decided to file all those negative, energy-draining elements away somewhere and look solely at the happy possibilities inherent in life?

He had made a career of doing just that, had preached hundreds of sermons about trusting God for health, prosperity, and success. It was what the members of his congregation expected of him; it was the "diet" he fed them each Sunday.

They've been malnourished all this time, he told himself. *What their souls needed, I was not giving them. They were starving for meat, and I fed them French pastry!*

And now ...

He reached for his concordance and started looking for references to Satan and his minions.

"The Spirit clearly says that in later times some will abandon the faith and follow deceiving spirits and things taught by demons."

He had preferred to treat such passages of Scripture superficially, going on to "more positive" ones.

"The god of this age has blinded the minds..."

The context referred to unbelievers, but he knew it could be applied to Christians whose minds were seduced by the things of the world and who allowed Satan to deceive them.

"...has blinded the minds..."

Satan was the master counterfeiter, the arch deceiver; he could fake virtually anything. He recalled something he had once read by British scholar, Dr. Martyn Lloyd-Jones: "There are other spirits, and these other spirits are very powerful, and can give wonderful gifts. Satan can counterfeit most of the gifts of the Holy Spirit."

But people have been healed in my church. Can that be false as well?

He sank to his knees for a much-needed time with the Lord.

* * *

He had fallen asleep on the floor of his study. When he awoke and looked at his watch, it was two o'clock in the morning.

"Lord?" he asked out loud, thinking he had heard a sound. He stood and walked out into the sanctuary.

Empty.

Of course it's empty, he told himself.

Of flesh-and-blood bodies, yes—but not memories.

My first sermon.... How clearly it returned to him.

"Salvation comes only by faith in Jesus Christ," he had told them. *"That is the sole foundation upon which we should build every day of our earthly existence.*

"As the song says, 'Alive in Christ, dead to the world'—that should be the cry of our spirits. And as the same song asks, 'How can we continue to be less than we can be?'

"A poor missionary working in the poverty-stricken suburbs of Calcutta, dedicating her life to the winning of the lost for Him, is being all that she can be in far greater measure than the head of a ministry who spends more on his wardrobe in a year than she gets in support during that same period of time."

When had he lost that imperative? Could it be pinpointed and, therefore, confronted and "exorcised"?

"We are called upon to take His light to a world where wrong seems right...."

Or had the vision become shrunken and wasted in little stages, so minute that they were indiscernible when they occurred?

And Mary...

Had even his love for her become something that stood between him and the Lord?

"Dear Lord!" he cried. "Lord, how could that be? Our love was good, pure. It was—"

The foundation for his life!

He wanted Mary to live in comfort, to have beautiful clothes; he wanted her to have all the modern conveniences designed to make life easier for her. He remembered her concern about all this and how he had reassured her that he hadn't lost sight of the purpose of his ministry.

And yet where was the sacrifice?

Used up and wasted for me... broken and spilled out and poured at my feet, in sweet abandon... spilled out and used up for me....

The tender words floated through his mind.

"Oh, dear Savior," he prayed softly, now on his knees in the center aisle, his face turned toward the ceiling, tears streaking his cheeks. "What did I give up for You?"

Not the increased weekly giving. Not the plans for new buildings.

Scott knew the answer when he came here that day!

"But I turned away, my ego offended!" he groaned. "I had his attention, and I threw it on some kind of emotional garbage heap. And did I also throw away his spirit for all eternity?"

He fell forward onto his face, his body shaking, every inch of it wet with perspiration.

Minutes passed as he remained in that position.

And then he felt a presence again.

Someone next to him.

He could feel an encompassing warmth, a gentle touch, words whispered into his ear.

Be not afraid...

Just those kind words, and then—

Be not weary in well-doing...

He opened his eyes.

For I shall never forsake you.

19

Media attention had switched from Valley Falls itself to the county courthouse, where there were no empty seats for the hearing of Mark Jacobson and Wayne Mulrooney. Most of the courtroom spectators were residents, but reporters and photographers filled the back rows.

As Paul DeKorte and Douglas Rogers entered, the minister stopped to speak with Edith Van Halen, who had parked her wheelchair on the left side of the center aisle beside the last row of seats.

"Terrible thing," she said.

"Yes it is," he agreed.

"Young people today. Just awful!"

She was wearing a now-familiar object on a chain around her neck.

"Edith, may I ask where you got that carving?" he said.

"Why, Scott Pennio sold it to me," she said. "I guess they're kind of a fad now. He was selling them to raise money for a new computer system, he said. I think he made a pretty good sale."

As the two men walked toward the front of the courtroom, DeKorte noticed that others indeed had the carvings, sticking out of shirt pockets or hanging around their necks.

"So Scott's in back of the carving phenomenon," Rogers said softly. "I wonder what that tells us."

"I don't know, but I have a feeling we won't like the answer."

Rogers nodded in agreement as they found two empty seats in the front row, directly behind the table where Wayne and Mark sat with their attorney.

"I've never had much contact with legal proceedings," DeKorte said. "I don't even watch 'L.A. Law'! So, am I right in thinking this is only a hearing to see if the boys should be bound over for trial? Nothing other than that will be decided today, will it?"

"Correct. They'll either be scheduled directly for trial or committed for psychiatric observation," Rogers said.

The judge entered just then, and after the preliminaries, each attorney made an opening statement. The defense attorney went first.

Tall, thin, in his late thirties, the man was a stranger to Valley Falls. None of the local attorneys had the experience to handle a criminal case of this nature, so the boys' parents had brought in legal help from out of town. Their advocate bristled with commitment and did a credible job, placing emphasis upon the bizarre nature of the case, but the hearing was strictly pro forma. There was never any doubt as to the inevitability of a trial.

The county prosecutor, Gary Harmon, a heavyset bear of a man pushing fifty, had a reputation for being exceptionally aggressive, and he lived up to it as he set the stage for the state's case.

"Your honor," he began, "certain facts are apparent. First, Scott Pennio has disappeared. Second, his parents have been murdered. And third, the only two connecting threads are the defendants."

DeKorte noticed that Mark kept moving around nervously in his chair.

"Their only defense," said Harmon, "that is, if you can call it a defense, is their claim that Scott told them he was the one who murdered his parents.

"And then, if we are to believe these two, Scott convinced his so-called buddies to murder him as part of some occult master plan he had allegedly concocted."

He turned to the crowd in the courtroom, then to the defendants, and finally back to the judge.

"But, I ask, where is the proof? Not one shred of hard evidence exists—except the murder weapon used on Scott himself.

"According to the defendants that is the very knife they used, but they claim the weapon used to murder the Pennios is at the bottom of Hidden Lake."

He chuckled with exaggerated sarcasm.

"And now, brace yourself—the confusion really starts! If we are to believe the defendants, they actually killed their buddy Scott not in obedience to his wishes, as supposedly planned, but out of self-defense because, it seems, suddenly he tried to murder them!"

Harmon paced back and forth as he spoke. Now he stopped abruptly and faced the judge.

"Was it murder? Or was it self-defense? Did Scott Pennio want to die, then inexplicably try to kill his friends instead? Just what are the defendants trying to tell us?

"They would have us believe that a plea of insanity conveniently covers this farce, else why would all this seem so irrational, which I must admit it does? Let me submit that it is a planned irrationality we are hearing, a presumption that this court will be gullible enough to believe the chaotic story these two have fabricated, as well as the hearsay statements of someone who may never be available to affirm or deny those very words in this courtroom!"

As DeKorte listened to the prosecutor's legal diatribe, he watched the two boys sitting directly in front of him. He noticed Mark becoming more and more agitated.

"Your honor," Harmon continued, "I for one—and I am quite sure I don't stand alone in this view—am becoming fed up with an overused insanity plea that, in this instance, is manipulated to allow the commission of three heinous murders to go without punishment. And yet that isn't even the full extent of what the defense has entered here; that isn't the limit to which credibility is being torturously stretched. They expect this court to lend decisive weight to a plea of insanity stemming from demonic possession!"

The smirking prosecutor had barely completed his last sarcastic sentence when Mark bolted from his chair and lunged for the man. Two guards tried to restrain the boy, but were unable to hold him. Though he was slighter than either of them, Mark seemed to toss the guards aside like toys. He grabbed Harmon by the neck and lifted him several inches off the floor, his fingers tightening around the man's throat.

DeKorte jumped to his feet and rushed forward. "Mark!" he shouted, "Mark, in the name of Jesus Christ, I command you not to harm that man. Leave him alone! Now!"

The teenager turned abruptly and stared at DeKorte, who instinctively stepped back as he saw the boy's expression. Veins bulged in his forehead, his eyes stared wide and wild, and saliva dripped from the corners of his open mouth.

In an instant, however, he changed. Looking fearful and ashamed, he dropped the prosecutor. Harmon fell to the floor with a thud and collapsed, burying his head in his hands and gasping for breath.

The two guards, now back on their feet, quickly handcuffed the teenager and took him back to his seat, then stood guard on either side of him.

The prosecutor managed to say, "Your honor, about that insanity plea—" when DeKorte interrupted and asked for permission to speak.

"Go ahead, Reverend DeKorte."

"Minutes ago, the notion of demonic possession was scoffed at here, your honor," he began. "After all, that is just a religious concept and has no bearing in a court of law which must base everything on the legal, not the supernatural. I can understand that, your honor. But in this case I think a larger issue is involved. If it is just a matter of insanity, then that is one thing. But let me pose a question: Have you ever known insanity to be an epidemic? Epidemics are caused by viruses and germs— biological causes— not by mental or emotional or spiritual causes."

"What is your point, Reverend DeKorte?" the judge asked.

"If this case before you now were just one of a handful, then insanity could be the right explanation. But it is not. Turn on your television. Pick up your newspaper, your national magazines. Study what you see, what you read, and you'll realize an epidemic is sweeping this country."

"Are you saying that this country is being taken over by demons?" the judge asked in a tone of disbelief and condescension.

"Your honor, may I interrupt?" said the prosecutor, who had now regained his composure and was seated once more.

"Yes, Mr. Harmon?" the judge asked.

"Your honor," the prosecutor continued, "this incident has caused me to revise my conclusions and recommendations about this case. What I saw in the defendant's eyes during his attack on me went far beyond insanity."

The judge turned to DeKorte. "Reverend DeKorte?"

"Your honor, may I propose this? Let me gather together a small group of clergymen from different denominations who understand the reality of demonic possession and its effects."

"For what purpose?"

"To spend time with the two defendants and objectively analyze just what has happened to them and to try and determine if any spiritual transformation can be brought about."

The judge paused for a minute or two, then said, "On one condition, Reverend DeKorte. That a court-appointed psychiatrist be present with these clergymen. I want the defendants' behavior assessed in that light as well."

The defense attorney and the prosecutor agreed that the proposal was acceptable, and the judge ruled that the boys were to be remanded to the Valley View, a nearby mental hospital. Then he adjourned the hearing.

Prosecutor Harmon approached DeKorte as the courtroom was clearing.

"Reverend, do you have any idea what I saw in that kid's eyes when he was trying to choke me?" he asked. "It was like I was looking through some sort of portal—"

"Into Hell?" DeKorte asked. "Is that about it?"

"Not about. That was it! I've seen a lot of troubled people in this job, Reverend—a lot of bad people. But I've never experienced anything like that. I feel as though I've looked into the very face of evil."

20

DeKorte left the courthouse and went home to eat his lunch. Then he headed for his study. Outside the church, he noticed a telephone company truck parked in the street. The serviceman was at the back of the vehicle, gathering his equipment together.

"What's the problem?"

"Lots of complaints," replied the man.

"Do I have time to make some calls? It's important."

"You've got maybe half an hour before I have to interrupt your service."

"Okay. Thanks."

Once he reached his study, DeKorte made five calls in rapid succession. All five ministers turned him down. One of them said he was taking a tour to China; another felt it was essentially a charismatic issue; the third didn't believe in demonic possession; the fourth was scheduled to be a guest speaker at a convention majoring on the crucial theme of evangelical unity and just couldn't change his plans; the fifth would have found the sessions fascinating, he said, but had a book deadline to meet for his publisher, who would be very upset if he took the time.

All that is necessary for evil to triumph is for good men to do nothing, he thought as he dialed one more number. The familiar quotation had never seemed more apt than at that moment.

"Harley Trent here," said the voice at the other end.

"Harley, this is Paul DeKorte."

"Paul, old friend, you've been having some problems down there, haven't you?"

"You've been reading the papers then?"

"Indeed I have. Sounds like quite a mess."

"It's more than that, Harley."

"You mean the media haven't over-sensationalized it for a change?"

"That's right. Satan is alive and well here in Valley Falls."

There was a second or two of silence at the other end. Then, "Paul, I confess to not taking everything I hear and read seriously anymore. I guess we all have reason to be skeptical about journalistic integrity these days. But I fully intended to call you and find out exactly what was happening. Please forgive me for not doing it sooner," he said. "Tell me what's happening."

DeKorte told him some of the details and of his attempt to bring in spiritual helpers.

"When do you want me there?" Trent asked.

"As soon as you can get here."

"This is Friday. I should be able to get away by next Saturday morning. How's that?"

"Thanks, Harley. That would be great! But what about your own church obligations?"

"Interestingly enough, we just brought an assistant pastor on board a couple months ago. The Lord's own timing, as it looks now."

"Praise the Lord," DeKorte remarked, breathing a sigh of relief.

"I get the impression you could use someone else as well."

"I could, I surely could."

"How about Bennett Chapman?"

DeKorte was astonished that he hadn't thought of the man himself. "Ideal!" he exclaimed. "We're having some problems with the phone lines here, so would you mind giving him a call?"

"Be glad to."

DeKorte thanked Trent again and said good-bye, feeling encouraged by the prospect of having two strong fellow believers by his side as he confronted the Prince of Darkness.

But not you, sweet Mary, he cried. *Is God trying to tell me that no crutch is acceptable in His eyes, no substitute source of strength? That I am to depend upon Him and Him only?*

How hard that was. How hard to feel whole, to feel strong, when part of his reason for living had died in his arms.

* * *

After DeKorte had broken the connection, Harley Trent hesitated, uneasiness colliding with skepticism.

What in the world has Paul gotten himself involved in down there? he asked himself. Thumbing through the Rolodex on his desk, he found the number he wanted and dialed it.

"Bennett?" he asked, barely able to make out the voice that answered. "Bennett Chapman?"

"Yes. Sorry about my voice. I'm just getting over a bad cold. Who's this?"

"Harley Trent."

"Harley!" said Chapman. "It's been a long time. How are you?"

"I'm fine, Bennett. But we've got a colleague in trouble."

"Who's that?"

"Remember Paul DeKorte?"

Silence.

"Bennett, are you still there?"

"Yes," he said.

"Do you remember Paul?"

Again silence.

"Bennett, are you okay? Can't you talk now?"

"No. Can't talk about it."

"About what?"

"Not over the phone."

Another pause.

"Let's meet at The Rendezvous. Tomorrow at noon."

"Bennett, that's an hour's drive from your church."

"I know."

"All right. I'll be there."

Chapman whispered a good-bye and hung up.

That was strange, Trent thought. Both Paul and Bennett had sounded very upset. Yet he had known both men for a long time, and neither was an alarmist. *What's going on?*

He rubbed his eyes briefly, stretched, and looked at his watch. Rosemary would be justifiably irritated at his lateness for dinner, especially since their parsonage was next door to the church!

Get moving. Think about it on the way.

Once outside, he shivered. *Cold*, he told himself. *Real autumn weather.*

* * *

The next morning Trent found a small package resting in the outside doorway of his study at the church. It was wrapped in brown paper, with no label or address on it.

He took the package in with him and placed it on his desk, then just sat there studying it a bit.

Just a package, guy, he told himself. *Don't be childish*. Then he unwrapped it and took out the contents.

A crystal pyramid!

"Where did this come from?" he asked out loud.

Suddenly he felt chilled to the bone, as though all the doors and windows were open.

He stood up, knocking the package onto the floor, and left the study with the pyramid. Out in back was a toolshed. There, he retrieved a hammer, found an empty grocery sack, ripped it open, and set the pyramid on top of the flattened heavy paper. Then he smashed the crystal into hundreds of pieces, and the pieces to dust.

He was shaking by the time he had finished.

He folded the paper, went into the church, and flushed the powdery bits and pieces down the toilet in the men's lavatory.

Back in the study, he noticed the package on the floor and bent down and picked it up. Something fell out.

"What in the world?"

It was a tiny wood carving.

Strange wood carvings are cropping up all over the place, Paul had said. *People are carrying them around like they're some kind of good-luck charm or fetish. They seem to have something to do with all this, but I don't know what.*

Trent studied the carving. *Hand-carved.* And then he realized that the face looked familiar. *Where have I seen it before?* He dropped it on top of his desk and walked down the hallway to the church library. *I'm sure it was here somewhere.* Then he spotted the title he was looking for: *Prince of Darkness: Satan in Scripture and History.*

Inside, the text was heavily illustrated with demonic images from various artists and cultures down through the ages. He stopped at one particular page that showed several of the Aztec devil gods.

That one in the middle. . . . A face reptilian in appearance, with a beak-like nose.

It was an exact likeness!

Trent was utterly unnerved. He had expected similarities, not duplication down to the last detail.

Dear Lord, he prayed. *Just what is happening?*

Then he noticed another title, *Demons in the World Today.* He leafed through it until he came upon one pertinent paragraph.

"A fetish is an object magically charged with protective powers . . . it has its roots in demon-energized idolatry and paganism."

Protection? he said to himself. *From what?*

Brushing that thought aside, he continued reading.

"Fetishism is much more than a manifestation of ancient primitive heathenism . . . supernatural feats performed through the use of a fetish are well-known in the history of occultism...these represent the intrusion of demonic deception."

A sense of oppression seemed to fill the small room, and he had to get out. He shut the door behind him.

Even in a church? he remarked to himself, not quite believing what he had felt, and more than a little ashamed that he had let it hit him so hard.

But there's nothing sacred about a church, he answered. *It's only a building, mortar and stone and glass. To think otherwise is idolatry. Satan can prowl its aisles as easily as he can any other building.*

He recalled Bennett Chapman's rather strange manner and wondered, with growing apprehension, if his friend would have anything similar to report.

* * *

The Rendezvous was a favorite spot for the luncheon crowd, for its dim lighting and rich medieval decor provided a relaxing quietness in the midst of a busy day.

Trent arrived at the restaurant before his friend and asked to be seated. The waiter had just brought him a cup a coffee when the hostess led Chapman to the table.

"I was about to say that you haven't changed much," Chapman said as he sat down, "but then it's been less than a year since I saw you last."

True, Trent told himself. *But what about you, my friend?* Bennett Chapman had aged considerably in those few months, his hair streaked with gray, his forehead lined with deep wrinkles, his skin pale.

Sensing Trent's reaction, Chapman tried to smile but failed. "You can tell, can't you?" he said.

"I can tell that something is very wrong."

"More than you realize, Harley," said Chapman. "Let me give you just one statistic: The suicide rate in my town has doubled in the past six months."

"Doubled?"

"You heard me. And all of the deaths have been teenagers," Chapman replied, placing a crumpled newspaper clipping on the table. "Look at this."

Trent read the headline.

Local Congregation Throws Out Its Pastor

Claims He Encouraged Occultic Practices

"That comes from the other end of the state, Harley. One of the deacons in that church is a friend of mine."

"Did you call him?" Trent asked.

"I did," Chapman said. "One of the things he told me was that they found a large box of wood carvings in the pastor's study, each an exact duplication of—"

"—an Aztec devil god," finished Trent as he pulled the small wooden carving from his pocket and laid it on the table.

Chapman reached into his own pocket and brought out its duplicate. The two men looked at each other with something like fear and horror in their eyes.

"Where did yours come from?" asked Chapman.

"I have no idea. It was outside my study this morning, with no name or markings on the wrapping paper. There was a crystal pyramid with it."

"Where's the pyramid?"

"Somewhere in the sewage system."

"Good!" said Chapman. "Harley, I did some research. Listen to this." He leafed through a small white pad filled with notes. " 'A fetish has been considered the material home of a demonic spirit, which can be unlocked and the demon freed when the individual becomes totally enslaved to it.' "

"What poppycock!" Trent said, though without conviction, in view of what his own preliminary research had uncovered.

"No, my friend, it's not. It may sound bizarre and unlikely, but when we condemn idol worship, aren't we suggesting that idols have been a means used by Satan to enslave his victims over the centuries? What's the difference? Even if a demon doesn't reside in these carvings, they can still provide a point of focus, a mind-set that demons can manipulate as a key to the soul."

"You're right," said Trent. "Sorry for that knee-jerk reaction. You see, I came across some similar data myself this morning. Please go on."

Chapman flipped the page and read, " 'Fetishes are not necessarily pieces of individual personal property.' " Then he paused, looked up at his friend, and continued in a hushed tone, " 'These may be considered as belonging to and entrapping an entire community.' "

He leaned back in his chair and pulled out another piece of paper—wrapping paper—and spread it out next to the carving.

"Look at the postmark, Harley."

Trent picked it up. "Valley Falls, Kansas."

Suddenly the significance of Chapman's notes hit him . . . *belonging to and entrapping an entire community.*

"But that's not all," Chapman continued. "What do you read on the sign in this Polaroid shot?"

The sign didn't register at first, but the mangled dog's carcass at its base did.

"Bennett, that dog's been cut apart."

"You bet it has, Harley. Now look at the sign. I think the locale must be a vacant lot."

FOR SALE
VALLEY FALLS REALTY
Phone: 765-4415

"Where did that photo come from?"

"In the same package as the carving," Chapman replied. "I should say, the carvings."

"You got more than one?"

"Try a dozen!"

"You think it was something like this that got that pastor hooked on the occult?"

"I'm certain of it," said Chapman grimly. "Now, tell me more about Paul DeKorte's situation."

Trent repeated everything DeKorte had told him, including what he hoped to do with the two boys.

"Do you think we can help him?" he asked when he had finished.

Chapman nodded, though he didn't speak at first.

"Harley?" he said finally.

"Yes?"

"There have been other places, you know, with similar stories, in a number of states."

"All traceable somehow to Valley Falls?" Trent asked with apprehension.

"No, I don't think so. Not as far as I can tell. And there is no denominational tie either. Some of the pastors are Pentecostal, some are Episcopalian, a few are Presbyterian, among others. But there does seem to be one common thread."

"What is it, Bennett?"

"I know some of the pastors," Chapman acknowledged. "And I've researched the others. And I've discovered that all of them are either pastoring ritualistic churches with no real evangelical core, or they are so far into the certain gifts of the spirit, especially tongues, that they have turned their backs on vibrant Bible teaching."

He paused for a moment as the waiter approached to take their order. Trent said they weren't ready to order yet and asked him to come back in a few minutes. After he left, Chapman continued.

"In the one instance, Harley, the focus on ritual leads to spiritual deadness. And in the other there is a constant struggling for emotional ecstasy."

"And the end result is the same," Trent concluded. "Wherever there is false doctrine or no real doctrine at all, Satan moves in to fill the vacuum."

"Without exception."

"And in each instance the wood carvings have been found?"

"Precisely," Chapman replied.

Trent let out a long sigh. "But I've not seen it in my congregation."

"Are you a Bible teacher, Harley?"

"You know the answer to that," Trent said, a touch of irritation in his voice.

"Right," said Chapman. "And you don't have to ask me that question either. You see, that carving and the Polaroid were found in the local high school, and the teenage girl involved wasn't a member of my church. I suspect yours may have come from a similar source."

The two men sat in silence for a few moments.

"So where does this leave us with the Valley Falls matter, Bennett?" Trent said finally.

"Well, whatever the explanation is, from what Paul has told you, things may be coming to a head in Valley Falls faster than in most places. "Bennett, I suspect I know the reason."

"What's that?"

"Think, my friend. How many other pastors have congregations in Valley Falls?"

"I imagine—" Chapman's eyes widened. "Wait a minute! Paul's is the only one!"

"Right."

"And if he stumbles and falls," Chapman spoke the words with heaviness, "there is no other shepherd ready to guard the flock."

They both lapsed into silence. The waiter did manage to get an order out of them, but it remained, uneaten, on the table.

21

"Doug, I have a special favor to ask," DeKorte said after his friend had answered the phone.

"Ask away," said Rogers.

"Would you attend the church service tomorrow morning?"

"Me?"

"Yes. It's important. I know how you feel about Christianity, and I wouldn't ask you if it weren't really important to me."

There was only a slight pause. "You know, with all this Hell breaking loose," Rogers said, "maybe it's not the worst thing I could be doing!"

"It would mean a lot to me."

"I'll be there."

"God bless you, Doug."

"You, too."

After he had hung up, he called Clement Albertson with the same request. The principal, too, promised to be there.

* * *

Filling the seats at Valley Falls Church of the Redeemer had never been a problem. Paul DeKorte's traditional peace-and-prosperity message was a popular one, hitting the most vulnerable areas in the lives of the town's citizens. Even in the midst of the tragedies that had occurred in the past weeks, the people of Valley Falls seemed to maintain their equilibrium. They turned out each Sunday well-dressed, with smiling faces and friendly manner.

DeKorte surveyed the faces he had known for more than a decade. There they sat, as they had on hundreds of Sunday mornings, joyfully singing one of the hymns he had picked earlier.

My hope is built on nothing less than Jesus' blood and righteousness.

The repetition of those words made him recoil inside, made him stand back and cry over the wasted time.

On Christ, the solid Rock I stand,
All other ground is sinking sand,

All other ground is sinking sand.

He looked up at the ceiling as the chorus concluded. *Lord, give me the words,* he prayed silently, then waited as the people settled themselves for the sermon.

"I've been your pastor for many years," he began, "and we have been blessed with some good times."

"Hallelujah!" someone shouted.

"Indeed hallelujah," he agreed. "But the good times—or rather the way we focused upon them—may have sown the seeds for what we are now experiencing."

He paused, looking at the congregation with as much honest love as he could project.

"It is entirely possible, beloved, to be too positive. To expect only the good and somehow try to wish away any of the bad. I am very much afraid that we have been living under a cloud for a long time now, a self-deceptive cloud of moral and spiritual cowardice."

No one was saying hallelujah now. No one was coughing. There was no movement of any kind.

"We live in a world cursed by the sin of Eden," he went on, "a world where everything was supposed to be the epitome of God's dream for mankind. But Satan entered that utopia and made it what we have today."

He held up several newspaper clippings.

"And what is it that we do have?" He pulled out individual clippings, one by one. "More than a million babies are aborted each year ... thousands of young people run away from home and end up on the streets of Los Angeles, Chicago, New York, and other cities where they sell their bodies to fill their stomachs with food or their veins with drugs ... meanwhile, our entire country is reaping the results of the rampant homosexual subculture. Our tolerance of their sin has allowed the AIDS epidemic to infect the weak and the helpless—the hemophiliac needing a blood transfusion, the unsuspecting mates of promiscuous spouses.

"This is the real world, beloved, a world of disease, crime, infidelity, media brainwashing, and much else that must cause our Lord to weep over us."

He put down the clippings and looked out earnestly over his congregation.

"Until recently we in Valley Falls have been insulated from most of what I have just mentioned. We have wrapped ourselves in the cocoon of our faith and counted on it to protect us from contamination. We have avoided, like the proverbial plague, any real grappling with the issues of the day."

Next, he held up a stack of cassettes.

"These are some of my sermons over the past five years. I have listened to many of them again. And out of nearly 200 hours of preaching I estimate that I have devoted less than 120 minutes to the central reason for our being Christians in the first place—our acceptance of the death, burial, and resurrection of Jesus Christ and our welcoming of Him into our lives as Savior and Lord."

He lowered his voice, softening the tone.

"Not everything in life is supposed to be handed to us on a silver platter. The early apostles were beaten, stoned, spat upon, cursed, and forced to live on the edge of poverty. Even Christ Himself had little that anyone could call material blessings."

Several in the congregation had begun to exchange uncertain glances.

"Yes, this is a prosperous town. We have much for which we can be thankful. But how many of us have fallen into the trap of being faithful, yes, of worshiping the Lord after a fashion, primarily for what He can do for us today, not for what He already did 2000 years ago?"

DeKorte's words were having an impact, but not in the way he intended. One man looked particularly annoyed as he whispered to his wife that he hoped DeKorte hadn't gone off the deep end.

"What I'm trying to say is that we should take our eyes off the banks of Heaven and direct ourselves toward the gates instead. We must examine the motives for our faith—and, therefore, the validity of our faith."

He leaned forward on the pulpit for emphasis.

"Five people we loved are dead—killed by a violent hand. And two more are at this moment confined to a mental institution to determine whether or not they are suffering from mental illness or—" He pounded his fist down. *"—demonic possession!"*

His face was red with anger now.

"There is no question in my mind that they would all be with us now if we had been more concerned about spiritual welfare and less about material welfare. Our priorities—and I put myself at the top of the list—have become distorted and misshapen. In the midst of our zeal for the gifts of the spirit, gifts that are entirely worthy in themselves, some of us may well have turned ourselves over to the wrong master. We have accepted Satan's counterfeits!

"That has got to change, beloved. That which is false has to be rooted out. We have no choice if we are to escape the sobering judgment of Almighty God.

"I'm going to be a different pastor from now on. This shepherd is no longer going to be leading you straight to the wolves!"

DeKorte was perspiring, and he pulled out his handkerchief to wipe his brow, his head bowed for a moment.

The congregation was silent—an oppressive silence.

Several seconds passed. Then, a voice came from the back of the auditorium.

"Pastor?" It was Lance Setterman.

"Yes, Lance?"

"Sir, I just wanted to say that I am concerned about what many of my friends have gotten into over the past few weeks. And I'm ashamed of those of us who have seen what has been happening and done nothing about it."

"Wait one minute!" said a middle-aged man, jumping to his feet. "What is all this alarmist stuff? We've got a happy town here."

"Mr. Earley, that's just not true," said Lance. "This town is like a Halloween party where all the guests are wearing masks to disguise what they're really like. Only this time the ugliness is underneath!"

"Lance Setterman, I never thought I'd—" Earley stopped in midsentence, turned his head strangely to the side, hesitated, then sat down.

"Pastor," the boy continued, "why don't we all join hands in prayer now? Ask the Lord for His guidance?"

"I think that's an excellent suggestion, Lance," agreed DeKorte. "Please stand and join hands."

The congregation stood, but they did not join hands. Instead, one by one they started to leave the sanctuary. He noticed Edith Van Halen's wheelchair heading toward the handicapped ramp at the side entrance. One man came up to the front and handed DeKorte a scribbled note: WE DON'T NEED A RELIGIOUS FANATIC HERE IN VALLEY FALLS. IF YOU KEEP THIS UP, WE'LL BE LOOKING FOR A NEW PREACHER!

DeKorte read it and sank to his knees behind the pulpit.

"Blessed Lord, please give me the gift of wisdom that I've so sorely lacked."

Someone touched his shoulder, and he looked up into Clement Albertson's eyes.

"Pastor, we're with you all the way," he said.

"We?"

"Yes."

As DeKorte was getting to his feet, he saw Lance and five other teenagers gathered in front of the altar.

"We don't know what we can do as yet," Lance told him. "Maybe we'll be like those who survived while Sodom and Gomorrah perished." The boy choked back tears.

"Paul, the kids and I are going on a retreat next weekend. We'll be thinking and praying about what we can be doing."

"I'd like to talk with you before you go, Clement," said DeKorte. "There are some more developments I think you should know about."

"I'll stop by during the week."

After they left, with DeKorte's promise to pray for them, he saw that he still was not alone.

Douglas Rogers was standing in the center aisle.

"Well, Paul, I think you finally found a message I just might listen to," said his friend. "I never did think religion by the checkbook was very honest or very satisfying! If I want that, I can go to the bank!"

O Lord, DeKorte found himself praying, *use me to reach Doug. Remove any remaining obstacles from his heart and mind, I beg You. Use these troubled times to bring about his salvation.*

22

Robbie Vachon knew that something was going on. He was in the locker room at school when he first noticed it. The jokes were raunchier, the gestures more obscene. And then he overheard two boys talking about their girlfriends, and it was not the usual sort of conversation; he could almost tolerate that, given the raging hormones of many of the guys.

But this time it was different. Violent. Perverted.

He heard talk of a gang rape, of a heavy metal drug party, and more.

Not normal locker-room banter.

And these were not the only clues.

Within a few days after Scott Pennio had disappeared and his buddies had been apprehended, Robbie noticed other little moments.

He worked as a cook at the local hamburger stand, and he started noticing....

Wood carvings.

Everyone who drove in seemed to have them. Most of the help, too.

There was a different "feel" about the place. He couldn't put his finger on what, but he knew he was right.

That night, in bed, before he went to sleep, he thought back and realized that "it" had started before the thing involving Scott, Wayne, and Mark, but he had done little more than shrug his shoulders and walk away.

Whispers in the school corridors, square plastic packets containing white powder being passed around, and more, more indeed.

But now, as he looked back, bits and pieces fell into place, along with chills that raced up and down his back.

The next morning after gym class when Robbie had showered and dressed, he was approached by his friend, Arnie Singer.

"After school," he said. "Could we meet at my house? I gotta talk to you, Robbie, please."

Robbie nodded.

Arnie was the school's reigning intellectual, but not at all an athlete. Not that Robbie himself was any great shakes in that department, but in comparison Arnie made him look like Olympic material.

Robbie was a gymnast, not quite good enough to be another Mitch Gaylord, but not bad either. He enjoyed sports, enjoyed the feeling of accomplishment they gave him, enjoyed being healthy and able to handle himself physically in just about any situation.

Robbie decided to skip lunch period and spend some time in the gym working out. Working into a good sweat was liberating for him, cleared his mind, freed his spirit.

He put on some earphones and listened to music while he was using the parallel bars. Again and again he swung on them, faster and faster.

Then something happened to shatter his momentum.

The music.

Open the door to Hell, and let the demons swoop in, and kill the mothers and the fathers of our torment....

The words hit him like a physical blow. He missed the bars and hit the floor, wrenching his left shoulder.

"I can't believe it," he said out loud.

Take the knife and do the deed....

He tore the earphones off his head.

He hugged himself, knowing his reaction went beyond the words themselves, as bad as those were.

"Oh, God," he prayed. "Oh, God, everybody in school listens to that station."

Everybody in school....

He was very glad he had a date with his girlfriend Cindy Simmons that evening. No one enabled him to relax like she did.

But first there was Arnie Singer.

* * *

Arnie let him in seconds after he rang the front doorbell.

"My room," Arnie said. "Follow me."

Once they were inside and Arnie had shut the door behind them, he hurried over to a desk next to his bed and took out a box, spreading the contents on the bed.

"Look at this," he said.

He handed Robbie a small sheet of paper.

12:30
The funeral home.
Party.

"What?" Robbie said, almost in a shout.

"I found it when I was emptying the wastebasket in homeroom, Robbie."

"A party at a funeral home?"

"And look at this," Arnie said, handing him a little booklet. "I found it in the locker room."

ANIMALS AND SEX—
HEIGHTENING THE PLEASURE

Robbie didn't have to look at more than the first couple of pages.

"There's a lot more," Arnie said. "There's something called ritual abuse."

"Just tell me. I don't want to look. I really don't."

"Girls are given drugs, then gotten pregnant. The baby they give birth to is literally a born addict."

"Here in Valley Falls?"

"Not yet. But that's the plan. The infant addict grows up with his own source of supply being the cult."

"And then what happens?"

"After the kid gets to be our age, he's turned loose on the world."

"Becomes a mass murderer, I bet."

"Oh, yes. They're shipped off to California and Texas and Florida and the New England states . . . everywhere."

"Time bombs."

"Ready to explode when somebody pulls the plug."

And then Robbie told his friend about his own suspicions.

"See!" Arnie slid off the bed, his eyes wide. "I thought I was going crazy, man, I really did."

"Have you told anyone else?" Robbie asked.

"My parents."

"What did they say?"

"They laughed at me. They said it was just a phase guys pass through. They hinted that if I was more red-blooded I would be doing the same thing."

"Red-blooded? Is that all they said?"

Arnie nodded.

"But what about the ritual abuse?"

"They chalk it up to some kind of fantasy on my part."

"But you don't have that kind of mind, Arnie."

"You know it. I know it. My own parents don't. We never talk. You know a lot more about me than they do."

"We've got to see Albertson. He has to know about this—this stuff."

"Agreed. Tomorrow."

"Keep it safe, Arnie."

Arnie smiled.

"Say hello to Cindy for me."

After his friend left, Arnie stood in the living room of the home in which he had lived all his life.

How normal everything was just a year ago, he thought. *None of this other stuff. Just a regular school in a regular town with regular kids.*

He remembered the weight lifting craze that had swept through the school. Every guy wanted to have bulging muscles. And there he was, a shrimp as always, his biceps more like pimples.

But not Robbie.

His friend had a killer build, great arms, well-formed pectorals, washboard stomach, strong thighs.

If only . . .

Arnie often compared himself with Robbie.

My mind in your body, guy! A combination to make history!

Arnie sighed.

He had other friends, but none like Robbie, who was more like a member of his family than—

Mom . . . Dad, Arnie said to himself. *If only you and I could—*

He shrugged his shoulders, knowing that few of his dreams would ever become reality.

"Say hello to Cindy for me," he said wistfully, thinking about the few girls he had dated, as awkward and homely and ill at ease as he was.

None like beautiful Cindy. . . .

And then he went up to his bedroom, to his books and his computer and the awful little notes and other disturbing things he had managed to collect.

He never got a chance to scream when he opened the door.

Robbie Vachon disappeared a couple of hours later. The last he was seen was as he was getting into his car to pick up his girlfriend.

Arnie Singer was dead by morning, officially listed as a suicide.

An investigation was begun.

But Valley Falls had less than a week remaining on Planet Earth before the holocaust.

Not much time.

Not much time at all.

23

"Reverend DeKorte?" said the caller when DeKorte answered the telephone on the second ring. "This is county prosecutor Gary Harmon."

DeKorte wondered for an instant if anything had gone wrong with the plan for Trent and Chapman to examine Wayne and Mark. But the prosecutor anticipated his concern and hastened to reassure him.

"Don't be concerned about what we arranged," Harmon said. "It's all set. Your minister friends are going to be picking up Elliott Gardner. He's one of the best specialists in the country and an expert on psychotic behavior."

"How can I help you?" asked DeKorte.

"Would you meet me at my office this afternoon?"

"I'd be glad to. What's the problem?"

"Let's just say that what I have to tell you may very well reinforce your beliefs about the supernatural."

DeKorte arrived a few minutes early, and Harmon's secretary showed him into the prosecutor's office.

As soon as he entered, DeKorte noticed the objects on the desk.

"You have five of the carvings yourself!" DeKorte exclaimed.

Harmon smiled slightly and said, "Look more closely, please."

DeKorte picked up one and rolled it between his fingers.

Pieces of dust—or something—flaked off.

"What in the world?"

"Precisely what I asked myself."

Harmon reached into a drawer, took something out, and placed it on the desktop.

"This is what you've been seeing ad nauseam, am I correct?" he said.

"Yes. But these others? What are they?"

"Examine them carefully but closely. They're very old."

What DeKorte saw were the remains of five little creatures, no larger than the carvings themselves.

"At first we thought they were the remains of some bat species," Harmon said. "But they're not bats at all, and they've been like that for a lot longer."

The prosecutor hesitated before adding, "This would seem to indicate that either the wood carvings were created totally out of someone's imagination and the resemblance is coincidental, or—"

"—or carved from real life?" said DeKorte.

"Right. And in that case, you happen to be holding one of the models."

Looking closely at the mouth of the creature, DeKorte observed, "The teeth are still intact."

"Our lab cut one of the things apart," said Harmon. "That's not as insensitive to the historical value as it may sound. You see, we've uncovered hundreds of the things."

"Where?"

"In the old cemetery outside Valley Falls. They were unearthed accidentally."

"Hundreds?"

"That's correct. Anyway, getting back to what the lab found... all of the internal organs were perfectly preserved."

"No deterioration?"

"None that mattered. They were in better shape than any of the mummies ever found in Egypt."

"So what do you make of them? What do you think they are?"

"I don't know, but a bunch of wild theories have cropped up. Would you like to hear some?"

"Yes," DeKorte said, sitting down across the desk from the prosecutor and resting the little object next to the others.

"One is that they're aborted fetuses from some ancient race of beings. I don't place any credence at all in that one," he said with a laugh. "Another is that they indeed may be a species of bat, and that centuries ago the spot where the cemetery is now was the place where they went to die, like the elephant graveyards in some African myths."

"Those are wild all right! Any other theories?"

"A crazy quilt of them. Perhaps the most absurd is the one that suggests they are not dead at all, but in some kind of dormant state, like a volcano. Appearing dead on the outside but actually capable of coming back to life. When I heard that one, as ridiculous as it sounds, I was tempted to keep them under lock and key twenty-four hours a day. Which is what I ended up doing."

Sensing that the man had more on his mind, DeKorte asked, "Is there something else?"

Harmon reached into his desk and pulled out a file folder filled with papers.

"Take a look at the contents."

DeKorte leafed through the papers, one after the other indicating almost exactly the same thing.

"Other grave sites like the one near Valley Falls."

"Many of them, Reverend DeKorte. Before the Pilgrims and the Puritans came to this nation, Indians and others lived here, of course."

"What do you mean by 'others'?"

"Some say the Aztecs, the Incas, the Mayans, and other races either originated here or established colonies at one time or another. The North American continent may even have seen communities of the ancient Phoenicians. Ironically we may have been on the receiving end of other nationalities and such long, long before we could ever have imagined."

"And all of them were pagan," DeKorte mused, "all worshiped the gods of the sun, the moon, and the earth itself."

"And Hades," Harmon reminded him.

"Yes, Hades."

"Those carvings and those bodies hardly seem the stuff of Heaven, wouldn't you say?"

DeKorte nodded absentmindedly.

"One of the sites was found ten years ago on the same property as the dismembered bodies of thirty-five teenage boys."

"That—that mass murderer, the one who's still in prison?"

"Exactly. On his land. To this day he claims to know nothing about it. And there's a report of a similar finding in Lizzie Borden's backyard."

"The ax murderess?"

"Right again. But listen to this."

Harmon flipped through the stack and brought out several sheets of paper stapled together. He read from the second page.

" 'Unreported to the general public for more than a century has been the following incident which occurred during the Civil War in a small town in Virginia. Yankees and Graycoats succumbed to the most abominable behavior, including mass slaughter of one another as well as cannibalistic atrocities right out of some pagan culture.' "

Harmon put the sheets back in the folder.

"There's more, but the details are, to say the least, rather gory. I don't have to tell you what was discovered in the general vicinity, do I?"

DeKorte shook his head.

"At Ford's Theatre one night," Harmon continued, "there was a gunshot, and then John Wilkes Booth fled from the scene. In his flight he accidentally dropped something that has never been reported in the history books."

"Not—"

"Yes, I'm afraid it was."

The atmosphere in the office seemed to grow oppressive, and DeKorte suddenly felt as though he couldn't breath.

"I must go now," he said.

"Before you do," said Harmon, "I have a favor to ask."

"What is it?"

Harmon stood and started pacing.

"I've been in this profession for many years, but never have I encountered people from whom it was harder to get any information. I'm talking about the Jacobsons and the Mulrooneys. They are very insular people, and I thought it might help if you spoke to them. Tell them I thought they might be more comfortable talking with you rather than strangers. They're going through an incredible series of traumas right now, I realize, and yet we desperately need their cooperation."

"To convict Wayne and Mark of murder?"

"That isn't my intention. After that encounter in the courtroom and uncovering those—those things, whatever they are, I've realized we have a case here beyond anything I've ever been involved in or heard about. I only want the truth. And perhaps that truth can set them free in the end. Will you help me?"

DeKorte nodded.

"Forgive me," he said. "I'm involved in this to such a degree that it has been traumatic for me as well."

"I understand. I've read the files on your wife's death, as well as that other boy."

"Patrick was clutching one of the carvings, you know," said DeKorte.

"He was?" remarked Harmon in surprise. "Now that wasn't in the report. I wonder why?"

DeKorte shook his head and shrugged his shoulders.

"You know, Reverend, I've probably seen more of the evil side of human nature than you have," said Harmon. "And evil is the only word to describe many of the crimes I've had to investigate over the years.

"I was a New York cop before I came here, and I can tell you that there are terrible things going on in the dark corners of every city.

But no matter how bad it all was, I'd convinced myself that it derived from psychological or emotional illness, certainly not the supernatural."

"And now you're not so sure?"

"You could say that. But then a minister who really studies the Bible can't be as overwhelmed as the rest of us—as stunned, I guess, by this sort of thing."

"Not by the idea," DeKorte agreed. "But the reality? Well, that's something else again. Certainly I've never encountered anything like this. Yet much that is applicable here is revealed in the Bible."

"Yes, I know. I bought a copy the other day and have been leafing through it," said the prosecutor. "One passage in particular hit me."

"Which one?"

"A section that mentions something about demons running to and fro over the earth. Now that is scary, Reverend."

As DeKorte was getting into his car a few minutes later, he repeated those words to himself.

Demons running to and fro over the earth.

Scary?

Oh, yes....

24

Albertson and the young people left directly from school after classes were over on Friday and arrived at the retreat center by dark. The was a privately run operation that catered to religious groups and organizations and was located in a heavily wooded area beside a small lake.

During the drive in the van they had borrowed from the school, Lance Setterman told Albertson about the curious feeling that had gripped him as he waved good-bye to several of his friends.

"Sad," the teenager said. "I felt a strange kind of sadness come over me."

"Any idea why, Lance?" Albertson asked.

"Not really. Except that some of my friends seemed to be avoiding me. Others just wouldn't look straight at me, like they were ashamed of something. Especially Jami Arlen," he said. "You know, we dated a couple times. But recently . . . well, I couldn't believe what she did at the songfest. And she's completely dropped out of the church youth group, as you know."

Lance fell silent after that, and Albertson thought about the boy's comments.

Like they were ashamed of something. . . .

Lance had been a strong witness for Christ during his high school years, never embarrassed about presenting the Gospel to those who would listen. At the same time, his movie-star handsomeness coupled with his athletic prowess, vibrant personality, and top grades made him popular with students and teachers alike.

So Albertson understood Lance's concern over the change in behavior of those with whom he had gotten along so well over the past few years.

Ashamed of something.

Speculating on just what that might be made Albertson more than a little uncomfortable.

* * *

After unpacking and settling in, Albertson went for a walk. The retreat was in the midst of a heavily wooded area, with a lake to the left and a portion of a small mountain range to the right. Autumn was a spectacular time of the year here, with so much color encircling the cabins that it was a blessing just to stand outside and look, smell the sweet air, and hear the natural music of a multitude of birds.

And that night he looked up at the sky, with a clear view of the stars, and he thanked God for the chance to recharge his spiritual and emotional batteries.

"Beautiful, isn't it?" A thin, old voice penetrated his thoughts.

Albertson turned and saw a skinny man of medium height in his late sixties or early seventies, his long bony face accented with a white goatee. He recognized Dr. Fritz Lorensen, the guest speaker for the weekend.

"Dr. Lorensen, welcome. I'm Clement Albertson, principal of Valley Falls High School."

"Ah, yes, I've been reading quite a bit about Valley Falls lately."

"I'm afraid you have."

The two of them walked together for a bit, talking, and finally came to the edge of the lake.

"You know, it's amazing how many people live their lives like the fish in those waters," Lorensen remarked.

"How is that, sir?"

"They go on blindly, swimming around in the currents, never understanding that someday they can be plucked right out without any warning. An accident can do it. A sudden heart attack. These days, even a terrorist bombing. And then it's all over. They make no plans for the future because they are oblivious to it."

"But there is a difference," Albertson pointed out. "Those fish can't do anything about their fate."

"That is it, my brother. And that's the particular tragedy of humans who live like those fish, because it means they are blind and have no interest in being given sight. For they do have choices, many, many times . . . choices that can better their lives, that can impact the lives of others . . . choices that determine their eternal destiny."

Lorensen sighed.

"And it would appear, if the media are accurate for a change, that three teenagers in your town made the wrong choice."

"I'm afraid it may go far beyond those kids," said Albertson and told Lorensen about his suspicions.

"I see," the man replied, rubbing his goatee thoughtfully. "Would you be interested in having me go back to Valley Falls with you for a few days?"

Albertson was taken aback.

"Of course. But do you have the time?"

"I'll make the time. Something is going on in Valley Falls, and if I can be of any help, then that's where I should be. You see, I've been concerned for some time about what the circumstances in Valley Falls and elsewhere seem to indicate."

"What's that, Dr. Lorensen?"

"It's all so devilishly clever, and I mean that literally. First, marriages are destroyed by promiscuity; then the unborn are aborted; then the young are hooked into drugs and Satanism; and finally the elderly are eliminated by euthanasia. And, of course, we mustn't forget the spread of homosexuality."

"All aimed at the destruction of the family."

"Precisely," Lorensen replied. "The foundation of so much of God's plan for the ages."

"And those young people who somehow survive are, in many cases, the worst possible candidates to resolidify the familial base when they are old enough," added Albertson, "and so the cancer-like deterioration goes on, generation after generation."

Lorensen folded his arms. "You are really quite good at this, my young friend."

When Albertson blushed, the older man said, "I mean it. I travel all over the United States, and I meet three kinds of people. They're either Rigid Controllers or Deaf Ignorers or Responsible Pilgrims. My sense is that you are definitely in the third group."

They were about to turn back toward the cabins when Lorensen hesitated a moment.

"What is it, sir?" Albertson asked.

"I thought—" he started to say, then stopped. "Never mind. It's late. The darkness sometimes plays tricks on aging intellects."

But Albertson noticed that while the evening air was cool, beads of perspiration had appeared on the older man's forehead.

25

Douglas Rogers occasionally sat back and analyzed why in the world he and Paul DeKorte had been such good friends for so long. At present they both were widowers. For Rogers the death of his wife went back many years; for DeKorte, it was recent. Losing the women they loved had only brought them closer together; it didn't form the basis for their friendship.

As he was getting dressed that morning, anticipating a full day of helping DeKorte dig into the Pennio Affair, as it had come to be called by the media, he looked in the mirror and saw a man in his late sixties, hair nearly gone, and what was left had become white a long time before.

Paul's some twenty years younger, he told himself. *And he's a man of faith. I have no faith. Never have had.*

Yet they were like brothers.

I would die for him.

That admission, coming so unexpectedly, took him aback.

Sounds almost Christian. Could that stuff be rubbing off on me without me being aware of it? He chuckled to himself. *I can't imagine what it would be like to pray to an empty void—*

He cut that thought in midstream because it wasn't quite true, he knew. There was a time when he had prayed daily, prayed that God would do something about his wife's cancer.

She died anyway, wasting away to only seventy-three pounds.

He remembered what she looked like that last day. He remembered the smile on her face less than an hour before she stopped breathing. He remembered being infuriated at a God who would deal with such a woman so cruelly.

After shaving and taking a shower, he got dressed, pausing for a moment at the photograph of his wife he still kept on the nightstand beside his bed.

Why were you smiling, my love? How could you be smiling?

Their house was quite small, and they'd never been parents, never been blessed with the sound of children around that house. They had only themselves over the years.

And then she was gone. God, how could You have done that?

He paused for a moment in the living room. Even so many years later, he could still imagine her scent lingering in the air . . . a hint of apple blossoms.

Something else.

Jesus, keep me near the cross,

The words were so familiar.

Free to all—a healing stream. Flows from Calvary's mountain.

How could she believe such a thing?

In the cross, in the cross,

Be my glory ever;

Till my raptured soul shall find

Rest beyond the river.

"My love," he said aloud, "you begged me to believe as you did. If only I could, dear, dear one. If only I could."

And then his manner changed.

"You took her from me," he said, his voice louder. "Why didn't You let her live longer? She might have been Your instrument to reach me. Why rip that wonderful woman from my life?"

He stopped then, making a conscious effort to control his emotions. Finally he had them back in check.

A little later, as he left to meet DeKorte, he realized how odd it was that he could feel continuing bitterness toward One who didn't exist.

*   *   *

Wayne Mulrooney's parents had agreed to meet with DeKorte and Rogers, so that was their first stop. As they sat in the Mulrooneys' family room and listened to Wayne's parents, Rogers thought they were still in a state of shock. All emotion seemed drained from them. Wayne's mother, Elizabeth, a high school teacher, spoke in a manner that suggested dispassionate television reporting, cold and clinical.

"I saw the three of them huddling with some other students in the hallway one day," she said, recounting a certain incident. "They were passing around some of those strange wood carvings. As soon as they noticed me, they stopped and went separate ways. But it stuck in my mind because it was so unlike Wayne to be secretive or evasive."

Betsy, Wayne's sister, spoke up then.

"It was all because of Scott," she said.

"How can you be so sure?" DeKorte asked.

"I just know."

"Can't you tell us more than that?"

She hesitated, then said, "Okay. I dated Scott a few times. At first he seemed real nice, sensitive and smart. I liked him. I liked him a lot. But after awhile he changed."

"In what way?" DeKorte asked.

"He became moody," she said. "And he started talking different... faster, harder to understand... saying really weird stuff. He played heavy metal music all the time in the car, turning it louder and louder. And he started to lose weight. He used to be a real hunk, but he got kind of skinny and flabby all at the same time. He seemed to lose interest in a lot of things that were once very important to him."

"When did you stop dating him?" asked Rogers.

"A couple of months ago. I did it because—because—"

Her father told her that she didn't have to continue, but she indicated that she wanted to do so.

"One night he asked me to watch while he—he did something awful with a dog."

"Mutilate it?" said DeKorte.

"No," she said, her face reddening. "Scott demanded that I watch while he—uh—while he had sex with it."

She looked down at the floor in embarrassment.

"I told him no! I told him it was sick... evil. And then—"

As she looked up at the adults, Rogers could see the tears in her eyes.

"Scott started cursing at me. He called me horrible names, dirty names, and he spoke to some kind of demon. Said it would come direct from Hell! But nothing happened. I didn't know whether to laugh or cry. But I'll tell you, I was scared. I made him take me home, and I never heard from him again. I didn't want to either. He was scary."

DeKorte thanked the girl for her honesty and asked if they could examine Wayne's room.

"Go ahead," said his father. "You'll hardly believe what you see. We haven't touched any of it. The police asked us to leave everything as it was."

As soon as the two of them entered, there was no further doubt about the direction in which Wayne had gone. Stapled or taped or nailed to all four walls were posters, not of beautiful women or regular rock music stars such as Springsteen, Manilow, and others, but those of Iron Maiden, Grateful Dead, and other heavy metal groups.

"Look at this," Rogers said, pointing to one of the posters where a man was brandishing a phallic symbol before a woman chained to a bed while another man was in the process of abusing her.

"Good God!" DeKorte said, not as an oath but a half-muttered prayer.

"There's more," Rogers said, surveying the others.

Both of them recoiled from the next image. A man with a helmet of what looked like chicken feathers was sitting in front of a baby out of whom he had just ripped the intestines.

"And all of this is protected by the Constitution!" Rogers muttered. "It boggles the mind!"

"Freedom of expression," said DeKorte. "But if yelling 'Fire!' in a theater isn't included, then how can this be rationalized?"

"Entire industries support this stuff," Rogers remarked. "Millions of posters on hundreds of thousands of walls. And yet the conventional wisdom is that it's all merely this generation's way of rebelling."

"But that's not the end of it, Doug," DeKorte added. "Look at the in-person concerts. The records themselves. The deejays serving as emissaries."

Rogers leafed through some of the record albums in a gold-tinted wall stand next to a sophisticated stereo unit, then turned to a stack of books on the nightstand beside the bed.

"What do you make of these, Paul?" he said. *Mysteries of the Ancient Americas.* What in the world has that got to do with rock music and demonic posters? And here's another: *Unearthing the Aztecs: A Look at Their Civilization.*"

"There are a lot of unanswered questions about the Aztecs, as well as the Mayans and Incas," DeKorte told him. "There is no way to account for all that they were able to accomplish, remarkable artisans and master builders and scientific geniuses that they were. But there was a dark side to them and their culture— sinister—and they all worshiped pagan deities. I wonder if that's what attracted Wayne and the others?"

He told Rogers about his conversation with the country prosecutor and the discovery of the mummified creatures in ancient graveyards and other sites.

"You know, Doug, something just clicked," he said suddenly. "Some say that the Aztecs, the Mayans, and the Incas either originated here in North America or established colonies here at one time. Suppose those creatures and carvings are from that era?"

As he spoke he had been examining the pile of books Rogers had found. Now he came upon a small brown pocket notebook.

"This looks like Wayne's diary," he said, scanning the first few pages. "Listen to this."

"I know it's all wrong, so wrong that I'm amazed I ever got into it this far. But what can I do? Music over the radio—my records—the rock magazines—it's there, all the time, the message, pounding, pounding, pounding at us."

DeKorte threw the diary on the floor in disgust.

Rogers bent down and picked it up, reading silently for a bit. Then he read another passage aloud.

"Scott has this odd hold over both Mark and me. There have been times when we are there, on the floor, so close together, and swaying back and forth, all sweaty, that I feel an attraction toward him, and suddenly I want to reach out and put my arms around..."

Rogers skipped to another section.

"Mark now seems to be totally enjoying this whole trip, especially trapping all those poor dogs, cats, and birds and smearing their blood on his..."

"Listen to this," Rogers said.

"If we didn't have some place to hide the remains and reuse some of them later, we would have to kill a lot more pets and that would generate a lot of talk—talk Scott tells us to avoid until everything is set."

"So that's the reason," Rogers remarked.

"The reason for what?"

"I've been reading in the county legal news that there is a rising incidence of animal disappearances."

"Not just in Valley Falls?"

"Correct!"

DeKorte had been flipping further through the diary. Now he paused.

"Listen to this, Doug!"

" 'There are times when I ask myself why we ever started this. And I really don't know. Looking for answers maybe? It all seemed so simple. Just a game. Now I think maybe it's just evil.

" 'But is it any less evil than everything around us? Violence as entertainment. Government and church leaders who shack up with prostitutes.

" 'I sure can't ask my parents, even if they would take time to listen. I mean really listen. I guess we only have each other. Maybe that's why it all started. At least the musicians know what's happening. Maybe their answers are the rights ones after all....' "

"Where in the world were their parents when these kids needed them?" said Rogers.

"I don't know, Doug. Maybe we should be thankful that we never had children. If we had, perhaps—"

"I don't believe that, Paul. Look at Scott's parents. They probably loved him more than you and I could ever imagine."

"And all three boys' parents are—well—supposedly Christians."

"Supposedly is probably the right word," said Rogers. "Supposedly I'm an agnostic, maybe even an atheist, and yet in the face of all this evil, here I am reexamining my ideas about all that."

He paused, then asked, "What does the Bible say about all this? Anything?"

"It says that in the latter days seducing spirits will descend upon the earth to deceive and destroy."

To deceive and destroy.

Rogers glanced about the room at the posters.

"Doug, you're—" DeKorte started to say, concerned.

"Yeah, I know. I'm shivering. And it's not because I'm coming down with something either."

The closet door was open, and DeKorte noticed a box of slides on the floor. It looked as though they had fallen from the top shelf and spilled out. He turned on the bedside lamp and held several up to the light.

"What's wrong?" Rogers asked when he saw his friend's face pale. DeKorte handed him the slides.

There were animal parts everywhere. Dogs, cats, birds. Intestines, severed heads, and what was left of the eviscerated bodies. Some hung from the ceiling at the end of thin ropes; others were strewn about on the floor. From the background, it appeared that the pictures had all been taken in the same room.

"Trophies," Rogers said.

"To be reused," DeKorte muttered.

"But where? Who would participate in such atrocities?"

A few seconds later, Rogers uncovered a shoe box filled with nearly twenty of the wood carvings.

"Here's something else," he said.

A sheet of paper.

He scanned it briefly.

"Paul, you know what this is?"

"Have no idea."

"A mailing list."

"To send the carvings elsewhere?"

"You got it!"

He handed the sheet to DeKorte.

"To the brothers and sisters of some of the kids in town—principally those away at college, it seems," DeKorte said as he glanced at it.

"As far west as Nevada and a host of other places around the country—from coast to coast!" said Rogers.

"Even Toronto, Canada," DeKorte added.

"See those little check marks?"

"I do."

"I think they signify the ones—"

"—already mailed," added DeKorte.

They both looked about the room but decided not to stay any longer. Though it might be the power of suggestion, there was a heaviness in the air that frequently seemed to hang noticeably in areas of supreme tragedy.

Downstairs, Betsy Mulrooney seemed nervous, prompting DeKorte to ask if anything were wrong.

"Nothing, Reverend DeKorte," her mother quickly answered for her, "nothing new, that is."

She wasn't very convincing, her voice a strange monotone, her expression the dull, lifeless stare of a mannequin.

The two men thanked the Mulrooneys for their cooperation and left, more unnerved than ever.

26

Elliott Gardner was ready when Trent and Chapman arrived at the clinic on Saturday morning. He was a tall, thin man in his late forties, completely bald, who seemed congenial despite the fact that he was giving up his weekend for this venture.

"Let me show you what we're doing here," he said after the two ministers had been shown to his office by a friendly receptionist. "I think you'll find it interesting."

Gardner personally conducted a tour of the facilities. His clinic proved to be modern in its approach to treating the mentally ill, a no-nonsense manner readily apparent. Patients with behavior categorized as nonviolent enjoyed rooms that were well-furnished and attractively decorated; attendants were unfailingly solicitous and efficient; and everything looked as though a cleaning crew went through several times a week.

There was also an attempt to make the clinic seem a bit less institutional. Potted flowers were in abundance, on window ledges and shelves, with tall green plants in the rooms as well as the corridors.

Patients had access to books, television, and plenty of video and board games.

"Everything on television is carefully selected," Gardner proudly told the two ministers.

"I suppose you do that because there is so much that is questionable on television," said Trent.

"Absolutely," Gardner replied. "If a patient with psychotic tendencies were to watch a violent crime show, for example, it could be very detrimental. In fact, we allow virtually no violence in their television diet."

"Everything they see has been videotaped then?" Trent asked.

"That's correct. We have a central communications room here on the grounds. Every TV set is tied in with it."

"Have you ever studied the effect of televised violence on normal viewers?" said Chapman.

"I have. And the answers I get are disquieting. But I'm afraid the effect of heavy metal music is even more disturbing."

"Do you feel there is some correlation between it and cases you have treated?" Chapman asked.

"Definitely. Watching a violent TV show or movie can be bad enough in itself, but it is often a rather casual experience, an isolated activity. With the heavy metal syndrome, the music becomes a way of life, an ever-present atmosphere. It is always there, somewhere in the background. The heavy metal devotee wears the clothes, speaks the language, and bands together with others who do the same. Then you add to that the fact that drugs are usually involved."

"I've just realized something," said Trent. "Every patient I've seen here is young."

"You're observant, sir. None of our patients are over nineteen," Gardner told them. "Twenty-five years ago there would have been no need for centers such as this. Today, there are dozens of them scattered across the country, and even that is not enough."

"Are most of them on drugs?" Trent inquired.

"That's the root of much of what we find, yes," Gardner replied. "I've seen a tremendous increase in cases over just the past year or so. What has made it worse is the mushrooming availability of so-called designer drugs created in home labs. They are sold for very little money but frequently contain the most damaging impurities."

They had come to a large room. Inside were half a dozen teenage boys and girls.

"This is going to break your heart, but it's only the tip of the iceberg, if you'll pardon the cliché," Gardner told them as he opened the door.

The room was pleasant and sunny, but the patients seemed totally unaware of their surroundings. They sat like statues, staring into space.

"Do they know we're here?" Chapman asked softly.

"Some do," Gardner told him.

They approached one boy who looked up at them and smiled. When Trent reached out to shake his hand, the boy extended his own hand but the movement was slow, like that of an elderly person crippled with arthritis.

They chatted briefly and then went on to the others. All were the same: young people whose movements and speech were like those of residents in a nursing home.

"What in the world is wrong with them?" asked Trent when they were once more out in the hallway. Both he and Chapman were close to tears. "I've never seen anything like that."

"Senility," Gardner replied.

"Senility in teenagers?" Chapman repeated in astonishment.

"A form of it, yes. Actually, the only difference is that with the elderly there is an accompanying deterioration in tissues and such. Those teenagers have the constitutions of their age group but the minds of their grandparents. What we have here seems very like Alzheimer's Disease; so much so, in fact, that the only good result to come out of this may be further insight into the root cause of Alzheimer's in adults."

The minds of their grandparents.

This seemed true of a majority of the patients they encountered at the clinic, and the two ministers were impressed with the doctor's obvious empathy for his young charges. His manner with them was gentle and sincere, and he was obviously dedicated to helping them.

"Your concern for these young people is reassuring," Trent told him at one point. "From what we hear, the two boys we'll be examining in Valley Falls will need every bit of your expertise."

* * *

The more violent patients were housed in a separate area of the clinic.

"We are unable to furnish their quarters as well as the others," Gardner pointed out.

The reason was obvious: any sharp-edged objects, for example, could be used to attack attendants or for self-inflicted damage.

"In other words, these patients can be calm one minute and violent the next?" said Chapman as they approached a heavy metal door at the end of the corridor.

"Very much so, I'm afraid," Gardner replied.

"Do you ever wonder about the intensity of their behavior?" Trent asked.

"You aren't going to suggest that we have a bunch of Linda Blairs here, are you?" Gardner countered.

"The Exorcist was Hollywood," said Trent. "We're talking about real life here."

Gardner nodded in appreciation.

"Thank you for that. I know many Christians who are convinced that Satan is behind everything."

"Nevertheless, while eschewing the superficiality of that film and others like it, I must be honest in adding that authentic demonic possession used to be quite rare but may be increasing."

"Not here, I assure you."

"How can you be certain?"

Gardner dodged an answer as he asked the two men to look at the patient behind the metal door.

"We keep Rodney sedated as much as possible," he told them.

Rodney was an exceptionally handsome teenager, this apparent despite the dark circles under his eyes and the scratch marks on his face and the awful look of fear that he manifested.

"Why are his arms bandaged?" Trent inquired.

"He was pulling off pieces of his own flesh."

"What will stop him from trying again?"

"More drugs. A straitjacket. That sort of thing."

"For the rest of his life?" Chapman asked.

"No one knows."

* * *

They were back in Gardner's office. He went over to the door and shut it and then turned to the two men.

"I must tell you straightaway," he said, "that I am not at all comfortable having clergymen involved in the process of studying those boys. I appreciate the attitudes I've sensed in both of you during the past hour, but I'm certain that when we confront the boys we have been asked to examine . . . well, that there will undoubtedly be the most disagreeable contention between us."

He returned to his desk and held up a hefty file folder.

"From what I have read about their actions, I can see nothing but schizophrenic behavior."

"We feel that each human being is not intellect only, not emotion only, not flesh only," Chapman reminded him, "but there is a spirit, a spirit that is the true battleground here. That's why we also are going to be examining them, as a balance."

"A balance? Your very presence perpetrates the root cause of their psychosis."

"How in the world do you arrive at that conclusion, Dr. Gardner?" Trent asked.

"A very large percentage of those boys and girls you just saw come from religious homes."

"But being religious isn't the point, Dr. Gardner," Trent told him. "Religion is ceremony, empty repetition of verses becomes meaningless. Redemption is something else altogether."

"Their problem by and large," Gardner went on, "is that they grew up believing in a fantasy, and when reality intruded, their psychological balloon burst and they couldn't cope. As I view all this, it would have been far more desirable having them reject the promise of Heaven so that they could better cope with the Hell of this life!"

"You view life in such a manner?" Chapman asked. "Where is the joy, Dr. Gardner? The hope?"

"I see mostly pain, the tragedy of lives going down some awful drain," he replied. "I see an entire generation throwing away its intellectual capacity. That's what drugs do to them. It destroys that which should be cherished, their ability to think cogently."

"We agree with you," Chapman said. "Our brightest kids are committing intellectual suicide. I've counseled with grief-stricken parents who dreamed great dreams for their sons and daughters, dreams of their using one of God's most wonderful gifts: the ability to reason, to discover, to think, to be able to achieve whatever they wanted.

"Instead, these fathers and mothers now visit their children in some institution where their only dreams are nightmare hallucinations of snakes crawling out of their skin, their hair bursting into flames, their—"

"I have encountered the same cases, I assure you," Gardner interrupted. "They snorted that first line of cocaine or smoked that first marijuana cigarette and there was no one they could confess it to, no way to relieve the guilt. Their parents wouldn't have understood. Their teachers would probably have called the police. So they turned to God and begged His forgiveness and got cold rejection in return."

"But what makes you think God turned His back on them?" Chapman retorted.

"Because He did nothing to help. And this drove them into one of two emotional blind alleys. Either He didn't care about them or He had never existed in the first place! And so they figured they might as well go all the way, get past the guilt and fear by embracing drugs as a way of life. So what if they died? In fact, death was desirable, for if there was no Heaven or Hell, death meant oblivion, and oblivion meant their pain would end."

"I notice you don't mention Satan at all," said Trent.

The doctor slammed his fist down on the desk, scattering papers in the process.

"That concept is the most damaging of all," he said, his voice trembling. "It's a cop-out. A means by which these kids can evade responsibility for their actions."

"But you implied that they do sense responsibility—that the biggest problem they have is guilt," Chapman reminded him. "And while I agree that the Devil-made-me-do-it mentality is dangerously simplistic, it seems to me that oppressive guilt is nothing but the other extreme: the state of accepting so much of that responsibility that it suffocates them."

When Gardner didn't respond immediately, Chapman continued, "How do you get past that guilt, doctor? Obviously thousands of young people are choosing the wrong answer. But what is the right one? Do you help them reason their way past it? Do you appeal to them through mere common sense? And if none of this works, what do you have left? Isn't your bag of psychological tricks empty at that point? I daresay it is, because you can offer them nothing to fill the very emptiness that drove them to drugs in the first place."

"And you think vacuous allusions to an afterlife will somehow magically do the trick?" Gardner snorted contemptuously.

"Only Christ can give them what they desperately need," replied Chapman. "Only through His sacrifice at Calvary do they, or the rest of us in fact, have any hope. Because, you see, there is a third alternative. It's not simply a matter of accepting God or rejecting Him. The third choice is that they can turn over their lives to Satan. You may view Satan as a delusion foisted upon everyone by religious fanatics, doctor, but the fact is that he exists. And increasing numbers of young people are embracing him with mind, body, and spirit."

Gardner's reply astonished both men.

"As my own son claimed to have done," he said with ill-disguised reluctance.

"Your son?" Trent asked in astonishment.

"That is what he told me I had forced him to do. Gentlemen, Robert is dead today because he felt that I did little to prepare him for the battle that he lost, making his last few months more hellish than you might be able to imagine."

The three men lapsed into silence for a moment or two.

"I do not feel that I am wrong," Gardner said softly then, his voice at the level of a whisper. "But, in all candor, there have been occasions when I considered, and rejected, the notion that the existence of God would confirm the existence of Satan because nothing else would explain the evil in this world. In any event, I consented to go to Valley Falls in order to help those boys, if possible, through whatever I may have learned as a result of failing with my own flesh and blood."

"Your son's case gave you some insights that could be helpful, I imagine," Chapman probed.

Gardner nodded, then cleared his throat, trying to rein in emotions he was unaccustomed to displaying before strangers.

"As I said, I believe the concept of Satan to be dangerous purely from a psychological standpoint because it permits one to avoid personal responsibility for certain acts and short-circuits any likelihood of their confronting the reality of their dilemma," he said, obviously unwilling to discuss his son any further. "But unlike you evangelicals, my views aren't etched in ancient stone, and I do not view this world in neat little squares like some gigantic chessboard. As far as I am concerned, it is more like a jigsaw puzzle, and I, for one, have no idea where all the pieces go."

He looked from Trent to Chapman, the hint of a friendly smile crossing his face.

"Shall we go on and somehow work together to help those boys in Valley Falls?"

Both men nodded their agreement without hesitation.

"I must say that I am relieved," Gardner admitted. "Perhaps I should call the institution to tell them when we can be expected? Wouldn't you agree, gentlemen?"

"Indeed," Trent told him, "and then I feel I should do the same as far as contacting Paul DeKorte."

"Ah, yes...Reverend DeKorte. Naturally he's in this file also. I'm eager to talk with him. He apparently assumes at least part of the blame for what happened. Such personal integrity as that is not so common these days."

Gardner reached for the phone on his desk after looking up the number of the sanitarium.

A frown creased his forehead.

He broke the connection and dialed again. Then a third time. Finally he gave up.

"That's strange."

"What's the problem?" asked Chapman.

"I can't get through to Valley Falls," he said, clearly nervous. "All the phone lines are dead."

"And God gave them up to uncleanness, in the lusts of their hearts, to dishonor their bodies among themselves...[and to indulge] vile passions."

—Romans 1:24,26

27

On Saturday morning, Clement Albertson and the young people left the dining hall after breakfast and headed toward the building where they were to hold their meetings.

Lance Setterman noticed a pay phone just inside the front door.

"Sir, I'd like to call home," he said. "Have I got time before we start?"

"Sure, go ahead," nodded Albertson.

Within a couple minutes he came up to the principal in the meeting room and said, "All the phone lines are out."

"Are you sure?"

"That's the recorded message I got. All the lines into Valley Falls are out."

Albertson shrugged his shoulders, trying to appear nonchalant. "Well, they'll probably have it fixed by this afternoon," he said. "You can try again then. Let's get started."

Since the retreat center catered to smaller groups, the meeting hall had a rather intimate feel to it. It was paneled in knotty pine, including the cathedral ceiling, and one wall was almost completely glass to bring the beauty of the surrounding forest inside.

As Fritz Lorensen walked to the podium, the principal recalled the elderly man's words of the night before. Words that had echoed in his mind as he drifted off to sleep.

The darkness plays tricks on aging intellects.

What could have prompted the man to—?

"My friends," the speaker's voice interrupted his thoughts, "let's pray that the Lord brought us here for a purpose and that we are fellowshipping because of Him and not out of some superficial social need to have a good time. There is nothing wrong with that, of course. Our Lord was in favor of it on occasion. But to quote a verse from the Old Testament, 'There is a time to weep and a time to laugh, a time to mourn and a time to dance.' "

He leaned forward.

"I have on my heart, now, a special message. Not the message I intended when I left for this retreat, but one the Lord has clearly placed on my heart since my arrival here last night," he said, then paused, looking out over the group of teenagers. "Today, dear young people, I want to talk about Satan."

Albertson felt a chill that seemed to come from deep inside. He looked to the left where a group of Latino young people sat together. They represented the youth group from a sister church in a nearby city, one that the Valley Falls church had helped support during its early days. The principal had seen this as an opportunity for these young people from two quite different cultures to learn from each other. However, the ice had not yet been broken, and even their body language isolated these inner-city kids from the others.

Lorensen was obviously thinking the same thing.

"One of Satan's tricks is to divide us. To erect an us-against-them mentality. He does that in the home, in the different neighborhoods representing different economic and racial groups, in the seats of government with opposing political parties, with unions against management, and in the church. I am not talking in the latter instance about the ecumenical movement which, in principle, is a fine idea, but in practice has resulted in a marshmallow type of Gospel. I am talking about those speaking in tongues at odds with those who don't, those who are of one ethnic group constantly experiencing friction with those of another, and so on.

"I am talking about—"

He stopped in mid-sentence and looked up at the ceiling.

The others followed his gaze.

And they all heard the same sounds.

Scratching sounds, like claws across tiles.

"Satan is constantly on the attack," he said, raising his voice, forcing their attention back to him. "But it is hard to convince someone living in a ghetto that Satan is the bad guy when, in his delusion, he has become convinced that God seemingly has given him nothing but economic deprivation, hunger, yes, a constant, grinding melancholy day after day."

Lorensen loosened his tie.

"So some Santarian voodoo chief in street dress comes in and sells that individual and his family a bill of goods about worship that is straight from the pit of Hell. It offers no easy way to riches— certain TV evangelists have a lock on that sort of thing—but it does promise emotional gratification, a release of certain carnal desires.

"And there is the alluring potential of power, if not over the offending economic classes above them, the ones with fancy Park

Avenue apartments while they live with roaches, the ones they see as the oppressors, then power over their friends, their neighbors."

One of the Latino boys near the front stood defiantly.

"Can you blame us?" he said. "My mother makes her living by selling her body at night so she can feed us during the day."

"No, I cannot," Lorensen replied, stepping away from the podium.

His shirt, Albertson noticed, *it's drenched in sweat!*

"But there is another way, son. It's hard for you to realize that because—"

"Because I have another god to worship!"

The teenager pulled something from his pocket.

It was a carving. A very familiar carving.

"I have a god who talks to me," said the boy as he stepped out into the aisle. "He *listens.* He gives me what I want."

"And what do you want?"

"Revenge!" he cried.

He was astonishingly fast and strong. Several of the other teenagers tried to stop him, but he outran them or pushed them aside.

Several of the girls screamed.

The boy plunged a knife into Lorensen, pulled it out and was about to stab again when the pain on the man's face momentarily passed, and he seemed to gather strength from deep within himself.

"I forgive you, son," he said softly, "and I love you."

And Lorensen collapsed.

The boy let out a cry so awful that those who heard it would, even in years hence, still awaken in the middle of the night from its echo in their sleep.

"It is time!" he cried, holding the knife up toward the ceiling. "It is time now!"

And then he turned the knife on himself, ripping it into his stomach and dying almost instantly.

Albertson rushed up to Lorensen just as the scratching sounds, which had been nearly forgotten, became louder, louder, louder.

"Be their shepherd," said the dying man.

For an instant, as his head fell back, his eyes widening, he saw the ceiling *being eaten through by*—

"Be their shepherd," he said once more. Then he, too, was gone.

Suddenly splinters and sawdust dropped from the ceiling as the origin of the sounds became visible.

Countless numbers of winged creatures.

The wood carvings come to life! thought Albertson.

The teenagers started running for the exits, along with their adult chaperons. After Albertson rested Lorensen's body back against the floor, he stood, not moving.

"Sir!"

It was Lance Setterman.

"Sir, hurry!"

But where do we run, Lance? Outside? They will pursue us. Into another building? They will eat their way into it as well. Back into the van? They will smash the windows.

Where do we run when we have nowhere to go?

The flying creatures had not as yet attacked, but merely hovered in the air above the panicked group, as though enjoying the screams, the fear.

Albertson stood in the middle of the hall, looking up at them.

"Take me now," he said. "And what is it that you will be destroying? Only this body. This fragile body that in time will deteriorate anyway and be increasingly useless. Go on! Take a piece of it now!"

Lance ran up to Albertson and tried to pull him away, toward the exit. At that point they were the only ones left in the building.

"Sir, you must—"

As though on cue, one of the creatures broke away from the others and flew directly for Albertson.

Lance jumped in front of him.

"Run, sir! Let them kill me! You have something to give. The world will never miss me."

The creature swung down and tore off part of Lance's earlobe. The teenager cried out in pain.

Albertson pushed him aside.

"He offered his life for mine," he yelled up at the swarming horde. "That's an act so noble that even you must reckon with it. *The same sort that spelled your doom 2000 years ago!*"

The creatures seemed to be stirring, getting ready to attack en masse.

Albertson glanced quickly at Lance who had fallen and was now getting to his feet.

"And now I challenge you to take me if you have the nerve!" Albertson said at the top of his voice. "My life instead of this boy's."

"Sir," Lance interrupted, "I can't let you—"

The creatures moved toward them, hundreds of flying monstrous bodies descending upon them, and the two were pushed to the floor by the sheer weight of their attackers.

For several seconds Clement Albertson and Lance Setterman fought as hard as they could, gagging from the stench that emanated from the creatures. And then their strength was gone.

Pain was pulling a curtain of darkness over them.

And then...the onslaught stopped.

Afraid to open their eyes, they lay there half-conscious.

A terrible cacophony of sound...shrieking...moaning...a growl like staccato thunder...together with a sensation of searing heat.

How much later was it that they came back to full consciousness? Perhaps neither would ever know. When they opened their eyes, the hall was littered with the bodies of the creatures.

They both stood.

"Sir, we've hardly been touched!" Lance exclaimed. "How could that be?"

Their shirts were torn in a couple of places, and their faces were smudged with dirt. Yet, except for Lance's ear which had stopped bleeding, that was all.

They started to walk through what looked like a grotesque miniature battlefield.

"Our Lord is protecting us," said Albertson. "And we have nothing to fear."

Many of the creatures were dead; others were dying, their bodies going through death tremors.

Albertson stopped before one.

It was holding up a claw-like hand toward him, making little piping sounds.

As he started to pass by, it grabbed his trouser leg. He reached down and pulled it away. He thought he saw, on that awful face, a single tear trickling down one side. While holding it in one hand, he broke its neck with the other and then tossed it to one side.

"And Satan shall be crushed under our feet," Albertson said softly.

"Romans 16:20," said Lance.

They looked knowingly at one another and walked out of the building.

"Look at this," Lance said as he picked up an object beside the front door.

A single white feather.

"Just like—" he started to say.

His eyes met Albertson's. Neither had to say anything at that point.

Outside, the other teenagers had gathered, astonishment on their faces.

A Latino girl came up to them.

"You'll never believe what happened!" she exclaimed. "You just won't."

"Don't be too sure about that," Albertson said, grinning a bit.

"Thousands of them, sir. It was as though the sky suddenly opened up and there they were...thousands of white doves!"

28

After they left the Mulrooney home, DeKorte and Rogers decided to stop at the local bookstore. During the short drive there, the minister turned on the car radio.

The music being broadcast was loud and brassy.

"I didn't think you liked that stuff!" Rogers exclaimed.

"What stuff?"

"That sounds like hard rock to me."

"Doug, KCMV is a Christian station," DeKorte told him.

"You must be kidding!"

"I'm not. But how does this sound?" *(a matter of personal music taste)*

DeKorte turned the dial to another station.

"Christ and Christ only—that should be the cry of every single Christian on Planet Earth, not the flash and dash of the secular world but the good old-fashioned Gospel of salvation that Christians have been martyred for over the many centuries since He took our sins upon Himself at Calvary."

"That seems much more appropriate," Rogers agreed. "That would speak to an aching heart far more deeply than that other nonsense."

"Absolutely, Doug."

Rogers fell silent, and DeKorte could tell that something was going on inside his friend.

As they drove down the main street of Valley Falls, DeKorte noticed an elderly man sitting on a bench and reading a newspaper upside down. He pointed it out to Rogers.

"Senility probably," his friend replied.

"I wonder...."

"Just a little thing like that?" Rogers asked.

"Lots of little things. The other night a lady was standing in the middle of her front lawn, hose in hand, as though she was watering the grass."

"What's wrong with that?"

"There was no water coming out of it," DeKorte said.

Rogers cleared his throat.

"I have noticed some things in my practice, I guess."

"Such as?"

"I give a patient some pills to take, and a cup to fill with water. They swallow the pills as they put the cup to their mouth, but without any water in it."

He moved around uncomfortably.

"Some of them have my home phone number," Rogers admitted. "And I've been getting calls in the middle of the night."

"About what?"

"Aches, pains, nothing serious."

"They wake you up for that?" DeKorte asked, surprised.

"That's the point, Paul."

"It didn't start until recently?"

"You got it!" Rogers exclaimed.

"Across the street," DeKorte said as they approached the store. "Park across the street."

"Why?"

"Trust me."

Rogers steered the car over to the curb on his right and turned off the ignition.

"What do you see?" he asked.

"Look," DeKorte said, pointing.

A teenage girl was coming out of the store, her arms piled high with books.

"Look at the left pocket in her jacket."

Rogers squinted.

Three of the wood carvings had been stuffed into her pocket!

A teenage boy went into the store, and a few minutes later came out holding one of the carvings.

"Sold in there?" Rogers asked.

"Along with the necessary instruction books, I suspect."

Along with the necessary instruction books. . . .

They both felt chilly just then, cold beads of perspiration breaking out on their backs.

"Right over the counter," Rogers said.

"With no restraints," DeKorte added.

They finally got out of the car, walked across the street, and entered the store.

DeKorte asked the manager if there was an occult section.

"Are you kidding?" the man replied. "It's one of our most popular."

"When did you start to notice this?" Rogers asked.

"A few months ago."

DeKorte and Rogers glanced at one another, then thanked him.

They started browsing through several shelves of books dealing with seances, astrology, demonology, reincarnation, and similar topics.

"People are really filling their minds with all this garbage!?" Rogers said as he started reading snatches from one of the books.

"Yeah," DeKorte agreed, "listen to this."

"The desire for power, the most dominant power imaginable, can only be satisfied, indeed realized, if the individual proclaims his total willingness to follow Satan—"

DeKorte hesitated, then finished the sentence.

"—even to the point of violent death."

"Good grief, Paul!" Rogers exclaimed. "Is that the kind of trash available to young people these days?"

"There's more . . . listen."

"Ancient truths indicate that when an individual dies thusly, preferably by his own hand, or by the act of one or more others who love him, he is able to return from beyond the grave, commanding legion after legion of ravenous demons with him at the very fore- front, in a metamorphosized version of his own fleshly body."

DeKorte glanced up at his friend.

"No word about Scott's body being found as yet, is there?" he said, his voice trembling.

"Nothing. I've been—"

Color drained from Rogers's face as he realized what DeKorte was implying with that observation.

"Let's get out of here," he said.

DeKorte nodded.

As they were leaving, Rogers noticed a magazine rack near the cash register. It was filled with heavy metal publications plus two or three occult titles.

"Wait a second, Paul," he said.

He picked up one of the magazines.

"I can't believe it," he muttered, handing it to DeKorte. "Look at that advertisement on the left page."

" 'Dial Creep Phone,' " DeKorte read. " 'Connect to the world of the occult. Talk to your own personal monster.' "

He turned to the manager who was standing behind the cash register.

"Don't you know what this is doing to the kids here in town?" he said, fighting to keep his voice in control.

"But it's what sells," the man replied lamely.

"What about your moral responsibilities?"

"My moral responsibility is to earn money to feed my family."

"Even if the youngsters in that family go down the drain?"

The manager's face reddened with anger or embarrassment.

DeKorte turned in disgust and walked out of the store, Rogers directly behind him.

After getting back into the car, they sat for a few minutes, stunned by what they had seen.

"I didn't show it to you, Paul, but there was also an ad that tied in crystal and pyramid worship and animal sacrifice. Can you believe that?"

"When you're drowning in a spiritual sense, you'll grab at anything that promises survival," DeKorte told him.

"But you've been the pastor here for a long time, my friend. And you never had a clue?"

DeKorte was silent for a moment.

"Doug—" he started to say, then hesitated.

"Spit it out."

"I—I think I've been part of the problem, not the solution."

"Why do you say that?"

"I got them all started on an emotional trip."

"There's nothing wrong with emotion, Paul."

"There is if it pushes the Bible to one side rather than keeping it at the center of every worship service."

He cleared his throat.

"I have the awful feeling that I've put emotional experiences on some kind of pedestal and that we've been worshiping them instead of the Lord Himself."

"Is it a little bit like taking a present at Christmas and saying to the one who gave it to you, 'I'm going to accept your gift, now get out of the way so I can enjoy it'?"

"That's about it, Doug," DeKorte admitted.

"I think you should go right now and talk to the boys," Rogers said. "I think you should lay it on the line with them. Break through their defenses with a confession of your own that they can't ignore. They'll respect you for it."

"And with that hopefully we can begin to communicate again?"

"Have you any choice, really?"

DeKorte shook his head.

"I'll be rummaging around here while you're gone," Rogers said. "There's a call from Edith Van Halen that I want to check out. Okay?"

DeKorte agreed.

"Good. I'll take you back to the house."

He dropped DeKorte off at the parsonage and then drove away. The minister went inside to get his car keys.

As he was coming out again, he looked up toward the sanitarium and couldn't avoid suddenly shivering.

29

Shortly before one o'clock that afternoon, Gardner, Trent, and Chapman stopped at a roadside diner for lunch.

"I'm used to flying everywhere," Gardner told them as he sipped the last of his coffee. "A long drive seems to take forever."

"That's interesting," Trent replied. "We travel mostly by car or church bus. A trip from one end of the state to the other isn't so unusual."

When the doctor excused himself to go to the restroom, the two ministers decided that they actually liked this man. People were not as easily won for Christ if needless barriers were erected between them. The fact that they got along with him was promising.

"He's extremely intelligent," Chapman mentioned. "If only God could use him—and us—as His instruments in this situation."

"I agree," Trent replied. "I've been praying that He will."

A few minutes later after they had finished their coffee and dessert, Chapman went up to the cashier to pay the bill.

The woman behind the register seemed nervous, and he asked, "Are you all right, ma'am?"

"Fine, fine," she said unconvincingly.

She took his money and handed back his change. As Chapman straightened the bills to put them in his wallet, he saw that she had stuck a piece of paper between them.

It read: *Be careful, please. The Lord has placed a terrible burden on my spirit for the three of you.*

When he showed it to the other men in the car, Gardner chuckled with undisguised skepticism. But Trent and Chapman looked at each other thoughtfully.

* * *

They were about an hour away from Valley Falls when Chapman asked the psychiatrist, "Would you mind telling us more about your son? It might give us a better idea of what we're facing."

Gardner looked uncertain for a moment, then nodded in agreement.

"Robert was going through a classic period of alienation," he began. "I should have recognized it, but I didn't."

"And your wife?"

"Margaret and I were divorced when Robert was quite young."

"You never remarried?"

"I began a number of relationships but wasn't very successful with any of them."

Gardner closed his eyes briefly, gathering his thoughts.

"I'm certainly stable enough as a personality to face the traumas of life. But Robert's death—" His voice trailed off. He stared into space, then shook his head, as though tearing himself away from another time and place. "It wasn't the fact of Robert's death that was so unendurable, though that was hard enough. It was the way he died."

"What happened?" Chapman asked gently. "Did he take his own life?"

"In a sense," Gardner said, and shivered. "Robert allowed the satanic cult he had joined to ceremonially decapitate and disembowel him."

"He was sacrificed?"

"Yes. Then they cut out his heart and ate it. They claimed they were carrying on an ancient rite practiced by the Aztecs."

Trent, who was driving, pulled over to the side of the road and stopped the car. His hands were shaking.

"And you don't think Satan had anything to do with that?" he asked incredulously.

"If I could believe that Satan was the cause, then he would find me a most formidable enemy. But in my twenty years as a psychiatrist, I have seen the depths to which mentally ill human beings can sink without the help of any supernatural influences. Let me show you the difference a year made in my son."

He pulled out his wallet, slipped two photos out of a plastic sleeve, and handed one to Chapman.

"That was Robert the year before he died."

Chapman looked at the picture of a handsome, tanned, muscular young man lifting weights.

"He worked to have every muscle in top shape, every inch of his chest and stomach sharply etched. The girls wouldn't stay away from him."

Chapman passed the photo to Trent, and Gardner handed him another.

"Now look at him at the end of that year," Gardner said.

Chapman would not have believed it was the same boy. This one sat slumped in a lawn chair, his eyes downcast, his skin pale and blotchy, his body thin to the point of appearing anorexic. But it wasn't that sight alone that riveted him. It was what Robert Gardner was holding.

"What's that in his hand?" Chapman asked, showing the photo to Trent.

"That little carving? What about it?"

"Where did he get it? Do you know?" asked Trent.

"From Central America. Robert and some friends spent several weeks down there. They were fascinated by the Aztec culture and the areas where they had lived. In fact, he made the trip about a month after that first picture was taken."

The two ministers exchanged glances, causing the doctor to ask, "Gentlemen, what is this all about?"

Trent told him.

"That wasn't in the report I was given," Gardner responded. "I would have picked up on it right away. What do you think they mean?"

"We believe they are the devices that Satan and his demons are using to gain control over individuals like Wayne and Mark," Trent told him.

Suddenly the blood drained from Gardner's face.

"What is it?" Chapman asked.

"Robert and his friends must have had a dozen boxes of those carvings. They passed them out as souvenirs to everyone they knew," he said. "I—"

Then he exclaimed, "Stop the car!"

When Trent had pulled the car over to the side of the road, the doctor opened the door and got out.

"The trunk," he said. "Open it for me, please."

Both ministers were out of the car in seconds.

"You brought one with you, didn't you?" Chapman asked abruptly.

"I—I did. I knew it had some significance and I wanted to see how the boys in Valley Falls would react. But I didn't realize—"

Trent put the key in the trunk, but had trouble turning it. Gardner impatiently grabbed the key and tried it himself. Successful, he started to lift the lid.

Suddenly he let out a cry of pain.

The metal handle had started glowing bright red!

"It's as hot as a furnace!" Gardner told them. "It would have burnt my fingers to a cinder in another few seconds."

"Look!" Trent exclaimed.

The trunk lid was rising of its own accord. Inside, their luggage was igniting, little geysers of flame shooting up from the material.

"The gasoline!" screamed Chapman. "We've got to—"

The three men turned and started to run, expecting to be knocked off their feet by an explosion.

Nothing.

They stopped. Turned back toward the car.

It was gone!

Gardner walked forward, slightly ahead of the others.

"We rode in it!" he exclaimed. "It was right here. It—"

He looked at Trent, and Trent in turn stared at him.

"I burned myself on the handle. I—"

He closed his eyes, his temples throbbing with pain.

"It's still there," Chapman said, his expression reflecting his own amazement as he looked back to where they had left the car.

"It is?" Trent exclaimed.

Gardner opened his eyes.

The car!

First it had disappeared, and now it was back.

What kind of optical illusion was this?

"But the three of us ran from it and then the three of us turned and saw that it was gone," Gardner reminded them.

"We all saw the same thing, yes," Trent replied, "but you were the only one hurt—not Harley or me."

"Is that supposed to mean something?"

"It could, frankly."

"But what? Why me? Why was I hurt?"

The two ministers were silent.

"Give it to me straight, please," he demanded.

"We are headed toward a town that may be in the midst of a demonic takeover," Trent replied. "We represent the spiritual, and you the psychological. If we are in fact effective together, then Satan will suffer an enormous defeat."

"You say 'if.' Are you hinting that I am the weak link? And therefore these forces, whatever they are, consider me—"

He swallowed once, twice.

"—easy prey?"

"I didn't say that. And I can't say it...at least for a while."

"But it's a possibility, isn't it?"

"Yes."

Gardner started laughing then.

"What utter nonsense!"

"Then give us an explanation for what just happened," Chapman insisted.

The laughter ended instantly.

"That is my problem," Gardner said. "I could offer half a dozen, I guess, if I really tried, but—"

"But what?" said Chapman.

"Never mind. Let's get back into the car and continue."

Trent had anticipated this and had already walked over to the driver's side.

"We can't," he told them.

"Why?" Chapman asked.

"The door's locked and the keys are in the ignition."

"No! I have them in my pocket," Chapman said as he reached in and took them out.

"But I saw the keys in—"

He tried the door again.

It opened.

"I think we're being played with," Chapman said. "It's an initial foray."

"Testing us?" Trent asked. "Seeing what we're made of?"

"I would say so. The closer we get to Valley Falls, the more intense all this will become."

*   *   *

"Look," Gardner said, pointing toward the side of the road.

Litter.

"What a mess!" Trent exclaimed.

There was litter everywhere. Piles of it. Garbage. Waste. Newspapers. Aluminum cans. Cardboard boxes.

The litter led into a small community.

"What's the name of this place?" Chapman asked.

"I didn't notice," Trent replied.

"Does it even have a name?" joked Gardner, trying to lighten the tension they all felt.

People were standing around or sitting—sometimes on curbs, sometimes on chairs or porches—and literally doing nothing else.

"Would you call them dispirited?" Chapman asked.

"Strangely so," the psychiatrist replied. "Let's stop here for a few minutes."

Trent pulled into a gas station, and the three men got out.

Gardner walked up to the attendant who was sitting on a wooden case just inside the open garage door. He had not moved when they drove up—hadn't even looked at them.

"Sir, I was wondering—" the psychiatrist started to ask.

The man turned and faced him.

His eyes! So blank! So—

"I was wondering," Gardner went on, forcing the words out, "how far is it to Valley Falls?"

The attendant held up the fingers of both hands, closed them into a fist, then spread them out again.

"Twenty miles?" he asked.

The attendant nodded.

"We've been noticing all this—" Gardner nodded toward the litter lining the curbs, "all this garbage and stuff. Has there been a trash collection strike or something?"

"What trash?" the attendant finally spoke. "I don't see no trash."

"But—"

The look on the attendant's face persuaded Gardner that there was no point in pursuing the matter, and he rejoined the others.

Odd how normal the little community seemed, except for the rubbish and the mystifying behavior of its inhabitants.

"You know what's really strange," Gardner observed.

"What?"

"That a close-mouthed gas station attendant could seem strange. that an elderly woman sitting in her rocking chair could seem strange. There's nothing strange about some guy taking it easy by sitting down on a curb—nothing at all. And yet it is just that...strange!"

They walked around, trying to engage some of the residents in conversation, but getting little response.

"Even that isn't unusual," Gardner told the others. "A certain provincial outlook is true of many country towns, particularly somewhat isolated ones. People they don't recognize are held at arm's length unless they are obviously tourists and vital to the local economy, which we obviously are not."

Trent's foot kicked something on the pavement.

A book, minus a cover, the pages torn and soiled.

He bent down and picked it up.

"A Bible!" he exclaimed.

"Thrown away like so much garbage?" said Chapman.

"Apparently."

He examined a few pages.

"Different verses have been circled," he observed.

"Any pattern?" asked Gardner.

"See for yourself." The minister handed the psychiatrist the tattered volume.

Gardner leafed through quickly, picking up a thread with an ease that impressed the two clergymen.

"Every one of these has to do with Satan."

"Correct," said Chapman.

Directly across the street was a tiny general store. They walked over to it, noticing the front.

"It's so brightly painted," Gardner said, voicing what they had all been thinking.

"Come to think of it, look at the other buildings here," said Trent. "A fresh coat of paint on each, it seems. And yet there's refuse everywhere."

Inside the store, Gardner approached the elderly man behind the counter and told him how nice the new paint looked on his store.

"Yes, we got together and made it a community project," the man replied.

"You repainted the whole town?"

"Yep. Wanted to look good when folks passed through."

"But what about all the garbage?"

"What garbage?"

"The cans, the newspapers, the dog droppings, the rest—it's everywhere."

"Whaddaya mean, mister? I don't see no dirt."

Gardner looked down at the magazine rack in front of the cash register.

Women without clothes, their bodies arched suggestively ... men together in intercourse ... men with young children. ...

"You sell this stuff?" he asked the clerk.

"What stuff, mister?"

"All these magazines?"

"Sure do. What about it?" The clerk smiled leeringly, revealing teeth black with decay, and a foul odor escaped from his mouth.

"But this is Bible country."

"Not no more, it ain't," he said. The coldness in his eyes and the monotone of his voice sent chills along every nerve in the psychiatrist's body.

Trent and Chapman had overheard and didn't require any persuasion to follow Gardner as he hastily left the store.

"What's wrong, Elliott?" Trent asked, noticing the doctor's pale face.

"That look, that voice—"

"What do you mean?"

"So much—so much like Robert's the last time I saw him."

30

Paul DeKorte had been to the Valley View Sanitarium several times over the years and had seen the number of patients fluctuate, but basically increase since the mid-seventies. Mental illness seemed endemic to modern society, as seemingly "normal" people found the pressures of daily life unendurable—even those not strung out on drugs or into Satanism or guilty of other bizarre habits or practices, even those who had once scorned such mental and emotional weakness in others, pointing the finger of doctrinal accusation with the admonishment, "There must be sin in your life." This mind-set labeled anything other than perfect health, mentally and physically, as evidence of Satanic intrusion or, at the very least, a rampant sin nature.

Under normal circumstances he would not have made the mistake of automatically equating manic depression, schizophrenia, or other forms of mental illness with demonic possession. To say that most of the people in mental hospitals across the nation were under the control of Satanic forces seemed to him irrational. It also served to weaken the cause for cases of genuine possession.

And yet as he checked into the brick-faced structure, he felt a sensation of darkness so strong that he almost turned around and went home.

"Is everything all right here?" he asked the intern who was taking him to see the boys.

The young man, a blond-haired surfer-type in his mid-twenties, snapped his head around and looked at DeKorte intently.

"Thank God someone else has noticed it," he said. "I thought some of the paranoia in this place had become contagious all of a sudden."

"I noticed it the moment I parked my car and started walking toward the entrance," said DeKorte.

"Things have been weird around here ever since those two kids were brought in," the intern told him.

"Like what?" asked DeKorte.

"Oh, a kind of dark, disturbing restlessness among the patients. Almost bordering on violence," he said, shivering a bit. Then he smiled, "Silly, I guess, isn't it?"

"I don't think so," said DeKorte.

They were outside Mark's room now, and the minister looked through the small window in the door. The boy was standing on the far side of the room, looking out through the barred window.

"He stands like that most of the time," said the intern. "Just staring outside. He seems to ignore everything else."

"Can I go in?"

"You'd better not. The doctor left orders that no one should go in without his permission," he said. "Frankly, sir, I think this kid is dangerous."

Apparently Mark had heard their voices, for now he turned toward the door.

DeKorte gasped.

"Looks bad, doesn't he? He won't wash himself, and we can barely handle him to clean him up."

"Can't you sedate him?"

"Drugs don't seem to have any effect on him, sir. It requires three of us just to take his food in to him. Not that he eats any of it."

"Three of you?"

"Yes. The second day he was here he attacked one of the attendants . . . nearly bit off the guy's middle finger."

DeKorte was stunned.

Mark's face was illuminated by the reflected light from a full moon.

"It's so dark in there," DeKorte commented.

"He won't let us keep the light on."

Heavy dark circles hung from the teenager's lower lids. There were scratches on his forehead and his cheeks, a bruise on his chin. But his eyes were the worst.

"They get to me, too, sir. So cold. So evil," the intern said.

"Are my reactions so transparent?"

"Probably because they're the same as mine—as well as anyone else who's seen him. The difference in the short time he's been here is astonishing."

Mark was walking slowly toward the door, his head at a slight angle. He seemed to be focusing on the minister.

"Mark, I—" DeKorte started to say.

The expression on the boy's face froze the rest of what he was going to say in his throat.

"Hatred, sir," said the intern. "What you're seeing is the blackest kind of pure hatred you've probably ever witnessed."

DeKorte stepped back from the door.

"You can't take more than a few seconds of it," the intern said knowingly.

DeKorte leaned against the wall.

"I'm trembling," he said in surprise.

"It's nothing to be ashamed of. I've been here for nearly a year, and there are times lately when I've felt such darkness, such oppression, that I end up having nightmares."

As they walked down the corridor, the intern reassured DeKorte that he would find Wayne Mulrooney an entirely different case. The minister found this difficult to believe, given what they had discovered in the boy's room earlier that day.

"The Mulrooney kid's on the second floor," the intern said, pushing through a metal door that divided off this section of the first floor.

DeKorte glanced in at some of the patients. Most seemed quite normal, a fact which he noted out loud.

"They all have lucid moments, sir. But, remember, not all mental illness manifests itself in bizarre behavior. Someone sitting quietly in a chair doesn't appear to be abnormal. But if he's been doing nothing else for days at a time, he's got a problem. So you have to see the whole picture."

Just then DeKorte heard a humming sound, a chanting.

"Sounds like one of those Hare Krishna groups," he said.

"That's been happening a lot lately," the intern told him, then stopped short. "Reverend DeKorte, while you're here, could I take you to see another patient?"

"Sure you can."

The intern led him down the corridor toward the sound. When he stopped in front of one of the rooms, DeKorte realized it wasn't chanting.

Tongues!

The young woman inside was speaking in tongues!

"We can go in," the intern suggested. "She's not violent."

He opened the door and said, "Maria, there's someone here to see you."

The attractive, dark-haired young woman, who appeared to be about eighteen, looked up from where she was kneeling with her hands held upward, palms toward the ceiling.

"This is Reverend DeKorte," he told her.

The girl smiled and stood up, holding out her hand.

"My name is Maria Esteban. I'm a member of Faith Chapel in Morgantown."

"I'm pleased to meet you, Maria," said DeKorte. "I pastor the community church in Valley Falls."

"You must wonder what I'm doing in a place like this," she said.

"Yes, Maria, that's true."

"They think I hear too many voices."

"Do you?"

"Yes. But they're from the Lord."

"How do you know?" asked DeKorte.

"They say so."

DeKorte started to tell her, carefully, gently, what the Bible said about demons posing as angels of light and the need for testing the spirits.

"No!" she said, her voice rising. "I heard the Lord speak to me. I know He's real."

"Yes, Maria, He is real. That is the foundational truth of our faith. Christ is alive today. But having a voice tell you that He is Christ isn't—"

"I don't want you here if you're going to talk like that," she said. "He brings me comfort. He gives me peace. What greater proof could there be?"

"Then why are you trembling?" DeKorte asked her.

"Because you're trying to rob me of my faith, just like the others in this place. You are the spirit of Antichrist, not the voices that come to me in the middle of the night."

"And do you speak to these voices in tongues?"

"Yes. All the time. Don't you believe in this gift?"

"I do. But —" He stopped.

Maria Esteban seemed so vulnerable as she waited to hear what he would say, her eyes wide, her body trembling.

"Maria, why are you here?" he asked gently. "Is it only the voices?"

He glanced at the intern, who nodded.

"Or is it what the voices ask you to do?"

Suddenly she began screaming and became increasingly violent so that the intern had to sedate her. In a few minutes she calmed down, and DeKorte held her hand as she drifted into sleep.

"What happened?" asked the intern when they were out in the hallway again. "She's never been violent before."

"I believe it is Satan who has been speaking to her, even though she may not realize it, and that his spirit recognized the Holy Spirit in me."

"Is that possible, sir?"

"It is, I'm afraid. Over the years there have been instances of believers being tricked by Satan in this manner. What they thought was heavenly language turned out to be incantations of evil. It's not frequent, and most of what has been bruited about is probably groundless rumor started by those who would detract from the charismatic movement. But there is no doubt that there have been some such cases."

"Sir, one other question?"

"What's that?"

"Is that girl a Christian?"

"I don't know enough about the young lady to have an opinion one way or the other."

"But suppose for a moment that she is," said the young man. "Then what is she doing in here? How can she listen to Satan and believe in God?"

"Being a believer doesn't mean that Satan can't cause us to suffer. And that suffering can be mental as well as physical. Obviously that young lady is suffering mentally."

"But what if she really is demonically possessed? How can that be?"

"The question is whether it is possession or oppression," said DeKorte. "Or perhaps she isn't saved. Perhaps she knows about God but has never made the deep spiritual commitment that is necessary. We just don't know right now, do we?"

The intern shook his head, and DeKorte was grateful that he didn't pursue the subject any further at that point.

* * *

Upstairs, Wayne Mulrooney was sitting in the chair in his room, reading a Bible. When DeKorte entered, he stood and shook hands. The intern seemed satisfied about the boy's mental state and left the two alone, saying that he would wait out in the hall.

After he left, Wayne offered the minister his chair and then sat down on the edge of the bed.

"I saw your folks today, Wayne," said DeKorte.

"Are they okay?" the boy asked, rubbing his hands nervously on the top of his legs.

"Well, they're worried about you," DeKorte replied. "As I am."

He had brought one of the wood carvings with him, and now he took it out of his pocket.

"What are these, Wayne?" he asked.

"We put them all over town."

"But why? What is their significance?"

"They're focal points. They unlock contact with the demonic forces, just as Christian and Jewish symbols are supposed to focus attention on God."

Wayne stood and started pacing.

"We were told that those wood figures were carved with the same knives used in ancient Aztec rituals," Wayne explained. "The knives were holy instruments they used for their blood sacrifices."

"Who told you this?" asked DeKorte.

"Scott did, sir. And I've done a lot of reading about the Aztecs. They believed there was a divine compact between themselves and the gods they worshiped, centered in the sacrifice of human hearts and blood that they pledged in exchange for the god's blessing on their corn and the other foods they needed for survival."

It didn't end there, thought DeKorte. *The Aztecs were not content with the mere shedding of blood. Directly after the sacrifice, pieces of the victim's flesh were dipped into stone pots of blood and fed to the worshipers.*

"When the Spaniards made contact with the Aztecs," Wayne continued, "their Catholic friars became convinced that these ceremonies were a satanic counterfeit of Holy Communion."

"Satan has always tried to counterfeit the holy, Wayne," interjected DeKorte, "twisting the Israelite shedding of the blood of lambs for his own purposes."

"But they didn't stop with periodic sacrifices, sir. In time, a general blood-lust took hold of them, and anyone was fair game for their devilish rites. Deranged priests sought out virgins, children, the elderly—anyone they could get their hands on. But it was the children and the young men who were considered the choice catches. Like the child pornography today."

"Satan has always played on man's natural desire to seduce and destroy innocence," said DeKorte.

"Scott filled his head with this stuff—and ours too. Then he became obsessed with another aspect of the Aztec worship that he read about in a history of the Aztecs, Mayans, and Incas."

"What was it?" DeKorte asked, dreading what he might hear as he recalled his own research.

*The Aztecs had a serpent god named Quetzalcoatl whose brother
was Tezcatlipoca. A ceremony honoring Tezcatlipoca was conducted in which a perfect young man was chosen as the epitome of
Aztec beauty, his hair long and straight, his eyes bright and
clear...his fingers long and sensitive, his body without scars,
wrinkles, or unsightly bulges.*

*During the ceremony four priests swiftly removed his heart and
offered it to the sun. Then his body was reverently carried down the
temple steps. The young man's head was severed, stripped of all
flesh, and placed at the pinnacle of a wooden rack called a tzom-
pantli, along with other skulls which were on lower levels, signi-
fying those who would become his subjects.*

"Scott became obsessed with this, sir. He began to see himself as
a perfect specimen and the ritual as a key to another world—a
world in which he would have a far more important role than any in
this life. He would no longer need to obey anybody. There everyone
would have to do his bidding and fear him."

"And only violent death—in other words, a modern version of
Aztec sacrifice—would accomplish all this?" DeKorte asked.

"That's what he believed," Wayne acknowledged, "and it crowded
out everything else in his life."

"When did these monstrous ideas begin, Wayne?"

The teenager fell silent.

"What's wrong?" DeKorte asked.

"I'm afraid the answer will make you angry, sir."

"Don't worry about that. You must tell me. I need to know."

"It began during a church service last year."

"What? How is that possible, Wayne?"

"It was one of those visualization services, sir, where you taught
us to open up our very souls."

"To God, yes!"

"No, sir, that wasn't all. You taught us to open up our souls to the
whole universe. That's what you said." Wayne's voice was trembling
now. "God is in that universe, sir, but so is Satan!"

"What are you telling me?"

"Well, at that point we'd begun playing around a bit with the
occult—Ouija boards and seances and stuff like that," Wayne said.
He began to perspire heavily. "Then one night at church as we
opened our minds up, we locked in on the same wavelength as an
ancient Aztec devil-god.

"We didn't know what it was at first. Like everybody else there
that night we were asked to confront our memories, to be open to
'spiritual communication.'

"I was remembering something that had happened when I young—something I had always felt guilty about.... One day when I was a little kid I took a can of hair spray into our backyard and found some praying mantises in one corner, behind a large bush.

"I sprayed all of them with the hair spray, and then I watched them struggling as they died. Only a few managed to escape.

"But that wasn't the worst part of it," Wayne recalled. "One of them flew up on my arm and stayed there...just looking at me.

"Something in the sight of that pitiful creature was devastating to me. I shook it off my arm and ran inside the house, sobbing so much that my sister came in to see what was wrong. And for years after that the guilt I felt came back to haunt me."

"So that night you confronted your guilt and were going to deal with it," said DeKorte. "I don't see—"

"Please, please, listen, sir. Don't you see? That was when I was at my weakest, and Satan moved in."

He was in some state between consciousness and a kind of sleep. Something cold and slimy touched his shoulder. He turned. A monstrous creature was smiling grotesquely at him, reaching out a taloned hand....

"Why didn't you come to me, Wayne?" DeKorte pleaded. "With God's help we could have—"

"We were in so deep by then, especially Scott," said the boy. "And quite honestly, sir, there was something attractive...compelling...about those dark forces...that power...."

He closed his eyes, his heart pounding as the memories surfaced.

"I remember the first time we killed anything...."

It was close to midnight.

The three of them had been prowling the streets, looking for a dog or a cat.

They had almost despaired of finding anything when they saw the dog walking across a vacant lot toward an old rusting tractor.

"That's the one," Scott said exultantly.

He stopped the car and they all got out and approached the tractor, under which the dog had crawled.

Wayne was the first to look at it.

The dog was a female that had obviously just recently given birth. She had crawled under the tractor to nurse her brood.

Wayne stood and faced Scott.

"Man, we can't do it," he protested.

"Why?" Scott asked.

"Listen up, guy! Look at her!"

Scott bent down and saw the mother and her pups.

"Hey, what's going on?" Mark wanted to know.

"She's nursing her puppies," Wayne said. "We can't—"

Scott stood up.

"We have to," he said, moonlight glistening off the perspiration on his face. "This is part of—"

"The christening?" said Wayne. "When we bathe ourselves in blood and pledge our allegiance to Satan?"

Scott didn't answer, his expression one of utter confusion.

"We can't do this. I think this should be the end, man," Wayne begged. "We should leave it all behind us."

But in the end, Scott...Satan...had won.

Wayne and Mark lured the mother dog out from under the tractor, pretending to have food for her.

Scott was standing to one side, holding a baseball bat. He clubbed the animal once. It fell to the ground, dazed but not dead.

"The pups first," Scott said, any hesitancy gone, a wild look in his eyes.

"But why?" Wayne asked.

"Because I think we can get high on the mother's reaction."

He was right. The mother dog tried to protect her puppies, tried to crawl forward, but the blow to her head had partially paralyzed her. She could do nothing but lie there, whimpering pitifully, as they killed her babies.

"Next!" Scott said excitedly. "Her!"

They took turns dismembering the animal with the knife Scott had brought. And then they started to feed....

Both the teller and the listener were white-faced and shaking now.

"In a few minutes we all seemed to wake up, as though coming out of a spell or something. We couldn't believe what we had done. We felt such guilt, such shame," Wayne continued. "I thought for a minute that Scott was going to use the knife on himself. But he started crying instead, and kept on crying until he was sick... we were all sick.

"We swore, then and there, that we would never do anything like that again."

Wayne cleared his throat.

"But I guess we had gone beyond a certain point...we didn't have any willpower of our own left. We had been taken over...and the second time it was easier, and the third...and the fourth...."

"So many?" DeKorte asked.

"Yes, sir... and I hate to tell you this, but we weren't the only ones... just the more readily susceptible. You see, later—"

"There were others, Wayne? Are you telling me that?"

"Yes, sir. That's correct. In fact... almost the entire congregation... and the rest of the town."

31

Nobody in Valley Falls paid much attention to Amy McCorkle. A short, thin spinster who kept to herself, she had few friends and did nothing to change her image as the town's mousey librarian. Shy and quiet, she went home alone to her apartment at the end of each day. Her social life consisted of an occasional church picnic or potluck, and her weekends were quiet and lonely, until the eventful day she bought a VCR. From then on, she would carry home an armful of movies for her weekend enjoyment.

On this particular Saturday afternoon, however, she had stayed late at the library, looking through the new books she had ordered for her special pride and joy, the religion section. A Christian for most of her adult life, Amy had great appreciation for the works of outstanding Christian thinkers like C.S. Lewis and Francis Schaeffer and made sure that the library carried a good selection of their works.

She was leafing through a new concordance when she heard voices outside. Though the windows were closed against the cool autumn air, the sound was loud enough to penetrate. She got up and walked over to the front door to investigate.

As she started to turn the knob, it was ripped out of her grip. Sheriff Wilburn stood in front of her.

"Join us, Amy," he said.

Beyond him, she could see a crowd of people walking past, heading toward the square.

"Sheriff, your mouth!" she exclaimed. "What's happened?"

His lips were smeared with blood.

"How sloppy," he said. "I just finished dinner."

Something in his eyes frightened Amy, and she stepped back, reaching to close the door on him.

He grabbed her shoulder.

"Join us, I said! That's an order."

She kicked him in the leg as hard as she could, and Wilburn fell back, his face contorted in pain.

Amy slammed the door, slid the dead-bolt lock into place, and twisted it closed.

A few seconds later a rock was hurled through one of the windows, missing her head by inches.

"Dear Lord," she prayed. "Dear Lord, it's true."

Amy may have been quiet and unassuming, but she was neither naive nor a fool. She was a mature and sensitive believer, and she had noticed strange changes in Valley Falls long before the recent deaths. Altered behavior in some of her fellow church members and neighbors. People who would no longer look her in the eye when they came into the library. A decrease in the circulation of Christian books; an increase in those dealing with the occult and related subjects. Even whispers about an increase in bizarre sexual practices, strange rituals, and disappearing animals.

Then she had discovered the mutilated body of her own pet cat and had started to piece together the different fragments of the puzzle.

"Why didn't I act sooner?" she said aloud. "I should have gone to Reverend DeKorte. What shall I do now, Lord?"

Suddenly the front door smashed inward, torn from its hinges.

She ran through the aisle between the bookshelves toward the back of the library where there was another exit. She could hear the sheriff shouting her name, other voices spouting profanities, and then the crash of books being pushed off shelves, and chairs and tables overturned.

"I don't know where to go, Lord, help me," she prayed, once she was outside the back door.

To your knees....

It wasn't a voice, she realized later, but a *sensation* of speech. The soft grass cushioned her as she knelt and began to pray.

Seconds passed.

Minutes....

She waited for whatever was to come, prepared to die for the One she loved. Not all the demons from a thousand black pits could make her renounce Him.

Finally she opened her eyes.

Sheriff Wilburn was standing there, alone, looking at her.

"Amy," he said, his voice a strained whisper.

"Help me, Amy!" he begged. "I'm damned. Help me!"

She stood then, looking intently at the man.

"You're alive!" she said. "As long as you have breath, you can still turn your back on Satan. It's not too late. Please, please believe that."

"It is," he cried. "Too late. I have nothing left that is honoring to Him. I serve another master now."

He held up his hands.

"Oh, what these have done." Sobs tore through his body. "What they have done in dark places of shame."

"In the name of the Lord Jesus Christ," she said, "I command you, Satan, to—"

The man clamped his hands over his ears and spun around.

"Lucifer won't let me hear what you have to say." Dark red liquid seeped through his fingers. "I can't hear you. I'm deaf. I'm—"

She hesitated.

"Go, woman! Now!"

Now, my beloved child. You can do no more here. Go now....

She ran.

As fast as she could.

To the outskirts of town and down one of the side roads until she was safely away.

Hours later she stumbled into a state trooper's post and told them about the demons in Valley Falls.

At first they refused to take her seriously....

32

Rogers rang the front doorbell of Edith Van Halen's modest bungalow near the center of town.

Nothing.

Again.

Still nothing.

He waited several seconds and was about to leave when he heard a creaky sound inside.

The door opened.

Edith Van Halen looked up at him from her wheelchair, smiling weakly.

"I'm glad you came," she said, wheeling the chair to one side so he could enter.

Instantly he noticed a strong odor, almost sickening in its intensity.

"You message sounded urgent, Edith," he began. "Is something wrong?"

"It's all over Valley Falls, you know," she replied.

"What is?"

"Pentagrams and rams' heads and inverted crosses—that stuff."

"How do you know?"

"Parents call me. I must be some kind of mother-confessor as far as they are concerned."

He had been standing, and the unsettling odor was making him a bit queasy. He asked if he might sit down, and she indicated the sofa a few feet away.

As he was sitting down, he quickly surveyed the living room. Though Edith Van Halen had been widowed for many years, she had obviously never lost her devotion to her husband. Photos of him sat atop the piano, on the mantel over the fireplace, and even on the round table next to him.

"How long has it been, Edith?" he asked kindly.

"That I've been a prisoner of this contraption?" she responded.

He nodded.

"Ever since I was a young woman," she told him. "I didn't break my neck, but there was enough damage to my spine to make a wheelchair necessary. Not even canes will do the job!"

She wheeled herself closer to him.

"Dr. Rogers, you and I have had less contact over the years than I have had with Reverend DeKorte. Yet I think sometimes he looks on me as just that poor old crippled woman. He may have kind thoughts toward me, yes, but I don't think he would take what I say very seriously."

"You may be misjudging him."

"Perhaps. But I thought you might listen more. I mean, I've been pretty healthy. I see my pastor two or three times a week, but I rarely see you."

"The last time may have been five or six months ago. You don't even come in for routine examinations. I wish you would, but you don't for some reason."

"Dr. Rogers, this town is going to Hell. Valley Falls is infected with a plague."

"I don't understand."

"That is the problem. Few people do."

She quickly pulled something out of a pocket in her dress.

One of the wood carvings, but this one was even more bizarre than the one she had dropped in the courtroom, and also quite obscene.

"At least one of these is in every home now, except yours and Reverend DeKorte's."

"But why do you have one?"

"Scott gave it to me."

"And you kept it?"

"Dr. Rogers, I can't get rid of it."

"You can't?"

"That's right. I've tried more than once. Something prevents its destruction each time. I've even started a fire over there and thrown it into the flames."

She had pointed toward the fireplace.

"What happened?" Rogers asked.

A deep frown appeared on her forehead.

"It would be there among the ashes, unharmed."

"Edith, I don't see how—"

"—such a thing could be?" she interrupted. "I thought that at first. And then I realized that Satan is not a puny enemy. If he were, then this world would be in much better shape than it is."

That odor was getting to Rogers. His impulse was to figure out an excuse and leave as soon as he could.

"I've got to—" he started to say.

"Tonight," she said. "It's tonight."

"Tonight for what?"

"Hell rises up!"

He would have left immediately then if it had not been for the phone call.

"Would you answer it for me?" she asked.

The phone was on the round table, and he picked up the receiver.

"Dr. Rogers, I'm glad I caught you, sir."

Sheriff Wilburn.

"Yes, sheriff, what is it?"

"Reverend DeKorte called. You're to meet him at the church in five minutes."

Perspiration drenched Rogers's back all of a sudden.

"Why didn't he call me directly?"

"He didn't know where you were."

"But how did you know?"

"Have to go now," Wilburn said without answering. "Talk to you later."

Rogers replaced the receiver and glanced at Mrs. Van Halen.

"I must leave now," he said. "Thank you for telling me this."

"But what about the town?" she asked, a desperate tone in her voice. "Valley Falls has been taken over by—"

He smiled weakly and headed for the door.

"Everyone!" she screamed. *"Everyone!"*

33

"You can't be unaware," Gardner told the two ministers after his nerves had settled down, "that what we've experienced thus far is playing havoc with my hard-nosed views about—"

"The supernatural?" Trent offered.

"And also that you both are playing havoc with my view of evangelical clergymen."

"The first doesn't surprise me, frankly, but the second? How so?" Trent asked as he made a turn from the state highway onto the road leading directly to Valley Falls.

"You don't seem quite so *loud* about your convictions."

"Loud? You mean we're not going about carrying signs proclaiming the end of the world and urging everyone to repent or be lost?"

"That's right. You seem more levelheaded, more reasonable."

"How do you define 'reasonable'?" Chapman interjected.

"I really am not sure at this point," Gardner told him.

"Could it be that you are more reasonable than many psychiatrists to whom we have been exposed over the years?" Chapman added.

"I am no less an agnostic."

"We are no less Christian."

Gardner nodded appreciatively.

"I think that that is a little of what I meant. You seem more tuned in than many Christians I have met. I heard an expression once."

"You can be so heavenly minded that you're no earthly good," Trent repeated.

"How in the world did you know?"

"I myself have met that type before. There's no doubt that they're going to Heaven, but in the meantime they seem to avoid fulfillment or satisfaction in this life, as though the Lord will accuse them of being less than dedicated."

"And they end up living miserably," Gardner said.

"And being such terrible examples that they drive people away from God in the process."

"Become a Christian and smother yourself in misery," Chapman said. "What a beacon to offer to the world."

"I think that is where I went wrong with Robert. Here I am, a psychiatrist devoting my life's work to helping others overcome their emotional and other problems, and I seemed to my own flesh and blood so dour, so insensitive, that it was easy for him to assume that I offered him nothing as a father...nothing at all."

"It's the same with P.K.s," Trent assured him.

"I suppose that means pastors' kids."

"Right. If we're not careful, we have our energies, our so-called wisdom drained away by the members of our congregations who come to us in a steady stream."

"None of us has an endless well at the center of his being. It's finite. It can become bone-dry if we go to it too often," Gardner agreed.

"Christ spoke of living waters. But He was the only source of that," Trent remarked. "You and I are more earthbound, I'm afraid."

Gardner was silent for a moment before saying, "I get the impression from that file I showed you that one of the principal problems with these two kids is not that they were raised in any kind of a liberal environment which I guess you both would call spiritually dead."

"You do your research, don't you?" Chapman said admiringly.

"It's essential, as far as I'm concerned. Anyway, we don't have a case here of spiritual deadness but rather religious excess, isn't that so?"

"I would have to agree with you. Bennett and I both believe in all the gifts mentioned in God's Word, but we don't covet any one gift. We are open to whatever the Lord cares to give us."

"But isn't it presumptuous to say, in effect, 'Okay, so I've done what You've asked, God. Now give me all those goodies I've been told You promise.'"

"That cuts to the heart of the problem, Elliott," Chapman continued. "There is a verse in the Old Testament that is pretty interesting in its implications. Put succinctly, it admonishes against making God some kind of good-luck charm to provide us with all our desires, or a kind of celestial guard dog to protect us against harm coming our way."

Gardner seemed to receive everything with interest; there was no sarcasm or disrespect whatever in his attitude or manner.

"You know, Elliott," Trent interjected, "it's interesting that you're not laughing in our faces."

"I might have ... at one time," the psychiatrist admitted.

"Not all Christians react similarly," Trent told him. "There are groups within my own denomination, for example, who ignore anyone who doesn't speak in tongues. They hide behind so many guises when they do this that I've lost count of how many, frankly."

"I remember the host of a Christian talk show berating a Christian journalist who was trying to be quite balanced in his outlook on the various gifts," Chapman remarked. "When he tried to tell her his own views, what resulted was a shouting match based at least partially on semantics and the twisting of words in which she was engaging. Not a scene that brought any glory to Christ, I can assure you! To make matters worse, she called his boss and tore him apart over the phone!"

"I'm afraid that many of my fellow psychiatrists are little exception to what you've indicated. Vain and insecure themselves, they view anything spiritual or religious as a threat. And that is what your talk show host's central problem happens to be, I suspect. Believe me when I say that I've dealt with that type of personality before. Their lives are so centered on the status quo, so stuck in preconceived notions no matter how false, that anyone who comes along and challenges any part of all that is viewed as the enemy."

"Even though he might be led of the Lord and, therefore, could be very helpful if she allowed that to be the case. But she found herself incapable of tolerating truth that played havoc with her preconceptions."

"In a manner of speaking, I suppose you could say that, yes."

Chapman and Trent more and more saw the potential in this agnostic psychiatrist. His spiritual perceptions were more germane than those of many Christians both men had known over the years.

Also obvious to the two ministers was how awkward Gardner was in opening himself up, especially under the circumstances, with those whose entire life views were contrary to that which he himself had embraced for a very long time. And they admired all the more his attempt at being straightforward with them and trying to understand their own outlook.

"Just as I carried my professional manner, I suppose, to an extreme with Robert, so it is that Reverend DeKorte may have—"

"—become immersed in the emotional extremes," Trent interrupted, "so that he lost sight of the biblical imperatives."

"In my instance, I lost a son as a result."

"And Paul lost someone who was in a sense a spiritual son," Trent pointed out, "while two others are hanging in the balance. And that's before we know the impact upon the rest of the town!"

"The pain we inflict upon those who look up to us!" Gardner exclaimed, sighing deeply.

The three men were silent for a few minutes.

Trent glanced at the odometer.

"How soon?" asked Chapman.

"About fifteen minutes I'd say."

Gardner cleared his throat.

"What I said back there, after we left that little store?"

"About how that clerk sounded so much like your son?" Trent said.

"That's right. It was true, you know. But how could that be?" Gardner asked. "And what's happened to that town?"

Gardner was well aware of what constituted mass panic or mob psychosis or mass delusion. But none of those classic psychological circumstances seemed applicable. Anything affecting a thousand people would surely have been reported by the news-hungry media.

"Let me suggest, Elliott, that what we saw was what remains of those who made that place their home."

"The others left, you mean?"

Trent was silent.

"Or were killed," interjected Chapman.

The possibility shook Gardner.

"Surely we're overreacting. It's probably just what we said before...one of those ingrown communities that don't welcome strangers."

"I don't think so," Trent said. "Because something obviously did happen back there. But what concerns me is another question: Why? After all, it's a little township of perhaps a few hundred people—a thousand at most—in the midst of an area of strong Christian heritage."

"And we're here because of Valley Falls," Chapman observed. "This sort of thing is, well, what we might expect there."

Gardner had brought along the Bible they had found and was leafing through it.

Suddenly he was silent for several minutes.

"Elliott, is there anything wrong?" Trent asked.

"I just came across the parable of Lazarus and the rich man in Hell," the psychiatrist answered. "I was wondering if it's going to be a little different in my case."

"What do you mean?"

"Oh, that perhaps Robert and I both will be in Hell and he will accuse me of not being a better example for him. And I will think back on all the patients whose needs may have gone beyond the purely psychological. I might even have helped them psychologically, in fact. But what if I merely wound them up like toys and sent them out into the world only to fall again and again when their 'mechanisms' wound down on them?"

He hesitated, then asked, "Am I making any sense?"

Chapman was about to answer when Trent slammed on the brakes.

"There!" he yelled. "Look!"

Ahead had been a rather steep upward curve in the road. As the car went over the top, they saw that a large crevasse had opened up straight across, and there was nothing anyone could do as they headed into it. Nothing but involuntarily surrender to the dark wave of unconsciousness that swept over the three of them.

34

While DeKorte was aware of Satan's ability to delude and deceive people by masquerading as the voice of God, as he had told the intern earlier, he had always assumed that instances of this were relatively rare. What he had never heard of during his years as a pastor was an entire congregation becoming entrapped by Satan.

His denomination's interpretation of Scripture clearly came down on the side of believing that Satan and the Holy Spirit couldn't inhabit someone's soul at the same time; it had to be one or the other.

But what about those who claimed to be Christians and yet frequently engaged in sin, compulsively so, the extent of their sin such that it must have had Satan and his demons cheering? In light of this contradictory behavior, could it be said that they were not saved in the first place? Or had they perhaps lost their salvation? And if the latter, then yet another supposedly definitive denominational doctrine would have to be questioned, since DeKorte and his fellow clergymen believed in the eternal security of every saved individual. On the other hand, it might be less wrenching to justify possession, despite the denomination's acknowledged traditional view, than to assume that salvation was so tentative a commitment on the Lord's part that He could withdraw it at any time, thereby making a mockery of John 3:16 and other verses.

But it was the possibility of that other explanation that sent shivers up and down his spine, which, if true, laid two decades of ministry to waste at his feet.

That many of the members of his congregation had never been saved in the first place!

True, they had professed acceptance of Christ as Savior and Lord, and yet how much of that was based upon devotion to the "blessings" He would bestow in time?

And then he remembered a clear-cut exception.

Patrick!

What about Patrick? The teenager whose gentle, Christ-loving spirit had sent a clear and certain signal to everyone who knew him that here was someone for whom salvation was real and vibrant, not just a "convenient" facade?

He shook himself out of momentary reverie and asked Wayne about the other teenager.

"Where in the world did he fit into all this?"

"Patrick was our first human experiment."

"Experiment?"

"Yes, sir. We wanted to discover if—" Wayne stopped briefly, the words coming with apparent difficulty. "Do you really want to hear any more of this, sir? I remember that you and your wife were real fond of Patrick."

"Yes, I must know. Tell me, Wayne!"

"Scott was obsessed with wanting to see if we could tear down a 'good' kid, and Patrick fit that description perfectly. So we invited him to go camping with us that last weekend. Scott said he knew Patrick would go so he could witness to us."

Tears filled Wayne's eyes as he looked straight at DeKorte.

"You would have been very proud of Patrick. We never destroyed his faith, no matter how hard we tried, no matter what we did to him...."

The boy stared into the distance for a moment, his eyes seeing terrible memories.

"We beat him with a baseball bat, and even though he was screaming with pain, he just kept repeating the Twenty-third Psalm...'though I walk through the valley of death, I shall fear no evil, for Thou art with me.'"

"The autopsy report said that Patrick had been sexually abused. Did you—"

Wayne threw his head back, letting out a cry of shame and regret.

"Yes, yes, yes, we did!" he cried. "But even in the midst of all that, the only thing he—he said—said to us was—was—"

Wayne collapsed, sobbing, into DeKorte's arms.

"He refused to curse us, refused to damn us all to Hell," he cried. "You know what he did? He asked God to forgive us."

Wayne pulled away, wiping his eyes with the back of his hand.

"That was when Scott saw that Patrick was proving too strong. His faith too deep. Scott said we had to kill him then!"

"But how did Patrick make it into town?" DeKorte asked. "What did you do to him?"

"We buried him alive and left him...at the old cemetery. There must have been an air pocket or something, and he was able to dig himself out and get back to town before...before he died."

"But the damage to his heart had already been done."

"Yes, sir. Patrick had a weak heart, you know. Scott was counting on that, even during the torture."

"And falling on his knees, he cried out with a loud voice, 'Lord, do not hold this sin against them!' And having said this, he fell asleep."

That verse about Stephen's martyrdom came to DeKorte's mind as the two sat in silence. Finally he managed to ask the question that had been eating at him for so long.

"Why, Wayne? Why all this horror? This evil?"

The boy had been sitting on the edge of the bed, his head bowed slightly. Now he looked up and smiled ironically.

"It was a thrill...the ultimate turn-on. It went far beyond anything drugs could offer. It was contact with real power."

"Was that why the three of you got involved?"

"Partly, I guess."

"But not all?"

"We were looking for answers. We weren't finding them at church, and our parents sure didn't have them," he said. "But with Scott it was more than that. He became convinced that occultism was some kind of supernatural passport to what he needed."

"But what did he need?" DeKorte asked.

"He wanted control, sir. He wanted to dominate everybody and everything. He wanted to have everyone in Valley Falls do his bidding."

Wayne paused. "It sounds crazy, sir, I know. And it was crazy. At the end we were all in a kind of crazy frenzy. The drugs...the music...the power..."

"But what about you, Wayne?"

"Oh, I'm not excusing myself, sir." He paused for emphasis, then said, "He couldn't do it alone, you see. At least not as effectively, he said. He needed three."

"An unholy trinity!" exclaimed DeKorte.

"Exactly, sir. And that meant the three of us, together."

"But Scott's dead now, and you and Mark are alive. So he failed."

"No, he hasn't. It's all gone according to plan."

"I don't understand."

"Scott said if he died violently, at the hands of the other members of his trinity, Satan would enable him to return as an all-powerful demonic spirit commanding legion after legion of fellow demons."

DeKorte was nearly in shock as he listened.

"Mark is, I suspect, next. And then he wants me."

"To join him? To become like him?"

"To become one with him, sir. It's called group soul. Scott read about it in a book by a renowned mystic. It's like what the Buddhists call karma, but much more powerful."

Wayne leaned over and opened a drawer in the nightstand next to the bed. He took out a sheet of paper and read from it.

"Sir, listen to this!" he said, his voice trembling a bit.

"*...a number of souls all bound together by one spirit, acting and reacting upon one another in the ascending scale of psychic evolution.*"

"I don't think you should read any more of that stuff, Wayne," DeKorte said. "I—"

"Just this, please. It's important."

"*...in the After-death, we become more and more aware of this group-soul...individual souls on various astral planes, various levels of consciousness in the After-death...separate and yet one, acting in harmony.*"

"Sir, I won't read anything else," Wayne said. "I know it's repugnant, the work of Satan. I just wanted to let you know what's happening. Notice the more than coincidental link with the Aztec deification rites."

"Bound together by one spirit, into one demonic entity?" DeKorte repeated reluctantly. "Which is Satan, of course."

"Not the Devil, sir. At least not right away. Not as far as Scott was concerned. He would have *his* day first, his glorious moment in the spotlight."

"Then what—?"

DeKorte's mouth dropped open. Seeing this, Wayne smiled ironically.

"That's right, sir. Satan may have been behind it all, but at the beginning that one spirit was to be—"

"Scott himself!"

"Yes, sir," said the boy. "But because we know that truth, because we cling to it in the midst of all this, because we can proclaim it to others, you and I stand in his way. We haven't succumbed to Satan's delusions. And Scott has to destroy us as a result. I bet he's especially enraged that I will not be part of his trinity. By now he realizes that he cannot touch my soul. But he can still play havoc with my body."

"As with Patrick?"

"As with Patrick."

How many are lost? DeKorte asked himself. *How many were unprepared for the onslaught because—*

"Sir!" Wayne's voice came through as though from a great distance. "Would you be willing to do a favor for me?"

DeKorte looked at him, his mind still on Patrick and Scott and—

"Anything, Wayne, anything at all," he was able to say, snapping out of that fleeting reverie.

"Would you please kneel and pray with me, sir?"

At precisely that moment the single light in the room flickered several times.

"Wayne, it's important that we call on God's strength right now," said DeKorte. "We must surround ourselves with His armies of protection."

The man and the boy knelt together on the floor, and DeKorte held out the Bible he had brought with him. They both placed their hands on it as they prayed.

"Lord, I have committed unspeakably evil acts, right out of the pit of darkness. I have served the Prince of Hell rather than You," Wayne began.

"Father, have mercy on me. Forgive me," he said. "I don't know how long I will survive. But whether it is an hour, a day, or a year, guide me to use that time so I can help to turn around this nightmare that I was partially responsible for creating in the first place."

Wayne prayed for several minutes, speaking with growing wisdom as he asked the Lord for forgiveness and guidance.

When he had finished, DeKorte prayed, "Oh, God, I have been blind. I confess that to You now. I have pushed for prosperity while sacrificing salvation. I have focused on the gifts instead of the Giver."

Then the lights went out completely.

DeKorte reached out and joined hands with Wayne.

"Lord, we cannot do any of this in our own strength. It must be in—"

A howling sound ripped through the air. They could hear people running...screaming....

"Lord, the enemy is here in our midst, even as we now turn to You!" Wayne exclaimed.

Tears came to his eyes.

"I ask Your forgiveness and cleansing. I confess my sins and claim the promises in Your Word."

They could feel the sanitarium tremble, as though caught in a moderate earthquake.

Suddenly someone knocked briefly and opened the door.

"Reverend DeKorte?"

DeKorte looked up at the rather rough-looking attendant standing in the doorway.

"Yes?" he said.

"We just received a call from Sheriff Wilburn. Something's going on in town. He says you're needed there."

DeKorte turned to Wayne and said, "Will you be all right?"

"Yes," he said. "And thanks for coming."

"I'll be back."

DeKorte took the boy in his arms and hugged him, hard. The teenager clung to him, as though reluctant to let him go.

Then DeKorte turned to the attendant, "Let's go—"

But the man had disappeared.

DeKorte walked out into the hallway and saw the intern he had talked with coming toward him.

"Are you leaving now?" the intern asked. "Is there anything else I can do?"

"No, there isn't. Your help is appreciated, son."

"Sir?"

"Yes?"

"Could I have just a couple of more minutes of your time?"

"No problem. What can I do for you?"

They walked down to a small office on the first floor. Piled on top were several books and magazines the intern had collected. He sat down in a chair behind the desk, and DeKorte in one in front of it.

"Listen to this!" the intern said, picking up a book from the pile.

"IRVING'S CHURCH, SPEAKING WITH TONGUES: In 1831 an outbreak of speaking with tongues occurred in the congregation of Edward Irving in London. For several years Irving had waited for such a visitation, and had instituted special early-morning services for the purpose of hastening it.

"And then, suddenly it happened, sir—people speaking in tongues throughout the congregation. But listen to this.

"The inspired speakers were often attended by physical symptoms, such as convulsions, and they spoke in loud, somewhat unnatural tones."

"Sir, does that remind you of something?" the intern asked.

DeKorte got his point, his mind hauled back to just a short while ago and his visit with Maria Esteban.

"But there's one last bit of information," the intern added. "Here it is!"

"At length, however, evil spirits began to appear in the congregation, some of the members admitting [later] that they had been possessed by false spirits."

The intern put the book aside.

"Convulsions, sir. Loud, unnatural tones. Possession by false, evil spirits. How could that be?"

An intercom on the wall next to them buzzed, and the intern excused himself to answer it.

"What's the cause?" he asked, after listening for a few seconds.

Finally, breaking the connection, he turned and looked at DeKorte.

"Sir, that was our switchboard operator."

"What's wrong?"

"All the phones in Valley Falls apparently have gone dead. Nobody can call in, and we can't get any outside lines."

They both looked at one another.

"Then how could I have received a call from Sheriff Wilburn?" DeKorte asked, apprehension gripping him.

"Who told you that?" the intern asked. "That man I saw leaving Wayne's room?"

"You referred to him as that man. I assumed he was an attendant. Are you saying he doesn't work here?"

The intern cleared his throat a couple of times before he told DeKorte, "Sir, I never saw him before."

35

The only illumination in the sanctuary was coming through the stained glass windows on either side as moonlight hit the panes, sending out shimmering rays of blue and gold and brown and other colors.

Douglas Rogers stood in the foyer, looking at the kaleidoscope, impressed by the scene which had an ethereal quality to it, the pews and the large cross hanging from the ceiling and the podium in the very front catching the color and bouncing it back off the shiny wood, especially the cross which had been coated a number of times with a varnish that made its surface sparkle like glass.

A splashing sound interrupted his thoughts.

He tried to sense the direction from which it was coming.

Ahead!

He walked forward slowly.

Kids playing in the baptismal, he said silently. *Mischievous little—*

He caught himself, cutting off that last word, chuckling a little.

He was up to the podium now.

The sound was nearer. . . .

Rogers jumped as, suddenly, the spotlight over the baptismal came on.

"What the—?" he said.

The liquid in the tub-like area cast a rippled reflection that was coloring the white walls.

Rogers stopped in his tracks.

Red!

Perspiration started soaking his clothes, and beads of sweat dripped from his forehead, stinging his eyes before he could wipe them.

Blood-red!

And that odor, one he had smelled many times during his years as a physician, especially at the scene of a serious accident.

But never this intense, never this pervasive. His lungs were filling with it, as though the sanctuary had been turned into a slaughterhouse.

He walked slowly forward, knowing he should turn and leave, the sensation of his skin crawling as though turned into a million slimy little—

Just a foot or two more.

There was water in the baptismal. The red color of a moment ago nothing more than an illusion.

And yet—

Shapes reflected on the walls, dark shapes amid the—

He peered over the edge, transfixed, reaching out, touching the surface, feeling the texture.

Instantly something misshapen, twisted, and ugly—resembling a hand, but with what would have been fingers merged together into a single talon—shot up from beneath the surface, grabbed his own hand, and pulled him forward. And into his mind there came a voice, guttural and profane.

"Behold, your children!"

And that was when the other hand shot up, gripping two tiny, squirming bodies. They turned, and he saw their faces.

Wayne and Mark!

Both bore expressions of pain so intense that it must have meant every nerve within them was sharing in their agony. Wayne reached out one miniature hand, and Rogers could hear a small piping voice pleading with him to set them free.

Then he saw a face below the surface, barely visible, eyes wide, mouth open.

Laughing!

He had seen that look once before, years earlier, when he visited a psychiatrist friend in the asylum where he worked. . . .

While they were touring the facilities, they had come to a specially reinforced cell that housed a patient who spent his waking hours screaming obscenities, reciting the most perverse incantations, and spitting at anyone who passed by.

Rogers still remembered the chill he had felt when their eyes met, madness apparent in the other's and yet something beyond that, something that seemed to reach up from deep within. And if the eyes were the mirror of a man's soul, then this particular man had an inner being that was born in the pit of Hell.

Suddenly, in a moment of astonishing speed, the man had rushed to the bars, reached through them, and grabbed his wrist, squeezing it until Rogers could feel tiny bones splintering, sending needles of pain into his brain.

Interns came at a rush. One managed to pry the man's fingers open while another injected a tranquilizer.

*That moment stayed with Douglas Rogers for a long time,
playing havoc with his agnostic approach to both God and Satan.
This had been enhanced by the fact that as he left the hospital he
had been approached by an elderly woman who looked up at him
with a strangely wise expression.*

*"Tell Satan to flee from you," she exhorted. "Admonish him as
God's Word tells us: 'Get thee behind me, Satan.' Order him to
return to Hell from whence he came."*

Those words came to the fore now, from some long-forgotten
corner of his subconscious.

"Get thee behind me, Satan! Flee from me, back to Hell!" Rogers
shouted, remembering the words as they filtered up to the surface
of his mind after being buried for a very long time, covered over by
decades of rationalistic hypothesis, long periods of denial and rejection and finally, or so he thought, a deadness, a coldness that had a
numbing finality to it.

And yet—!

He shook his head.

Without warning, he found himself looking down at clear water,
the dangling bodies gone, his hand free.

He turned and glanced around.

Everything was as before, the sanctuary suspended in the glow
from the stained glass windows.

Breathing a sigh of relief, and pushing aside any conjecture
about that moment, he walked toward the center aisle, his heart
pounding so loudly that he wouldn't have been surprised to hear it
echoing back at him from the emptiness of that large room.

The leather sole of his right shoe touched something wet on the
floor, and he nearly fell. Steadying himself, he bent down to see
what he had slipped on.

Blood!

A puddle of blood!

Suddenly he heard a cacophony of sounds, voices as though in a
bazaar, merging together chaotically, different languages colliding
with one another.

*"Only those who truly believe can say effectively what you did. I
do not respond to empty platitudes, dear Dr. Rogers!"*

And then he was picked up by some invisible force and thrown
the entire length of the sanctuary, landing on a table of tracts and
pamphlets which scattered in a dozen directions as the table collapsed under the impact of even his modest weight.

He heard the faint sound of bones cracking, and a wave of pain
washed over him, nearly causing him to black out.

He got to his feet falteringly.

A second later, the three stained glass windows on each side of the sanctuary shattered inward, shards of colors flying through the air.

"Help me!" he shouted. "Oh, God, help me!"

He started toward one of the side exits.

"Please, help me get out of here!"

Then he stopped.

Something seemed to close over him like a shroud. Even then, he knew, he had no real faith; even then the words were just a kind of desperate ritual.

He hurried toward the exit, perspiration drenching him afresh, pain lacerating him.

The door was ajar.

Only inches away he could feel the chill night breezes. He was almost there. Thank God, he was—

"God has nothing to do with you now, Dr. Rogers!"

That voice again, louder, more accusatory.

He reached out his hand, and it was no longer the strong limb of an athletic, healthy man. He reached out an ancient, liver-spotted hand, twisted by arthritis, joints knobby and enlarged, veins protruding, infected sores dotting the surface. A hand that—

* * *

After thanking the intern and hurriedly leaving the sanitarium, DeKorte headed back to town, his mind swirling with all that Wayne had told him and with what the intern had discovered.

As soon as he was within sight of the church, he saw that the windows were gone!

"God help us!" he cried.

Slamming on the brakes, he jumped out of the car and ran to the front entrance.

Locked.

And he didn't have his church keys with him!

He went around the side, hoping one of the other doors would not be locked.

One indeed was unlocked and partly open.

He started to go inside.

A stench greeted his nostrils.

He had smelled something like it only once before, during a vacation in England, as Mary and he had entered a room in Windsor Castle on the outskirts of London. They noticed it immediately, like centuries of death compressed together in a single moment, so pervasive that they had to leave after just a few seconds.

But what was it doing in his church?

Amid the scattered piles of glass in the sanctuary he spied a small pile of white powder and bent down to examine it. Some of it seemed to be finely ground, some quite coarse, and there were chunks of what looked like—

Bone!

He picked up one piece and turned it around between his fingers.

Finally, standing, he muttered, "Better turn on the light so I don't trip over anything."

"No! Don't!" a voice said. It was a voice both familiar and strange. It sounded old; no, it sounded ancient.

"You mustn't turn on the light."

"I won't then. Who are you? Where are you?"

"Oh, Paul!"

"Do I know you, sir?"

"You tried to take care of their souls, and I did my best with their bodies. We both failed!"

And then, of course, he knew.

"Doug? What's wrong with your voice? What—"

He heard movement ahead.

A shape moving. Just beyond the doorway into the foyer.

"For the love of God, Paul, don't come any closer!" the voice pleaded.

"But I—"

Then in the faint slivers of moonlight beginning to sift through the window frames, Paul DeKorte saw what was left of his friend.

"Doug!" DeKorte exclaimed.

"I can feel myself disintegrating inch by inch," Rogers said in a raspy whisper. "My bones are becoming more brittle by the second."

His body was hunched over, the bones twisted, one hand missing. As he turned his head to look up at DeKorte, who was now standing next to him, thin clouds of flesh-become-dust puffed out into the air.

"I commanded Satan to flee, but he...or Scott or whoever it is...wouldn't listen. I tried, Paul, I really tried."

DeKorte bent down close to his friend.

"I don't want you to—" he started to say.

"You don't want me to go into that great beyond you keep preaching about without accepting Christ as my Savior?"

DeKorte nodded sadly.

Tears were streaming down Rogers's face.

"Please, Paul, please...help me...before it's too late."

"Oh, Lord, my friend wants to come to You now," Paul prayed, "to allow Your Son's shed blood to cover him and cleanse him from all sin, bringing the redemption promised in Your Word."

After each phrase, Rogers whispered, "Yes, Lord."

Paul could feel a hand on his wrist, a hand with the grip of a feather, so light, the texture of its flesh so dry.

"Lord, take him to You now, on wings of—"

"Yes," and he heard his friend whisper something about the scent of apple blossoms.

DeKorte opened his eyes.

A pale, wrinkled countenance was just inches from his face. The mouth opened for a final cry of pain, and then the figure fell forward against him. He put his arms around it and could feel it caving in. Chalky dust spurted out—into his eyes, his nose, down his throat.

"No! No!"

DeKorte's scream tore through the sanctuary, bouncing back at him in ghostly echoes. He scrambled to his feet, shaking his fist at the air.

"No more, Scott! You will not claim another life. This is your last victory!"

DeKorte rushed to a pew, grabbed a Bible, and opened it to Revelation.

"And the Beast and Satan and all the demons shall be cast into the lake of fire forever and—"

Immediately the book burst into flames. Letting out a cry, he dropped it, and it was consumed at his feet.

DeKorte spun around, his eyes darting about the darkness.

"Scott! You're nothing more than a coward, hiding behind your demonic lackeys! You made Mark drink your blood. You killed helpless animals. You killed Patrick! That's not power, Scott! That's sinful sickness...evil—"

Grinding, tearing sounds came from beneath him, and he felt the floor buckling and twisting under his feet.

Scores of talon-hands popped up through the planking, flinging chunks of splintered wood into the air. One grabbed DeKorte's foot, but he shook himself loose. Another clamped onto his trouser leg.

Searching in his pockets, he found his small pocket knife and jabbed it into the misshapen thing, which slithered back through a hole in the floor.

Just then the whole building shook violently and visibly before his eyes, and a section of the roof started to cave in, pieces of it plunging down into the sanctuary.

He turned and ran toward the exit. Seconds after he was outside, the building shuddered and the entire roof collapsed, together with the west wall.

He backed away, in shock, and bumped into someone.

"Hello, Pastor DeKorte," Sheriff Wilburn said in an eerie monotone. "Having a pleasant evening?"

36

Elliott Gardner regained consciousness slowly, pain assailing every limb. He had been thrown from the front seat into the back, and beside him lay the still body of Bennett Chapman, barely breathing.

Harley must have gone for help, Gardner told himself.

Somehow he managed to climb out through the open door on the driver's side, but the pain made him vomit at one point.

He was so weak! The simple act of standing required uncommon effort.

He glanced around at the crevasse.

We should all be dead. What could have caused this?

The crevasse was wide at the top but quickly narrowed, sloping to a secondary fissure not more than a foot wide. He could not see the bottom.

As he leaned over to look, he felt . . . heat.

Heat coming up from the crack in the earth.

And something else!

He could hear movement.

"What in the world?!" he exclaimed and, despite the pain in his body, bent over to get a closer look.

Several pairs of eyes stared up at him!

He jumped back, lost his balance, and fell against sharp pieces of rock. He almost passed out again, but with an extra surge of adrenaline he was surprised he had, willed himself to cling to consciousness.

When a hand deformed into the shape of a talon thrust up over the edge of the secondary crevasse, he instinctively groped for a large rock.

Another hand appeared.

He raised the primitive weapon.

"Dad, don't, it's—"

Every muscle in his body froze as he recognized the voice.

Robert's voice.

But the forehead appearing over the edge was not his son's, nor were the blood-red eyes, nor the fangs dripping with—

His heart seemed to stop for an instant as those eyes locked into his own.

"God, help me, please help me!" Gardner cried.

Unable to meet that awful gaze any longer, he closed his eyes. Seconds later when he opened them—

Gone!

Whatever he had seen was no longer there.

And yet that had been his son's voice. There was no way in the world he could have mistaken it. No way....

* * *

At the county medical hospital near Valley Falls, the lack of telephone service had initially created massive problems. But these were forgotten in the wake of the behavior manifested by certain members of the staff.

A female nurse on the second floor, in a ward confined to those on life-support systems, went up to each and turned off the machine connected to that individual and laughed ecstatically.

"I've been wanting to do that for ages!" she screamed.

One by one the patients gasped their lives away, some falling out of bed in the process, ripping plastic tubing from their veins. Some had massive coronaries and died in agony. Others—

The nurse paused for a moment by one of the beds.

On it was an elderly woman, who looked up in terror.

"Nadina, I'm your—"

The nurse slid the pillow out from under the woman's head and put it over her face.

She suffocated in less than a minute.

And then the nurse stood in the middle of the large ward, the air filled with fading cries.

"I killed them all!" she cried, looking around her, recoiling from the horror of her actions. "It's what the Master demanded of me! What was I to do?"

Her next stop was the operating room on that same floor, where she headed straight for a generous supply of disinfected scalpels.

Trembling, she held up her hands in front of her face.

"These offend me because they have the blood of the innocent on them. I must—"

And she did.

* * *

Walking down the bare gray-toned corridor toward the nursery at the end was a young male intern. Somewhat out of breath because of what he was lugging, he approached the double doors, swung them open, surveyed the incubators and open cribs.

"Inside the womb or here now," he said to the tiny, uncomprehending forms. "Does it really matter?"

That movie one night on cable television ... about this guy and his chain saw ...

The intern bought one right afterward—real expensive, and almost too heavy to carry for very long, but with lots of power!

* * *

A handful of doctors, nurses, and interns managed to escape. Considerably outnumbered, they could do little or nothing inside the hospital itself.

"Into town!" a young doctor screamed as the rest started to head in the opposite direction. "To get help!"

"Not *there!*" a middle-aged nurse said. "It's going to be worse there."

"I don't understand," he said. "I—"

She held up a leather-bound Bible.

"You will," she replied simply. "You will."

* * *

Gardner was shaking, his body soaked with perspiration, dizziness playing at the corners of his equilibrium.

Directly ahead, beyond the crevasse, the road to Valley Falls stretched out straight and level. To his left, a narrow trail led into a thickly wooded area. To his right, the trees gave way to level farmland, now slashed by the ugly gash that crossed the road and terminated in the woods, where trees had toppled over into it.

He glanced down at the car, tilted at a 45-degree angle at the bottom of the first crevasse level. Chapman still had not stirred, but Gardner didn't dare try to move him. There was no tell-tale odor of gasoline, so there seemed no danger of an explosion.

And there was still no sign of Trent.

Gardner stumbled along the side of the road for about half a mile before his fragile strength played out and he had to sit down on the bare ground.

No cars had passed him, and the countryside was strangely quiet.

So still, he told himself. *Nothing stirring at all.*

He rested his head in his hands, shivering with the suddenness of what had happened.

Something touched his cheek. He brushed it away.

Again.

As he was raising his hand a second time, he looked up.

Floating through the air were wafer-thin pieces of debris.

One landed on his hand. He examined it closely. It was whitish-grey, the edges singed black. Like skin that had flaked after a bad case of sunburn!

Like skin ...

He blanched at the thought, wiping his hand clear of the stuff.

Ahead of him, in the night sky, he could see a reddish tinge hovering over what must be Valley Falls.

He looked at himself then, saw his torn clothes, his bloody shirt.

Walking toward a town that—

He stopped momentarily, no longer able to look back and see the crevasse but suddenly not wanting to continue ahead either.

That was when he noticed, through the trees, what remained of a neglected cemetery.

And the sound of weeping coming from that same direction....

It was an old burial ground, neglected. An odor of mustiness was in the air, an ancient "feel" that was well-nigh palpable.

Examining several of the headstones, he saw that most of the graves dated back to the time of the American Revolution.

He could still hear the weeping ahead, and he stumbled forward, tripping on the underbrush that had grown up over the years. He fell just a short distance from a body lying facedown on the ground.

A body!

Gardner got to his feet and approached the still, small form.

It's a youngster.

His foot touched a bony hand, breaking off one of the fingers.

"Dad!"

The voice again!

Robert's voice!

And then the body in front of him moved!

Old bones rustled like dead leaves, and the form stood and turned ever so slowly to face him. It was wearing the tattered remains of a child's school outfit.

"Dad!"

Dreadful odors came from the figure. And the voice was like the hissing of a serpent, and yet it was Robert's voice.

The figure walked toward him, holding out each hand, the jawbone opening and closing, opening and closing.

Out of the eye sockets slithered graveyard worms, their slimy forms glistening in the moonlight.

"You were older when you died," Gardner screamed, backing away from the thing. "You were a man!"

You destroyed me long before then, Dad. You killed my spirit in my youth, and it was only decay afterward.

"I—I loved you, Robert," Gardner cried, his voice quivering. "I gave you—"

You took God from me, Dad. And you gave me the empty shell of your unbelief in return.

"But God wasn't real. God was a fantasy. I gave you reality."

Indeed, Dad. You gave me the reality of Hell.

And with that the form collapsed, the bones unhinging and turning to dust, the skull splintering in half as it hit a rock.

The reality of Hell . . .

Gardner felt something burn his cheek.

Cinders.

Falling from the sky.

Cinders like grotesque burning hailstones, reaching his clothes, igniting them in tiny sections of flame.

Frantically he tried to pat these out and failed. He tore off his coat, then his shirt, and the cinders burned his flesh, turning it red.

Strands of his hair caught fire, and he sank to his knees to throw dirt on his head, managing to extinguish one flame only to have another flare, and then—

There was movement among the surrounding trees.

"Harley!" he yelled. "Thank God!"

Not God, Dad. Not God at all. You cannot thank One you refuse to acknowledge.

Gardner cringed at the sound of his son's voice again.

Out from the trees came the Robert he remembered, just after he had gotten into drugs and Satanism, a son with a haunted face of pain and guilt and—

And changing before his eyes!

You abused me. You—

"I did no such thing," Gardner protested. "I never laid a hand on you, Robert."

Up here.

A finger touched the forehead and poked on through.

And here.

The finger withdrew from the forehead, leaving a hole where it had been, and touched the chest.

You abused my mind. You tore apart my emotions. I lost my soul because of what you did to me.

The figure took both hands and tore open its chest.

Nothing left, Dad. Nothing but another master.

And inside, as though coming from a demonic and twisted womb, was another figure. Shredding the now useless shell of Robert Gardner in hellish rage, it spouted obscenities as it strode toward him on cloven feet.

Bring your hands together in prayer.

Another voice! On the fringes of his hearing. Unfamiliar, but quite different in its purpose. And along with the words there was a feeling of—

Joy—sudden and profound.

In the midst of the deepest, most chilling terror!

"I don't know what to say," he whispered, his nerve ends alive with the sensation of it. "I—I—God doesn't listen to people like me. He—"

Open your heart. Speak My name. Surrender yourself.

The creature was now standing directly in front of him. Its skin was littered with boils, and these erupted, sending their foul-smelling filth into the air.

"O God!" Gardner cried from the heart.

Go on, Elliott Gardner. Not in vain do you now speak My holy name.

"I don't deserve to live any longer."

Mottled green liquid slobbered from the creature's mouth.

"But in death, I pray, take me from this awfulness into Your arms."

He fell, prostrate, on the ground.

Accept My Son, Elliott Gardner. Accept My Son as your Redeemer.

"Jesus!" he cried, tasting the dirt of the ground with his tongue. "Jesus, enter my life—and forgive me."

Several seconds passed.

He waited, steeling himself for the pain, waiting for the taloned hand to rip him open.

It never came.

Dad!

Robert's voice. Gentler, kinder than before. As though from a great distance.

Gardner raised his head.

The creature had backed away.

Dad, listen to me, please!

Gardner started weeping.

Oh, Dad. That was all demonic trickery. I'm not in Hell, Dad. I asked God to forgive me. That's why the cult sacrificed me. I was rejecting them . . . and Satan.

"Robert," Gardner said, "oh, my son!"

Gardner felt the soft touch of a gentle breeze cooling his burning flesh.

Suddenly the creature snarled ferociously, a fist raised toward the sky in pathetic defiance.

And just as suddenly the ground split open around it and—

That was when darkness overwhelmed Elliott Gardner again, and he fell into it—but not with fear this time.

* * *

When Gardner opened his eyes, he was lying flat on his back and Harley Trent and Bennett Chapman were hovering over him.

"What?!"

"We had to pull you from the wreckage," Trent said.

"We didn't know how badly you were hurt," Chapman added, "but we had to get you out of there."

"But—but—I saw you still there when I left," Gardner told him. "And you, Harley, you were gone."

"You were unconscious," Trent told him. "But you mumbled a great deal. We could get bits and pieces of what was going on in your mind."

"In my mind!" Gardner said a bit angrily. "You make it sound as though I should be one of my own patients."

He hesitated, then added, "But you must be right, of course."

He started to sit up, was dizzy for a second or two, then managed to get to his feet.

They were only a few yards from the crevasse.

"I have never had such a vivid nightmare," he said. "In it I stumbled upon an old cemetery just down the road a ways."

Trent nodded. "We got that much from what you were saying."

He was holding something in his hand.

"Does this look familiar?" he asked.

It was a medallion.

"It looks like—" Gardner started to say, gasping as he turned it over and read the inscription on the back. "But here? In this place?"

For Robert, with love that is real—Dad.

He looked helplessly from Trent to Chapman.

"He never believed those words," Gardner said finally. "I did everything I knew how, but—" He cleared his throat, then added, "How could this be?"

"Elliott," Chapman interrupted, "as an evangelical I look with the greatest skepticism on dreams and what we are supposed to learn from them. That sort of thing is more often than not abused to the point of actually being quite evil. But I cannot rule out the intervention of Almighty God, from time to time, in such a manner, through such a vehicle."

"If God was glorified, if what you dreamed elevated His love and forgiveness," Trent added, "and gave some hope of your son's redemption, then, my friend, I would rejoice if I were you."

"But I turned my back on Him a long time ago. How could He possibly still care about someone like me?"

"Because He never stops caring," Trent said. "That is precisely why Christ died. An unforgiving, stone-hearted God would never have allowed His Son to go through the agony of Calvary."

Elliott Gardner began sobbing then, weeping away years of bitterness, hatred, guilt, and defiance.

When he had finished, minutes later, he looked at his two companions and said, "Weren't we on the way to Valley Falls, gentlemen?"

They both nodded.

The sky above them was red now with the hint of flame, and human flesh fell upon them in flakes like confetti.

The one part that Elliott Gardner had not dreamed.

37

Later, as DeKorte looked back on those moments directly after discovering Douglas Rogers in the church, his recollections would be quite confused, the circumstances proving so bizarre that there was no way he could view them with any degree of normal coherence.

He remembered running from Sheriff Wilburn, running from a growing mass of people gathering around, looking at him, their normal human expressions transformed, lips twisted up into sneers, saliva drooling from the corners of their mouths, eyes wide, bloodshot.

Undoubtedly he saw a great deal also ... *a man he knew taking a knife and opening his own wrists, screaming ecstatically ... children being herded toward the center of the square, frightened, crying* ... but so brutal, ugly, and demonic that he could tolerate no more, the memories mercifully blotted from his mind.

Running ...

Things became a little clearer for him. He remembered ending up at Edith Van Halen's front door, remembered banging on it but getting no answer, remembered finding it unlocked and then going inside.

Remembered—

That ghastly odor!

He had never encountered anything like it, so intense that it seemed almost palpable in the air.

He walked through the foyer into the living room.

In the dining room he found a tea service outlined in the moonlight which was coming through the delicate lace curtains on the single small window in the room. Steam was coming out of the pot; two cups were ready to be filled.

He entered a hallway.

The door to his right was slightly ajar.

Stronger here ... rotten ... almost overwhelming ...

He opened the door further and flicked the light switch to his left.

It's the scene from the photo in Wayne Mulrooney's room!

Animal parts everywhere. Legs of dogs and cats. The severed head of a spider monkey, degutted robins and crows. Some hung from the ceiling at the end of thin ropes; others were strewn about on the floor, a windowsill. Dozens of pieces, most in an advanced state of decay.

DeKorte staggered back into the hallway.

He heard a creaking sound. It seemed to be coming from the kitchen just ahead. He was nearly at the doorway to the kitchen when he discovered that the sound was coming from a room immediately to his right.

The door was wide open.

Outlined in moonlight was a rocking chair. As he walked slowly up to it, he saw a folded wheelchair to one side, as though it had been thrown there.

He reached the rocker.

"Edith?" he said hesitantly.

He walked over and leaned down, placing one hand on the right arm of the chair.

Edith Van Halen turned and smiled at him.

"Nice of you to visit my humble house, Reverend DeKorte," she said, her tone innocuous.

In an action so swift that he was totally unprepared for it, she took a knife she had been holding and stabbed it through his hand and into the wooden arm of her rocking chair, effectively trapping him in that spot.

DeKorte almost passed out. He could barely see the woman as she slowly stood.

"Crippled for nearly fifty years," she said.

She staggered toward the wheelchair and fell inches away from it.

"Chained to a wheelchair for most of my life," she continued, "a prisoner every bit as though I was actually behind bars."

She slapped her leg.

"Useless . . . might as well have been made of stone."

She started weeping.

"Other women could do so much—walk, dance, make love, bear children."

She managed to get the wheelchair set up and climbed into it. Then she wheeled over to DeKorte, who had slumped to the floor.

With mocking sarcasm she said, "And that Christ of yours refused to heal me! That wonderful Lord who's supposed to be so kind and loving."

She fumbled for something in the pocket of her dress.

"But not my new master!"

She pulled her hand out of the pocket.

"Lucifer, yes! Satan . . . the Devil! He has not yet given me back the use of my legs, but I can begin to feel needles of pain where there has been only paralysis. Soon I will have their full use back. And in the meantime he has made me powerful in another way: I now serve him as the High Priestess of one of his most powerful demons, one who has been trapped without a body for many centuries. But soon he will claim a new one!"

She shoved the object in front of his face.

"And a new form for me as well!"

It was one of the wood carvings but different, even uglier, and more unsettling by far.

"He didn't want to frighten anyone at first, you know. He didn't want to show them his anger! He has good sense, this demon. So the early ones were curiosities. But there is no longer any need for that deception. You see, Reverend DeKorte, my lord, the Lord of Darkness, is coming into his own at last!"

She broke out in hysterical laughter.

"I'll be back," she said. "I've worked up quite a hunger."

DeKorte fought not to lose consciousness. He could feel his stomach turning sour, and he spit up some fluid.

He got to his knees, reached out, took the handle of the knife, and in one quick, awful motion pulled it up out of the wooden arm and his hand.

Father, help me, he prayed. *Help me, Lord.*

The creaking of the wheelchair.

Down the hallway.

Closer. Closer. Clo—

DeKorte staggered to his feet, holding the knife in his good hand, clasping the other one, bleeding, against his stomach. He made it to the doorway, stood to one side, and raised the knife.

The woman came back into the room, holding something that squirmed in her hands, something unrecognizably bloody and whimpering.

"Dinner is served," she said, approaching the rocker, then screaming as she saw that he was no longer there.

She spun around.

Moonlight flashed off the knife.

Her expression changed for an instant.

"Do it," she said. "Please, pastor . . . before I wallow in worse things than—"

The moment passed.

She started cackling, raising whatever it was in her hands to her mouth and ripping at it like a frenzied animal.

He stood there, horrified at what he was seeing . . . hardly able to believe that he was not in the midst of some terrible nightmare.

"I do what he says, you know," she said pitiably, tears coming from her eyes. "I am his slave."

He dropped the knife.

"Aren't you going to kill me?" she asked.

He was feeling very dizzy, extremely nauseous. He knew he was going to pass out at any moment.

"You look so pale," she said. "Here's some red meat—take it."

He backed away, barely able to stand. She was within inches of him, holding out her abominable offering. The head of the small creature, now unrecognizable, turned toward him, the mouth frozen open as it finally died.

"Look at what's happened," she said. "Look—"

He slugged her with his good fist, and she flew backward. The wheelchair toppled over and she fell out, hitting the opposite wall.

Her eyes angry, she started to stand, then fell.

"My legs, my legs!" she screamed. "The feeling's gone. They're dead again."

She took the wood carving from her dress and bowed her head.

"Master of Darkness and Evil, please let me know that pain again, the pain of life returning to my—"

DeKorte had fallen to his knees, too weak to stand.

She noticed the knife lying on the floor and began pulling herself toward it with her hands and arms.

His vision was fading rapidly. He couldn't reach the knife himself.

Her hand closed around the handle, and she turned in DeKorte's direction muttering a stream of obscenities, her eyes wild with rage.

I can't move, DeKorte thought in his fetal-like helplessness. *She's going to sacrifice me to some demonic god, and I can't defend myself.*

"Lord, help me," he prayed aloud. "Give me strength to—"

Abruptly something crashed through the window, the sound of breaking glass reaching his ears.

He saw Edith Van Halen lash out with the knife at a blurry form.

And then she dropped the weapon, wracking sobs suddenly tearing her body.

"Oh, Lord Jesus, set me free," he heard her voice, as though coming from a great distance.

The form hovered in front of her.

"Forgive me, Lord...save me!"

Chills gripped DeKorte, not from what he was seeing but from the loss of blood and the pain.

Movement...the woman reaching out...the sound of...wings?

He heard her talking, at first with great frenzy, and finally in the sweetest manifestation of—

Unconsciousness came quickly then, but not before he could detect, faintly, Edith Van Halen close to him, so close that he could feel her breath on his face and hear her voice, vibrant, in his ears.

"Reverend DeKorte, I'm free!"

* * *

Something warm in his mouth.

He tried to move but couldn't. He opened his eyes.

"Easy," Edith Van Halen said, smiling sympathetically. "You're very weak."

DeKorte leaned back against the wall. From her wheelchair, she was holding a cup of tea to his mouth.

"Your legs?"

"As useless as ever," she said sadly. "When I withdrew from Satan, I lost what little feeling had returned, probably for good."

Several minutes passed.

Then, in a quiet tone, she was telling him what had happened.

That strange sensation, very much like sensing the presence of Someone who had stepped in front of her, blocking her path, though she could see no one, no one except DeKorte who would soon feel the wrath—

Pain shot through her body.

Words. Whispered.

"I could hear words but not clearly, no matter how much I strained," she said. "I thought at first that it might be the presence of a demon, and yet I knew no demon could give me the kind of overflowing love, the kind of peace that settled upon me."

She could hear the sound of singing, not a dozen voices or even a hundred but thousands.

A hymn!

They were singing a beautiful old hymn.

And then the sound of wings. Suddenly through the window, shattering the pane of glass, came—

"And there it was, on my hand, its eyes piercing through to my very soul. A dove—"

"A dove?" he asked incredulously.

"A dove, Reverend DeKorte. Its wings were spotted with blood... I guess because of all the glass from the window."

"Where is it now?"

"I don't know. It just disappeared, except for this."

She held up a single white feather.

Those tiny eyes seemed to lock in on her own. She could not turn her head away. She could only feel the Presence.

"Lord?" she asked. "Lord, is that You?"

And then she touched her forehead.

A single drop of blood.

"I knew, even then, even in the midst of the awful acts I had committed, that according to His Word, God would not withhold His forgiveness if I came to Him. And I knew I indeed was in His Almighty Presence, and that my sin could not stand before Him. 'Take away this ghastly curse that has overrun my life,' I cried. And He did!"

She smiled sweetly, and it was difficult for DeKorte to believe that only a short time before this face had been twisted with demonic hate and evil as she plunged a knife into his hand.

"I wanted to walk so badly," she said, almost wistfully, "and Satan used that desire to gain entry into my life, as he has enticed so many others."

Then she frowned.

"Satan will try to tempt me again I know," she admitted. "I've tasted the kind of thrill, I guess you could call it, that has enticed so many others. But he will not make me succumb ever again."

She paused, memories yet haunting her.

"How I could have done those awful—"

"Please, you don't have to say any more," DeKorte interrupted.

"But I do, pastor. I need to confess what I have done to someone with spiritual understanding. Satan indwelt me for longer than you could ever guess, his evil twisting my very spirit."

Closing her eyes momentarily, she said, "I'm the one who provided Scott with the carvings."

"Why?"

"Revenge! I hated life! I could hardly bear to see people who called themselves Christians walking around healthy and happy. I wanted to strike back at them and, through them, at God Himself."

"Where did you get the carvings?"

"From an occult mail-order catalogue."

"As easily as that?"

"Yes. It came in with my junk mail one day."

She opened her eyes slowly.

They fell into silence for a bit. Then DeKorte, feeling somewhat stronger, got to his feet. Once more a dizzy spell incapacitated him briefly.

"You'll need to have Dr. Rogers take a look at that hand," she said. "And you've lost quite a bit of blood."

Memories swept over him at her words.

"Doug Rogers is dead," he said, and told her what had happened at the church.

She fell back against the chair, her expression troubled.

"All because of me," she said, banging her fists down on the arms. "Satan thought he could possess me, forever, as one of his own and through me—"

She was interrupted by the sound of chanting.

DeKorte walked cautiously over to the window.

Townspeople were gathered outside, their figures ghostly-looking in the glow from the overhead moon.

Suddenly one of them threw a rock, and DeKorte jumped aside as it crashed through the window.

A note was attached.

Come outside. We will not harm you. We will protect you.

He saw their faces, people he had known for so many years. Just weeks before they had seemed so happy, so dedicated.

Then he noticed something that made him stumble back in shock.

"What is it?" Edith Van Halen asked.

"A tornado," he said. "But not like any I've ever seen before."

She wheeled herself over to the window.

In the distance, a telltale funnel, but not of rebelling air waves . . . rather, a funnel of flame so bright, so hot though still some distance away, that it began to cast a reddish glow on the faces of the townspeople. They seemed to have been transplanted from Hell itself.

"I grew up with most of them," she said.

"And I was their pastor," he said sadly. "They worshiped in my church. They—"

She looked at him, smiling knowingly.

"Doesn't the Bible teach that not all of those who appear to be godly are necessarily His own?"

He had officiated at weddings for several of them, baptized others, and taught them almost every Sunday for ten years. And now they were gathered together, waiting to—

The funnel was closer, just a block away. It was huge, its heat worse than any desert at high noon.

"Look at it!" Mrs. Van Halen said, adjusting her glasses. "Are my old eyes deceiving me?"

"No, I see it too!"

Shapes.

Will-o'-the-wisp shapes among the blazing flames.

Suddenly one of the townspeople was pulled, screaming, into the whirling inferno.

The others backed away, terrified but unable to run, transfixed by the evil that had possessed them as well as its visible manifestation directly before them.

"I'm going out there!" DeKorte said.

"Not alone," Edith Van Halen insisted.

"But—"

"I have just recently come from the enemy's grasp, you're probably thinking. An easy target. Well, don't bet on it, buster!"

He had to smile at her in spite of the circumstances, and quickly nodded. Together, they went outside.

The townspeople had gathered in a packed little group, huddling together like frightened sheep.

Directly in front of them was the swirling funnel of flame.

There was no ferocity on their faces now, fear replacing it.

Where could they go? Ahead were the flames, behind them the town square, more than a hint of the frenzy there.

Sounds of screaming...a dog's awful howl...and something else, something he couldn't quite identify just then, though it reminded him somewhat of—

He stepped in front of the dozen or more men and women, stood between them and the funnel.

Now that he was so close, he could see much more clearly.

Those shapes.

The shapes appeared briefly, seen for only a split second and then replaced by others, hardly distinguishable from the flames but visible enough to send chills of the most gut-wrenching terror through his body.

Every nightmare vision he had ever dreamt in the darkness when his defenses were down, every lustful desire, every perversion planted by the wiles of satanic emissaries—embodied in those shapes, like the drawings on the walls of a modern Pompeii, only infinitely more unsettling because instead of being filtered through the veil of men themselves, diluted by their finite limitations, *these sprang forth from the very source!*

And there were in his mind . . . words . . . voices . . . scenes. . . .

Washing over him, enveloping every pore, every nerve, every sense he possessed—he saw, he heard—

And was touched . . . a woman's hand caressing every part of his body.

Whispering . . . so close . . . yes, now an inch from his ear . . . words beguiling him to sin.

Join US . . . take OUR hand . . . and let US give you more ecstasy than you've ever imagined.

He brought his hands to his ears, trying to block out the filthy sounds.

Strip it ALL away. All that mercy and salvation you talk about. None of it is real. It's all phony. Only what we can bestow is real.

Then—

Thunder.

DeKorte froze at the unexpected sound . . . thunder so loud that it shook the ground with near-earthquake intensity.

Lightning.

Bolt after bolt of it lashed out from the sky toward the earth. One bright spear hit the house directly behind him.

Edith Van Halen's house.

She screamed as it caught fire.

And then the tenuous veil between the natural and the supernatural worlds was torn asunder, and there was no longer any question of seeing through a glass darkly.

Demon hordes were stunned, gibbering in their confusion.

The veil had been rent!

Nothing separated them from the physical world.

"This cannot be!" they exclaimed as a group. "The mask of our deception no longer—"

Even the Master shuddered, his fist clenched in fury. . . .

DeKorte saw what had been only whispered about over the ages. Four thousand years before, Isaiah had seen the angels in a moment of extraordinary revelation. For DeKorte it was altogether different.

He saw the powers of darkness.

Countless thousands of creatures, misshapen, some with gnarled faces and arms, taloned hands, bodies exploding with gangrenous pus, eyes red with the rage they had felt for all of time, ever since being denied what they lusted for—the subjection of Heaven and Earth to their beck and call, even God Himself, Creator subservient to His creation—as they tried with awful dedication to displace Him from the Throne.

And in their midst their supreme ruler, one so unholy that at the sight DeKorte stumbled back, falling, but not before their eyes met, not before he felt hatred beyond comprehension.

"No!"

The voice seemed at once old and thin and weak and yet as loud, as commanding as a trumpet blown by young and vibrant lungs.

Edith Van Halen was standing slowly, pain on her face, but standing just the same, and leaving her wheelchair behind.

DeKorte gasped, as did most of the others, seeing this woman who had been wheelchair-bound for as long as they had known her—

Walking!

She approached the very edge of the funnel.

"I am old. I may live only a few years longer before I join my Lord. But I dedicate every second I have left to protecting this man in prayer. He will have *a mission, a mission against which all the powers of darkness cannot prevail!*"

At that, she took the wood carving from her pocket.

"No longer!" she shouted, her voice possessed of a strength even she must have found surprising.

She had thrown back her head triumphantly.

Holding the carving out in front of her, she thrust it and her hand into the flames.

But she did not cry out in pain.

Instead—

She started singing triumphantly.

There they are, the witnesses of Jesus take their stand....

The townspeople were no longer huddling together. They were joining hands, one of them reaching down and helping DeKorte stand.

We once were dead but now raised to life....

They began to sing that hymn, swaying back and forth, the dirt on their cheeks mixing with the tears from their eyes.

The brokenhearted sing....

Shaking mightily, like a giant wounded beast, the funnel rose back into the air and then proceeded over their heads... toward the town square, where they could hear the shrieking cries from help-less men and women who ignited instantly as it whirled through their midst.

"No!" DeKorte shouted as he saw the direction it was taking. "Not Wayne and Mark! Not—"

A man handed him a set of keys.

"Take my car," the man urged him. "It's parked in the next block, at 29438 Promontory Place."

DeKorte hesitated.

"Go! And may the Lord be at your side."

DeKorte knew he had no choice.

That shimmering mass of flame, now changing shape and becoming bigger, was headed straight for the sanitarium!

The administrator was working in his office when he felt the heat.

Unusual, he thought. *This is autumn, not the middle of summer.*

He attempted to ignore it, trying instead to concentrate on the report on his desk.

Flickering.

"What the—?" he started to say, the reflection on the papers puzzling.

Then it started to fill the room, flickering, dancing forms on the walls and the ceiling.

He stood and looked out the window.

A raging wall of fire, stretching as far as he could see, apparently surrounding the entire building!

And in the flames he saw....

No one knew he was a pedophile, no one except the children. He had managed to keep that part of his life secret. Often he had chuckled at the irony, the irony that he headed an institution dedicated to treating people with psychiatric problems.

He would go away, to a convention or on a vacation, and he would cruise streets where he was a stranger, finding child after child, enticing them with the emotional games he had learned in his profession.

And that is precisely what he saw in the inferno ... the vision of an innocent child, a pleading expression on his face, arms outstretched.

* * *

An intern had been outside when he saw the funnel approaching and tried to run back into the sanitarium to warn others.

Locked.

Every door he tried was locked.

He banged on each one.

Nobody came.

The funnel had expanded, stretching, encircling the building and the grounds, trapping him.

He heard someone scream and looked up as the administrator jumped from the window in his office on the third floor, hurtling down.

Their bodies met in an instant, bones snapping, muscles tearing, and death came quickly.

* * *

One of the patients stood in the doorway, watching as the administrator went berserk and jumped.

He rushed to the window and saw the flames.

In another life I was a cheetah. I roamed the jungles, and the Serengeti. No one could trap me. I was free. When I was reincarnated, it was here, in a human body, behind these walls.

The extent of his insanity was to the degree that he had involved himself in the reincarnation movement. He saw himself as a wild animal, racing with the wind. When he was closed in a room, any room, he could not endure it, and so his mind snapped.

And this time it snapped again as he tore off his clothes and ran from that office.

Animals were terrified of fire.

* * *

Besieged by the sudden and vivid manifestation of evil, the behavior of the patients changed almost immediately, since their defenses were already down and they were largely incapable of resisting the massive demonic surge.

Nearly all went on a rampage.

The handful who tried to stay out of the way, tried to avoid participation in what was happening, inevitably became victims, literally torn to pieces or beaten to death. Hapless staff members were slaughtered as well.

Windows were broken, tables smashed apart.

Those patients who were locked away in padded cells clawed the walls to shreds, then banged their heads bloody on the hard concrete blocks underneath.

A few screamed that they saw demons....

* * *

... and Satan will probably use the debris of this transformed and debased House for the fuel to heat his Hell.

No one in the sanitarium had probably ever read those words, but it had become a prophecy that doomed virtually all of them as, outside, there was an extraordinary occurrence: like a geyser from Hell itself, the surrounding wall of flame enveloped the building, pouring over it in lave-like fashion ... seeping in through windows, door frames, cracks. Furniture and curtains ignited, and in the kitchen, a stove, left unattended in the mushrooming confusion, leaked gas out into the air.

Wayne was on his knees, holding his Bible as he prayed, the sounds of chaos getting louder, the heat from burning wood and other materials and the awful smoke nearly suffocating.

"Wayne!"

He looked up.

The door was flung open, and the young intern who had brought Reverend DeKorte to see him was standing in the doorway.

"All Hell has broken loose," he said. "Get out of here! Hurry!"

Next the intern went down that corridor and then another to Mark's room.

He opened the door and stepped inside.

There was no illumination except that shed by the moon, which didn't reach into the corners of the room.

He squinted, trying to see.

Two shapes.

The intern walked forward.

He heard a hissing sound, and something else, like old leather.

A face thrust out of the darkness into the silvery light.

Mark's face! But there was something else underneath!

Something pushing through, emerging like a grotesque butterfly from a slimy cocoon, shaking itself violently as it cast aside whatever was left of Mark like an old suit of clothes.

Something like—

The wood carving....

Whatever it was that had possessed Mark was no longer merely vaporous spirit.

"Run, Wayne, run!" screamed the intern as a taloned hand reached for his throat.

Seconds later the ceiling was torn into shredded plaster and wood, and moonlight shone through from the huge gash that led out into the clear night air.

* * *

An inmate, rushing outside, heard a sound like that of helicopter blades and looked up at the sky.

A dark shape directly above him, growing larger before his eyes.

* * *

For Wayne, survival was as immediate as getting out before the building collapsed on him.

Attendants and patients alike were running in every direction, panicked, out of control. A burly body bumped into Wayne and sent him sprawling.

He got to his feet and made it to an exit at the end of the corridor. He was about to open the door when it was torn off its hinges *from the opposite side*.

He was thrown across the corridor by the force, his back slamming painfully against the wall.

For a second or two his vision wavered, and then he saw three small children at the top of the stairs leading to the ground floor.

They were thin and pale, their gaunt faces littered with cuts and bruises.

"Please, mister, help us!" they cried in unison. "Our father has beaten us terribly and we—"

But the voices weren't human. The counterfeit images themselves were remarkably lifelike, but not those voices, more like synthesized recordings than—

He turned and ran.

Behind him there was a squishing sound, followed by a scream.

He turned, briefly, and saw three medusa-like demons vent their rage and frustration by cornering a patient who had just approached the same exit. They were proceeding to—

He could do nothing and continued running, managing to reach another exit, which wasn't blocked, and from there escaped to the ground floor.

He had to race down yet another corridor and then one after that before he could reach the entrance to the sanitarium. All the side exits on that floor were blocked by debris or bodies or both.

He ran past the kitchen, the odor of gas strong.

An explosion threw him through the glass-paned front entrance, shards cutting into his back and neck and hands.

With strength that surprised him, he was able to crawl frantically up to a large tree on the grounds and lean against it as he pulled himself to his feet, and then he continued running. He had reached the gate when four explosions in a row shook the ground, and—

* * *

Flames from the hospital were reflected on the windshield of the car, and the night breeze carried embers that landed on the hood.

Wayne and Mark are gone, DeKorte told himself, the presumption chilling him. *I've lost all three! Dear God, how can I ever live with that?*

Ahead of him, trees were igniting, and he found himself hurtling along the winding road through a bizarre landscape of fire and smoke and intensifying heat.

Someone running....

He squinted, trying to see who it was.

Wayne!

The boy had escaped from the inferno and was obviously heading toward a footpath through the woods that would lead him back to town.

"*N-o!*" DeKorte screamed. "Not there! Wayne—"

But the boy was too far away to hear him.

DeKorte was about to stop the car and run after him when something in the middle of the road ahead of him caught his attention.

Another figure.

Just standing there, barely visible amid the fog-like curtain of smoke issuing from the building behind—

Her!

A woman. Probably one of the nurses.

He swerved, trying to avoid her, but couldn't. The fender caught her, knocking her into the ditch beside the road. In the process he lost control of the car and it headed toward a large tree directly ahead, colliding with it and throwing him back against the seat.

Somehow he managed to scramble out before the car burst into flame, but was knocked down by the force of the explosion. He momentarily lost consciousness, but extreme pain revived him, along with the taste of blood dripping into his mouth.

The woman—where was she?

He falteringly got to his feet, his vision fading in and out, his eyes watering from the density of the smoke.

Ahead!

He saw, faintly, a still form, the smoke nearly obscuring her altogether. She was lying in the ditch, facedown.

He limped to her side, pain shooting through his left leg.

The back of her blouse was stained with splotches of red.

No sound. No groaning. Nothing. Perhaps she was dead.

He bent down beside the body, touched her shoulder gently.

She moved. Thank God she moved.

He turned her over as carefully as possible, then stumbled back immediately, tripping and landing flat on his back.

The woman lifted her head slightly and looked over at him, smiling weakly.

"Paul, dear, dear Paul."

Words of response came to his lips with enormous difficulty.

"Mary! In the name of Heaven—"

Despite apparent injuries, she got to her feet with surprising agility and hurried over to him, helping him to stand as well.

"You've been cut," she said as she tenderly touched the edges of a gash across his forehead. "You'll be all right, Paul. This is nothing."

This is some kind of accident-induced hallucination. I must be unconscious. I'll wake up in a minute.

"Let's walk over there," she said, pointing to a promontory of grass on the other side of the road next to the footpath Wayne had taken minutes before.

When they got there, she sat down, and he did the same.

Lord, what is happening? Did I die, and are You now welcoming me into Your kingdom, with Mary the one to greet me? Dearest Savior—

"I've returned, my love," she told him. "We're together again. That's all that matters."

"But I buried you," he managed to say, his voice quite hoarse. "I threw a handful of dirt onto your coffin."

She reached out and hugged him—flesh and blood, not spirit at all. But she seemed so very cold, her flesh almost clammy. Gone was her familiar sweet odor, replaced by something stale and unpleasant.

She stood then and walked over to the edge of the promontory. He noticed how plump she seemed.

"Look, Paul! Look at what's going on below."

He got to his feet and joined her.

Far below he could see the town square. A large crowd had gathered, their numbers steadily growing. Some of the townspeople were dancing. Several of the women were only partially clothed. Being led into their midst was a group of very young children. Several men were hauling square slabs of concrete toward a pile of bricks in the center.

As he watched, it became clear that they were building an altar!

"It's really glorious," Mary spoke. "The Master is actually taking over, first right here in our town, in good old Valley Falls, and then that other town down the road from here, and then later—"

DeKorte looked at her in disbelief.

"Glorious? It's satanic, Mary. Evil. Why do you call it anything but that?"

Her back was turned toward him. He saw her shiver abruptly, the sound of her voice changing.

"Evil is good," she said. "Evil is—"

She spun around.

Still quite recognizable as Mary, she was nevertheless changing, a serpentine tongue darting out from a lipless mouth, the skin at the edges turning darker and darker green.

"Mary, your—"

Eyes. Those eyes. Blood-red from edge to edge.

"The Master gave me a choice. I never wanted to be Eve in the Garden. Eve was weak. Make me something else, I asked. Make me . . . *Eden's serpent!*"

The change was becoming more pronounced by the second. Mary now half-snake, half-lizard, with human features less and less apparent.

DeKorte grabbed a large, fallen tree branch and hit her across the face with it. She fell to her knees, then stood once again, hissing, as she sprang at him.

The two of them struggled violently as she tried to wrap herself around him. DeKorte managed to grab her neck and an arm, and with enormous effort, flung what Mary was becoming over the edge of the promontory. Halfway down, a bare, rusty pipe protruded from the cliff. In less than a second, she was impaled on it, her transformation halted—part of her human, the rest reptilian.

"*P-a-u-l!*"

One claw-tipped hand reached out frantically toward him, her voice a blood-chilling mixture of the human and the demonic.

"*T-h-e-b-a-b-y's-c-o-m-i-n-g-n-o-w-a-n-d-S-c-o-t-t's-t-h-e—*"

She thrashed around frenziedly, but to no avail, and died before his eyes.

Then before he could turn to run back to the road, he staggered in utter shock at what he witnessed next.

Mary's belly was splitting open.

No! No! It wasn't Mary at all. Mary hadn't left the golden streets to torment him.

One talon-hand appeared, then another, ripping their way out. In seconds, a perfectly formed humanoid-lizard creature fell to the bare dirt, its eyes still closed. The miniature form rolled from one side to another, uttering tiny gurgling sounds.

DeKorte started down the slope. Not far from the twisted, demonic body he found a large rock and picked it up. The creature seemed to hear him and instantly turned in his direction.

Suddenly its eyes were open, making contact with his own. Blood-red eyes with only a thin black pupil in the center.

God help me! DeKorte's mind screamed. *This is a preview of damnation!*

It started crawling toward him, groaning, then stopped near his feet, reaching out to him, but not in any threatening manner, its toothless mouth barely moving. He saw what might have been tears streaming down its face.

Forgive me....

He stepped back and dropped the rock.

39

Wayne leaned against a tree, watching what was taking place before him, his mind reeling from the massive unleashing of pure evil.

A man stood only a hundred feet away, his hands outstretched, palms up, as he swayed back and forth, back and forth, blood seeping from deep cuts in his wrists. In his frenzy he seemed oblivious to the fact that his injuries could prove fatal if the bleeding weren't stopped. Instead he acted so turned on by the pain that it was as though he had taken a very large dose of magic mushrooms.

Suddenly he turned and saw Wayne.

"Dad!" the boy screamed as he saw his father's face.

Mulrooney stumbled toward his son, eyes wild, body covered with blood, clothes tattered. His forehead was pulsating, his cheek muscles twitching.

The next instant his body puffed up from within and exploded like a rotten melon, drenching Wayne with sickening residue.

Wayne fainted but was comatose only for a few seconds, unwelcome consciousness returning, the reality around him more and more intense.

The town square pulsated with movement.

And sound.

Fires were burning, dead bodies being put on these and roasted like in some grotesque community barbecue. Crackling noises, like those emitted from a whole slew of downed electrical wires. Every few feet, ethereal shapes appeared in the air, each mocking, slavering, blasphemous presence, spectral presence gone almost instantly, yes, but indelible just the same, the whole scene overlaid with great surging masses of them, wave after wave, like a monstrous army of devilish and misshapen fireflies, fluttering here, there, in and out of view, released from the satanic awfulness of Hades.

And in the center of the square . . . an altar.

Children were grouped near it, frightened, faces dirty, clothes torn, bodies covered with cuts and bruises.

Wayne's foot kicked against something as he walked forward, shouting. He almost hated to look down to see what it was.

A pistol.

He picked it up and fired several shots into the air.

People spun around, startled.

"Stop!" he shouted. "You must stop. In the name of the Lord I forbid you to go on in this—"

Suddenly a dull pain shot through his back, and he spun around.

His sister, Betsy, stood there, a knife in her hand.

She swung at him again, burying the blade in his shoulder, and then pulled it out and—

He backed away from her.

All around him, people he had known all of his life were pressing in on him threateningly.

Several lashed out at him with knives, cutting his cheek, his hands, lopping off part of his left ear.

The odor of their sweat mingled with the stench of burning flesh and the sweet-musty scent of blood.

He turned and saw the church, staggered toward it, and fell as he reached the first step. Through the opened entrance the darkness inside was punctuated by fire that had begun in the pews and reached upward toward the cathedral ceiling. Moonlight poured through the open roof and empty window frames.

Wayne looked up at the cross above the entrance and the Figure on it and started sobbing.

"Lord, forgive me for opening the door to Satan," he cried.

Again pain. In his back.

He turned.

"Mother!" he said, his voice scarcely above a whisper.

The blade of a long knife caught the moonlight as it was raised in the air.

Wayne looked toward that Figure again, his eyes squinting for an instant as he thought he saw the head move and that kind face, wise and yet with so much anguish mirrored on it, look at him with an expression of joy transcendent, and then peace encompassed him as, so briefly, torn and bloody and pain over his entire body, he stood on the edge of eternity beckoning.

* * *

As DeKorte started back up the slope, he felt the air become suddenly very warm. Perspiration drenched him.

He reached the top and glanced back at the rusty pipe and the impaled body, now completely limp, strange little twirls of steam arising from the mottled skin. It was not without a strange and momentary pity that he gazed at the misshapen form and its offspring lying underneath the rock he had dropped.

Oh, Lord, he said, his head turned toward the dark sky. *Lord and Savior, please protect me from Satan and his demons.*

He knew it was all tricks played upon both the conscious and the subconscious parts of his mind. Satan was very good at that. But he was good because of how real he could make it all seem, more so than if a film producer had spent ten million on that scene alone in a motion picture.

He came to the road, saw the still smoldering wreck that had been his car, and realized with profound irony that this was the exact spot where his beloved Mary had died—

—the first time!

Those words formed in his mind but not on his lips, and he knew how satanic they were. The Bible stated clearly that human beings, created in God's image, died only once, but even then it was merely their physical bodies that died, for their eternal souls went either to Heaven or to Hell . . . and never back again.

The delusion that the living could contact departed loved ones and spend just a few more minutes with them was a standard twisting of the truth straight from the lips of the Deceiver, one he used often to gain entrance to the souls of countless victims. It was a second cousin to the notion of reincarnation, a "doctrine" increasingly fashionable and at least as repellent.

Straight from the lips of the Deceiver. . . .

Mary.

The prince of darkness and deceit had taken the purity of his beloved's memory and corrupted it into some kind of monstrosity.

"I never saw her like that, did I?" he shouted. "It was all a lie spawned by the father of reprobate minds, isn't that right? Aren't I very close to the truth when I—"

Suddenly from somewhere nearby . . . a voice.

Of course you saw her.

"No! My beloved Mary is in Heaven. That loathsome creature's a demonic counterfeit, it—" he said as he spun around, to see who had spoken.

Nothing.

He was quite alone.

You mustn't lose any more time.

He froze in his tracks.

That same voice again!

Go to the edge.

He walked back to the promontory, where he could see shadows and forms and frenzied activity from the square far below.

Throw yourself down. If God is with you, no harm will come to you.

DeKorte hesitated.

The rocks will be soft pillows to cushion your body.

His feet were at the very rim of the precipice, the toe of each shoe edging over. It would be so simple just to trust in the Lord and—

But he knew, with a certainty founded on Scripture itself, that the Lord had not been speaking to him, and he drew back, chills gripping his body at the nearness of that seduction, its tempting call almost lulling him into Satan's control.

"Deceiver!" he shouted, a hidden reservoir of strength welling up inside him. "You wanted Christ to throw Himself over the edge, and He didn't. Nor shall I!"

Weakling!

"Yes I am weak," he said. "I cannot deny that."

Too weak to resist my power.

"No, I—" he started to say, then happened to glance down toward the rusty pipe where only minutes before—

The *thing* impaled on it no longer bore *any* resemblance to the woman he—

And it no longer merely hung there, suspended, seemingly all the life gone from its pitiable body.

Moving.

It was moving now, squirming, trying to pry itself off the pipe.

My night, Paul DeKorte.

"No!" he screamed.

Yes, my puny one! A night straight from Hell!

He felt something crawling up his leg then.

He looked down.

The creature he thought he had killed with the rock—

He stood, transfixed, as it reached his waist, its greenish scales cold even through the material of his suit.

The odor! Foul and—

It was at his neck, wrapping its ghastly arms around him, forcing him to turn his head back in the direction of the promontory.

"Momma! Momma! Momma!"

A tiny voice came from between its scaled lips, its red-tinted eyes widening in anger.

And as he looked, the other creature turned toward them, its face torn with pain, foam slavering out of its mouth. It raised one taloned hand, which it shook several times.

Even from that distance, he heard a single ferocious word, magnified until it seemed like thunder in his ears.

"Kill!"

And right next to him, a response, cold breath against his cheek, the smell as from an ancient crypt clogging his nose.

"Yes, Momma!"

And then pain as a razor-sharp talon cut his flesh.

DeKorte tried to pull the creature off.

He couldn't.

Surprisingly strong, it had wrapped one arm around his neck, as though hugging him, hissing sounds emanating from its mouth.

DeKorte became dizzy and fell to his knees, almost passing out.

"Lord—" he said simply, in his physical weakness.

He realized how often he had used that name in a repetitious fashion, in mechanical prayers of habit or routine. Or worse perhaps, the times when he called upon the Lord for blessings, blessings, and more blessings—not always giving thanks when petitions were answered, but accepting them as some kind of right or privilege that the Lord owed him.

How often . . .

And now when life and death were at issue, would God choose to hear?

"Praise Your holy name, Lord," DeKorte whispered the words, gathering what little strength he had left, "whatever Your . . . answer . . . my Lord."

My Lord. . . .

How joyous to say that not just from the lips, but from deep within him.

The creature started screaming, its grip on his neck loosening. As it fell from him, the expression on what he took to be its face, though a face of such distorted countenance that he couldn't be certain, was a mixture of anger and defiance, but both were undermined by fear so intense that it—

Full consciousness momentarily faded for DeKorte, although he was still able to see, indistinctly, luminous shapes, their outlines blurred but giving an impression of apparently pure whiteness.

Then something soft brushed his cheek.

It could not have been a more tender touch, far beyond anything he had experienced prior to then.

He reached out, quite blindly, but whatever had touched him was gone. Yet he realized that that touch, the memory of it, would remain with him for the rest of whatever life the Lord granted him.

When DeKorte came back to full awareness again, seconds or minutes later, the creature was lying a foot or two away; it shuddered for a moment, and then was still. Next to the misshapen body was a single white feather.

DeKorte staggered to his feet and looked down at the pipe. Once again the figure on it was still, one taloned hand frozen in death as it reached outward.

And below, the scene being played out in the town square had reached a frenzied height so evil, so chilling and bizarre, that he had to turn away, his entire body shaking.

Go. . . .

This time the word came not from a voice of scorn and blasphemous intent, but in tones so gentle, so kind, so filled with an extraordinary sense of love that he suddenly was driven to tears.

"Father?" he asked, sobbing, uttering the name with a certain tentativeness of which he felt more than a little ashamed. Then, "My God . . . my Savior."

Go, and guardians will be at your side.

"But I am one man, Lord," he said.

For some seconds he couldn't be sure, really, that he had heard those words, couldn't be sure that it had been more than a kind of sanctified wishful thinking on his part:

As with Elisha, so it will be with you.

Again!

A slight smile crossed his face.

"I did hear You, Lord!" he said in sudden triumphant assurance.

As that knowledge caught hold, he realized that his doubts were as shifting sand at his feet. He had only to walk through them, and then take off his shoes and brush them away.

He started down the footpath to the square.

* * *

Bizarre rites and other activity had intensified.

Those whose bodies had been ignited by the funnel passing through their midst had long since died, and the others, consumed by their own lusts, went about their bacchanalian frenzy.

The children continued to huddle near the altar in the center of the square. One little girl clung tightly to her doll.

A possessed man, looking in that direction, saw the child, rushed up to her, and ripped the doll out of her arms.

"This is what we will do to you," he laughed, tearing the toy apart and throwing the pieces on a nearby pile of smoldering coals, the remains of someone who had burned to death right before the little girl's eyes.

"You know," he said, scratching his head, "why wait? I can have the pleasure now."

He grabbed her and—

"No, no," she screamed, remembering a verse from her Sunday school class, "you can't hurt me. Jesus says I am precious to Him. He will take me on His knee and protect me."

The man roared with amusement as he slapped her across the face.

"I have hurt you," he screamed.

She fell to the ground, and he kicked her in the side.

"I have hurt you a second time!" he exclaimed. "And I will—"

He started to raise his hand, which he had doubled up into a fist, when his eyes widened in horror.

A cut had appeared, circling his wrist as he watched . . . a very deep cut.

He held up his other hand.

Another cut, also around his wrist.

In seconds he started screaming in agony, advancing toward the little girl, holding out the bleeding stumps of his arms where his hands had fallen off.

Another cut started around his neck. He could feel it slicing into his flesh, like someone was taking a razor and—

"Dear God, please—!" he said, his words lost in a gurgle of pain, his body falling forward, hitting the ground with a thud.

All the adults had turned and seen what had happened. All were frantically examining their own bodies.

And then a woman came running toward the children, not threateningly, but with fear apparent on a face that had started to develop boils, lesions, open sores.

"Tell Him to stop!" she begged. "Tell Him to—"

She fell to her knees because, in just those few seconds, her body's bone structure had begun turning soft like wet spaghetti, collapsing in on itself.

Panic spread.

"We must obey the Master!" arose a scream. "He will help us if we obey him!"

It was coming from one of the men who managed to make it to the children and grabbed a little boy and dragged him to the altar, where he took the long knife that rested on top and raised it above the squirming form.

Several of the other children grabbed him by the legs and tried to topple him, but the man was far too strong and kicked them off.

"Little boy, little boy," he said, slobbering with anticipation, "the Master thanks you for the sacrifice of your heart to him."

And then a sound, immediately audible, coming from nowhere in an instant.

Wings.

The beating of thousands of wings.

The man hesitated, looking up.

White shapes piercing the suffocating smoke.

The man dropped the knife, stumbled back.

Within seconds, the group of children was surrounded by legion after legion of pure white doves.

40

Trent, Chapman, and Gardner were only a couple of miles from Valley Falls.

"It never lets up, does it?" Gardner observed.

"Never," Chapman told him.

As they walked, Gardner told them about his son and the encounter in the old cemetery.

"I thought he was gone," the psychiatrist said.

"He is dead," Trent agreed. "What you first saw was a demonic manifestation."

"And, later ... that voice?"

"If it proclaimed victory in Christ, then it was of Him."

"I see. I—"

He never finished that sentence.

"Look!"

Chapman screamed, looking upward.

The sky had turned blood-red.

Suddenly a wave of heat washed over them, and in seconds their clothes were drenched with perspiration.

Gardner sniffed the air.

"Burning rubber," he mused.

"Also rotten eggs," Chapman said, grimacing.

Abruptly the ground shook as the sound of an explosion shattered the air.

"What was that?" Trent yelled.

Flame and smoke filled the sky. But that wasn't all.

As they continued walking, a deepening sense of oppression enveloped them.

"Feel it?" Gardner asked.

The others muttered agreement.

"Before today I would have labeled this the beginning fringes of severe depression," Gardner said. "But now?"

"It's more than that, I'm afraid," Trent told him. "Look straight ahead, my friends."

They stood still.

A few hundred feet ahead they saw shapes....

"What the—?" Gardner started to say.

Accompanied by a buzzing sound, like that of a thousand hornets...coming toward them.

But not hornets or flies or locusts or bees.

Something quite different.

Something—

"Right out of Hell!" Trent exclaimed.

"Join hands," Chapman shouted above the growing noise. "In God's name, join hands!"

Gardner was clumsy in doing this, but a second or two later they were clinging to each other.

Thousands of creatures hovered in the air now, surrounding them, each no bigger than a sparrow.

Wings beating a thousand times a second.

Heads so ugly, so cruel-looking, so evil...

"I'm going to be sick," Gardner said. "Please forgive me, but I'm going to be very sick."

"Don't break contact with us," Trent begged. "When two or three are gathered together—"

"They're in my mind," cried Gardner, "poking around, digging up awful...oh, no, awful things."

"Think pure thoughts...holy, kind. Think—" Trent said.

One of the small flying creatures landed on Gardner's shoulder, two on Trent's, but a dozen or more on Chapman's.

"Weak links," Trent said. "They're testing us."

Chapman's eyes widened.

Years before, during his seminary days, he had had to confront a part of himself that had been buried since then, but now was being forced to the surface...his attraction to another male student.

"This is wrong, Lord," he had said then. "I know it. Please, I commit this burden to You."

And it seemed to end. He had married, was the father of three children.

But now—

In his mind he saw that student again: tall, blond, athletic. He saw the two of them together. He—

"No!" Chapman shouted. "No, you cannot use that against me. The Lord has taken that yoke from me."

Gone.

The thought, the vision, the memory gone as though it had never been.

For Trent it was something else.

Power.

He had wanted power for a long time. Wanted to become the most influential pastor in his denomination, wanted total control of the church he shepherded.

His was not simple, everyday desire but a consuming lust for power, everything in his ministry geared toward that end.

"You can have it," the voice in his mind promised. "You can move into an executive capacity at the denomination's headquarters. You can have everyone eating out of your hand."

"Lord, forgive me," Trent said, realizing that he had asked for forgiveness for all his sins except that one, keeping it in a special "room" in his life, the door locked . . . a game room where he could play with the enticement of power as much as he wanted.

"Lord, take it all away." he prayed. "I turn all that over to You."

And a feeling of steadfast peace took hold of him so that he was able to smile.

And so was Chapman.

Now the creatures turned to Gardner, surrounding him in force.

"Stand firm," he could hear Trent's voice saying. "Call upon the Lord—"

So many wings beat so rapidly that a blur seemed to encompass him, and he broke physical contact with Trent and Chapman, stumbling backward.

"We can't help!" Trent shouted. "There are thousands of them now."

Gardner fell to his knees.

The odor sucked up into his nostrils was overwhelming, an odor of decaying flesh, and with it a mental image of worms routing around in gangrenous pulp.

But then something quite unexpected happened.

Into his mind came a verse from his childhood, a verse he had not recalled for years. . . .

For this purpose the Son of God was manifested, that He might destroy the works of the devil.

"Jesus," he said ever so softly, but from deep within himself. "Jesus my Lord."

He closed his eyes then, and another odor became apparent, one he had breathed in years ago in the midst of a field in the country, a field with thousands of brightly colored flowers.

That He might destroy the works of the devil.

Something touched his left shoulder, then his right.

He opened his eyes.

Trent and Chapman were embracing him.

"Where—?" he tried to ask.

"Gone," Trent told him. "They formed a group, like ducks going south for the winter, and disappeared."

"Just like that?"

"Just like that."

"But it's not over, my friend," said Chapman in reply to the relief on Gardner's face. "Valley Falls is still before us. And I suspect all this has been child's play compared to that."

He pointed ahead.

The sky was still blood-red. But there was something else now...a hovering outline, a shape they couldn't discern clearly except to see that it was huge.

41

The closer DeKorte got to the town square, the more he noticed something apart from the orgy of violence in front of him, apart from the children at the altar, apart even from the extraordinary sight of thousands of doves descending upon the spot, forming a nearly solid wall around the little ones.

Something else . . .

A shape, somehow out of sight, looming there in the darkness, its presence faintly perceptible. So faint in fact that he was about to chalk it up to an imagination understandably heightened by events that would have seemed wild fantasy days earlier. About to dismiss it altogether.

Surrounded by the doves, and led by them, the children were walking forward, away from the altar, toward the edge of the square, toward the main street that led out of town.

No longer a vague image, no longer something on the frazzled edges of reality, the shape appeared directly in their path, all two stories of it, dwarfing the adults, the children, the doves.

It had *flown* in from where it had been hovering, like a puppet-master offstage.

The creature confronting them was a personification of all the centuries-old depictions of demonic evil: huge leathery wings flapping with unbridled rage, cloven feet stamping the ground, taloned hands reaching down toward the children, fang-like teeth protruding from the mouth, forked tongue flicking the air, pronounced cheekbones, and eyes blood-red and maniacal.

The creature contemptuously brushed scores of the doves aside with one sweep of its left talon. Hundreds of them landed on its arm, trying to inflict wounds severe enough to make it stop, but it disposed them with a roar, a kind of ear-splitting laughter.

DeKorte looked frantically around.

Lord, Lord, please provide me with the means to destroy this beast. . . .

An ax. To his left.

He grabbed it and rushed forward.

The creature had taken one of the children and started to lift her off the ground.

DeKorte screamed wildly as he approached, imbedding the blade in the creature's leg...once...twice...a third time, swinging the ax as fast and as often as he could.

The creature bellowed in agony and lashed out one huge talon at the minister, knocking him to the ground. The ax fell from his grip.

The monstrosity bent toward him, its mouth full of jagged teeth opening wide.

"Scott!" DeKorte called out. "Scott, I love you, son."

The creature hesitated ever so slightly.

Tears filled DeKorte's eyes.

Just then he heard another voice.

"The Master you serve will not stand behind you!"

Harley Trent and Bennett Chapman, followed by a man he did not recognize, stepped into the square. It was the stranger who had spoken.

The creature turned and faced the newcomers.

"A short while ago I would have been ripe for your plucking," the stranger said. "But no longer!"

He reached into a pocket of his slacks.

"You feed on hatred. You gloat on ignorance and pain. You exist out of infamy and deceit and filth."

He pulled out a medallion and held it up before the creature.

"You made me think my son hated me. You tricked me into thinking he was lost forever, burning in that monstrous place of torment created because of you and the rest of your kind *who are damned for all eternity!*"

The creature swung a talon and ripped off the arm that held the medallion.

The man staggered from the pain but didn't fall.

"Only my body!" he screamed defiantly. "You can no longer touch my immortal spirit!"

The next blow hit the side of his head, and he collapsed.

As the creature prepared to rip him apart, Trent and Chapman rushed forward.

"Join hands!" Trent yelled to DeKorte. "Surround our brother!"

They formed a circle, with the stranger in the middle.

"You have Mary's blood on your hands," DeKorte cried. "But she died wanting me to forgive you. *I do! I forgive you!*"

The creature drew back a bit.

Suddenly scores of the doves attacked its eyes, piercing one. Partially blinded, it stumbled backward.

More doves descended on the other eye.

The creature held up its gnarled arms, trying to ward them off, backing away from hundreds, then thousands of doves, until it stopped in front of the church.

Suddenly the doves pulled back.

What is happening? DeKorte thought.

The creature reached out a huge talon toward the *empty* cross above the entrance.

DeKorte gasped...stunned.

The figure of Christ was gone. Only the nails that had held the hanging form remained.

Nails that were being loosened from the wood... turning, turning, turning...then being flung through the air, impaling themselves in the creature's forehead, neck, and chest.

It staggered back.

DeKorte broke away from the three men and rushed toward the creature.

"Scott!" he screamed, trying to be heard above the cries of those in the square who were now running in utter panic and fear. "Look at me. I claim you for the kingdom of God. I—"

The creature stopped suddenly and turned toward DeKorte, shaking its massive head, then falling to its knees.

Its mouth opened, and it seemed to be trying to speak.

DeKorte had stopped only a few feet from it.

The creature looked at him just once, reaching out a taloned hand, but with no menace this time.

DeKorte extended his hand also.

They nearly touched, but then the creature withdrew, raising that same hand toward the sky in a final gesture of defiance before it fell forward and hit the ground, a single loud gasp coming from its lips, a shudder rippling through its huge body, the wings fluttering, and finally it was still.

DeKorte, who had had to jump out of the way when the creature toppled, now fell to his knees, bowing his head, sobbing.

A hand touched his shoulder.

He looked up.

A teenage girl, familiar, so—

"I'm Jami Arlen," she said.

The girl from the songfest!

"I belong to Christ now," she said, as though answering his thoughts. "He gained control of my spirit. When I wouldn't join in with the rest, they dragged me here. They were going to do awful things to me. But I had given everything over to Him, without holding back any of it, including my very life. If He wanted to take it then and there, I would not protest out of my trust and love for Him, and, you know, He spared me."

She smiled, her eyes sparkling, her face radiant.

"Won't you join us, sir?" she asked. "I think it's quite safe now."

She helped him to his feet.

"Praise God always," she whispered.

He nodded.

Trent and Chapman were holding the stranger upright between them.

"This is our dear friend, Elliott Gardner," Chapman said.

Gardner, very weak now from loss of blood, tried to smile but didn't do a very good job of it.

"We've got to get to a functioning telephone as soon as we can," said Trent. "The sound of an ambulance's siren would be music to Elliott's ears, and ours, too."

As the group was weaving its way through the fringes of that awful scene, DeKorte thought he heard someone crying.

He stopped a moment, listening, quite aware of the fact that the conditions around them could easily create deception, demonic or otherwise.

A voice!

He turned his head, trying to detect the location.

They were near the church, part of the structure eaten away by flame, now shooting out through the roof.

And he saw Wayne's body where it had fallen on the steps in front.

He broke away from the others and went over to it, knelt down and lifted the body, hugging the—

Life!

He could feel Wayne breathing. Just barely, but breathing nonetheless.

"Thank God," DeKorte cried.

Wayne's eyes opened.

"I just did," the teenager said, "and His hand is reaching out toward me."

"If only I had been wiser," DeKorte sobbed. "If only I had not been blinded by—"

"I see my Lord," Wayne said. "He's forgiven me . . . I have lost nothing and gained . . . everything."

Smiling with a radiance that astonished DeKorte, he reached up one hand and wiped away the tears from the minister's left cheek.

"Rejoice, sir."

He swallowed several times, forcing the next words from his constricting throat.

"Tell them, sir...tell everyone...proclaim His love...His mercy. Warn them...you must warn them...*of what waits in the awful darkness.*"

And then he died.

DeKorte held Wayne's body, as he had held Mary's and Patrick's, reluctant to let go.

A hand rested lightly, comfortingly, on his shoulder.

"That's only his body now, you know," Jami said softly. "The Lord's protecting Him now, for all eternity."

With profound tenderness, DeKorte lowered Wayne's body to the debris-littered ground. As he was doing so, he noticed something sticking out of the boy's trouser pocket.

It was the small leather-bound Bible the two had held onto together in Wayne's hospital room earlier that day.

He took it and clasped his hands around it.

"Lord," he prayed, "make me Your instrument. May I never forget what has happened here. Use me to help free souls from Satan's enslavement. Give me Your strength and wisdom."

He stood and rejoined the group of children, Jami by his side, the doves surrounding them as they walked the rest of the way through the square, smoldering piles of ash everywhere, bodies half-consumed, a knife here, an ax there, hands frozen in their death throes as they reached too late toward the sky.

DeKorte turned once, briefly, looking back to where he had found Wayne, and tears trickled down his cheeks again as he said good-bye.

'Twas to save thee, child, from dying,
Save my dear from burning flame,
Bitter groans and endless crying,
That thy Blest Redeemer came.

—Isaac Watts
from *Divine Songs for Children*

Satan will never conquer heaven.... He will have nothing more of our universe than the material carcass. And Satan will probably use the debris of this transformed and debased House for the fuel to heat his hell.

—Denis de Rougemont

42

The area around the falls showed the touch of autumn, with multicolored leaves that lent to that spot one of the ingredients that made it an isolated wonderland for the children as they gathered beside the little lake, their laughter filling the air, along with a slight mist generated by the spray from the falls.

None noticed, at first, the State Police cars. Half a dozen stopped a few hundred yards away on the single dirt road leading up to where the children were sitting, listening to Paul DeKorte and Jami Arlen telling them Bible stories.

"And if any try to hurt the least of these my little ones," he was saying, "it would be better that a millstone be hung about their neck, and that they be cast into the deepest sea."

"Is that why we're here?" one of the children asked.

"Yes," replied DeKorte. "It is in God's mercy that we are."

The troopers approached them in amazement.

"Look at how happy they are!" one of them said, his tone hushed.

"My G—" another started to say.

"—goodness," he finished, when a fellow officer gave him a cautioning look. "How could they seem so—so peaceful? After what they've been through!"

And happy was the word to describe the dozen youngsters. In fact, their faces were joyous, eagerly taking in the familiar stories as though they were entirely fresh and, indeed, thoroughly captivating.

"This is where the Pennio kid was murdered," a fourth officer recalled.

"All things become as new," whispered his partner.

"What's that supposed to mean?" the other asked.

"I'll explain sometime."

Nor were DeKorte and the teenage girl any less serene, it seemed. Every so often she would pitch in and read several verses.

All of the officers took off their helmets and sat down on the grass and listened.

Several minutes passed. The morning mist had started to dissipate, and the sun was poking through an overhead canopy of autumn leaves.

"So quiet here," an officer said.

"Yes," another agreed.

Eventually, though, the men stood, and one of them approached DeKorte and told him that everyone would have to go to the county medical hospital.

"Indeed," DeKorte said.

A little girl pulled at the same officer's trouser leg.

"Mister, I'm real tired," she said. "Would you carry me?"

Realizing that her parents were probably dead, but unaccustomed to showing any real tenderness on the job, the young man hesitated for an awkward moment.

"Don't be afraid," the child said. "I won't hurt you."

One by one, the children got into the cars. A little boy grabbed a tiny wood carving he had found in some bushes and rushed off with it.

DeKorte and Jami were the last to go.

"Would you check for me about the three men who were with us?" he asked one of the officers in the car. "One of them was in pretty bad shape."

"We'll check as soon as we get to the hospital," said the officer. Then he nodded toward the cars ahead, filled with the children. "How will they ever deal with what happened to their parents?"

"With pain and anguish," replied DeKorte, "but eventually with victory."

"Thank God they survived," the officer added.

DeKorte, a slight smile on his face, said, "Yes, my friend, that's right . . . thank God."

* * *

Back in Valley Falls, the entire town was on fire. The smaller, more combustible homes had already burnt down to ashes, and thick, black smoke mixed with the red flame of those structures yet standing, however tenuously. Helicopters circled overhead, dropping the same kinds of chemicals used to contain and extinguish forest fires.

Firemen from four counties had joined in to try and salvage some of the buildings, and a dozen or more fire trucks were still on the scene. Reporters and photographers were nearly as plentiful as those battling the numerous blazes, but most of them stayed far back, grouped outside the tent that women volunteers from the various firemen's auxiliaries had set up as a station for food and first aid for the weary rescuers.

Countless mounds of ashes in vaguely human shapes were everywhere, scattered with bits and pieces of bones that had not been incinerated—stark reminders of the human toll taken in the holocaust.

And the heat!

With the town a mass of flame from one end to the other, the heat grew so intense that several fire fighters collapsed.

"It's as hot as Hell!" one of the men exclaimed.

"I wonder if Hell could be any worse than this," the one next to him added.

To many, the scene indeed seemed like age-old depictions of that place of torment, especially early on when they had found some citizens in the town square still alive, though barely so.

Later, a fireman named Ralph Sloane would recount a particularly awful moment.

"I could hardly believe my eyes. There was this guy, standing in the middle of an area of intense flame, looking at me, and laughing! Yeah, he was laughing. Finally he dropped, and I thought I heard him say something. I thought I heard him say, 'It's not over.'

"I rushed up to him. He was nothing more than a charred piece of meat, but his eyes were open—I could see them still white amid the burnt skin of the rest of his face—and he spit at me before he died. That's right...he spit at me. And then he turned to simmering coals and smoking ashes before my eyes.

"You know, even all these months later, I sometimes wake up screaming at night, hearing that laughter, wild and hoarse, and seeing those eyes of his filled with something so intense, so terrible that I couldn't describe how they made me feel, except that my skin crawls whenever they come back into my mind, day or night, and I start to shiver. Even with my wife holding me, I still shiver."

Other firemen reported equally bizarre behavior of other dying victims. One told of a woman writhing and moaning almost in erotic ecstasy and screaming obscenities as she died, clasping a small wooden carving in her right hand. Another woman actually walked into a wall of flame, holding her hands out, palms upward, as though entering some rite of infernal baptism.

* * *

Clement Albertson and Lance Setterman had left the retreat center as soon as they could. The other teenagers from Valley Falls wanted to join them, but Albertson said no.

"We don't know what's happening back there," he said, "but if what happened here is an example, we may not survive this time."

Someone needed to remain to tell what had happened.

"That's important," he told them. "The message must be spread, to every teenager like yourselves in this country . . . to every adult. They must listen while there's still time!"

The principal made sure they were in good hands with the other adults at the retreat, and then he and Lance climbed into the van and began the journey back to Valley Falls. . . .

They stood before the high school in which they had spent so much time over the past few years. It had not been set ablaze, but as they approached the entrance they could see hints of what had happened inside.

Shattered glass covered the lawn. Bits and pieces of furniture as well. And bodies.

One was still alive.

Lance knelt beside him.

"John," he cried. "John, what happened?"

The dying teenager tried to talk but the words were jumbled.

"Take my hand, John," Lance begged, "we'll talk to the Lord together."

"I—I—pain," the boy managed to say, "and awful, awful things in my mind."

"Lord," Lance said, closing his eyes and bowing his head as he took the boy's hand, "Lord, I offer up to You—"

The boy's grip tightened around his own.

"Already did," the words came, "though too late . . . for . . . my . . . my body."

"But not your spirit, John, *not your spirit!*"

"The pain . . . gone . . . now. . . ."

Lance opened his eyes and looked at his friend. For a split second, his face smeared with blood and dirt, John seemed to be smiling. And then his eyelids closed and his arm fell back against the soft grass.

"I think he's at peace now," Lance said to Albertson who was standing behind him.

Albertson nodded.

"You don't have to go inside, you know," he remarked. "We have no idea what we'll encounter there."

"I want to," Lance told him, tears trickling down his cheeks. "What is death, sir? What is the grave anyway? There is no sting in any of it for us, isn't that what the Bible teaches, sir?"

Inside, they almost immediately saw the carnage.

A body with glass shards piercing nearly every inch of flesh, the early morning light bouncing off it like a perverse kaleidoscope.

Other bodies in doorways. Along the corridors. Teenage boys and girls with their necks broken or their chests torn to shreds. Or worse....

The auditorium offered the most graphic testimony to what had happened.

Albertson went in first, then backed out immediately.

Bits and pieces of bodies ... arms and legs ...

"No need to go in there," he said, visibly shaken.

"I can handle it, sir," Lance commented.

"I can't handle it, son. Don't subject *your* mind to—"

Bodies stripped of flesh ... white bone ...

"Forgive me," he said as he hung his head and started crying.

"Sir?" Lance asked. "Can I—?"

The teenager walked up to him and put his arms gently around the man and held him until the sobs ran their course.

Then, strangely not ashamed of himself for this display in front of his student, Albertson looked up and said, "I think we should leave now. I—"

"Sir, look!" Lance interrupted, pointing down to the end of the corridor where it angled off into another wing. Turning the corner ... coming toward them ... were shapes, only dimly seen through the darkness.

"Shall we run?" Lance asked.

"Where to?" said Albertson, as he had told himself earlier at the retreat.

So they stood there together and linked hands, repeating familiar words that suddenly seemed to gain new meaning and power.

Yea, though I walk through the valley of the shadow of death ...

The shapes were moving slowly, haltingly.

I shall fear no evil....

Sounds were coming from some of them, though nothing that made any sense.

For Thou art with me....

"Mr. Albertson, look!" Lance yelled, suddenly realizing what he was seeing. "They're the kids from the Special Ed class. They're okay ... all of them."

The group of nine retarded children of varying ages was beside them now. One of the boys was smiling broadly.

"We did it!" he exclaimed, running up to them.

"What did you do?" Albertson asked gently.

"We claimed the name of Jesus, yes, we did, we did. We said Jesus, Jesus, over and over. And you know what happened?"

"What was that?" Albertson responded, tears in his eyes and, he noticed, in Lance's as well.

"Some mean faces just went away. They were all around us, saying mean things, and they scared us. But as soon as we said Jesus and told Him how much we loved Him, the faces disappeared just like that."

He snapped his fingers proudly.

"They didn't come back. They didn't!"

Albertson reached out and hugged the boy, looking around at the sweet trust on the other young faces.

* * *

A few miles from town, two state troopers who were combing the area for any injured survivors found a dozen adults huddling in a barn. The doors were pocked with holes, as though the wood had been eaten away by voracious termites.

One of the men told them what had happened.

"We were protected, officer. We got down on our knees and asked Him to protect us, and He did."

"Protected?"

"Yes, from those . . . creatures."

The officer bent down and picked up one of the tiny bodies. It turned to powder in his hands.

Like it had been dead for a hundred years!

"We had escaped from town and taken refuge in here when we heard them out there," the man continued, "gnawing at the door, screaming, frantic in their eagerness to get at us. . . ."

One by one the creatures came in through the holes, saliva dripping from their decay-encrusted fangs.

The townspeople hurried up a ladder to the second level of the barn. One woman slipped and fell, and the creatures were all over her. Two of the men managed to beat them off, and helped her climb the ladder as the creatures regrouped.

Suddenly they heard a wrenching, creaking sound, as though the door to the barn was being torn off its hinges.

A ghastly battle seemed to be taking place on the ground below.

"Lord," they prayed, holding tightly to each other, surrounded by bales of hay, "what is happening? What have we done?

"We confess our awful sinfulness before you. We were willing to follow the Prince of Darkness," one of the men said. "We—"

Darkness.

It was truly dark for them at that moment, sounds of terror and horror beneath them, nerve-chilling manifestations of demonic fury.

"We ask Your forgiveness, Lord," another took up the prayer. And all joined in.

"Forgive us, Father. Surround us with Your love ... Your mercy—"

And then—

Light.

A great wave of it suffusing the interior of the barn.

The sounds sputtered away, the shrieking dying off, then gone. Followed by utter quiet.

Several minutes passed. Finally one of the men crawled to the edge of the haymow.

He lingered there, taking in what he saw, and then he turned to the rest, his eyes wet with tears.

"Come!" he exclaimed. "Look!"

Through a curtain of near-blinding light they saw a figure standing in the midst of hundreds of the creatures' bodies. It had the appearance of a man, and yet it was more than that. Wings protruded from its back. Its hair was golden, its garment silky-white. And it looked up at them with a wonderful, radiant smile on its face.

"They will not harm you now," the voice washed over them.

They climbed down then and gathered before the majestic figure, so tall, so pure.

"Gabriel?" an elderly woman asked.

The figure nodded.

"You are Gabriel, sent by God to help us?"

"I am the one of whom you speak."

The voice was beyond description—kinder, gentler than any they had heard before.

An iridescent hand reached down and picked up one of the creatures.

This one was not quite dead.

It tried to shield itself from the light, from the—

"They have power only so long as they can feed on your weakness," said the angel sent from God.

As the creature's arms fell back and it faced that sublime light, it died. Its body shuddered once . . . twice . . . a third time, and then was still.

"Wait here," said the heavenly figure. "Wait here without fear. Be not ashamed. Remember only that He shall never forsake you. Not now . . . not through all of eternity."

They bowed their heads in prayer, and when they looked up again, the figure was gone. . . .

The two troopers listened in amazement, and the one who had spoken first took off his helmet.

"You know, I accepted Christ as Savior and Lord a few years ago," he said. "And I've seen the awfulness of sin in my work—elderly people robbed and murdered; women raped and scarred, psychologically, for life; things I can't even begin to describe . . . the bodies of aborted babies kept as trophies, like animals bagged in some awful hunt. . . ."

He cleared his throat as he added, "I encounter so little out and out *victory* anymore, as evil intensifies. But here, now, what joy to learn of it!"

His partner had been standing a few feet away, looking at him with amazement and respect, listening intently.

"I suggest we tell the Lord how grateful we all are," the first trooper said.

And they joined hands and lifted up their voices in praise.

A short while later, after the troopers had called for other squad cars to help transport the townspeople, the second trooper approached his partner.

"You know," he said, "when I saw you get down with them and start praying, I wanted to resist. That's not the sort of thing I'm used to doing. And then, when I joined you, I realized I had never felt so happy, so secure, in my life."

The other smiled as he put his helmet back on.

"That's the way it is, partner," he said. "That's the way it is."

* * *

But the most remarkable encounter occurred at the small two-story general hospital on the outskirts of Valley Falls.

"It's hopeless," Justin Mason, a volunteer fireman, observed, the flames reflecting off his face. "How could anyone survive in there?"

"Quiet!" his friend Arnie Gates said. "Listen!"

Both were holding hoses, spraying highly pressured streams of water at the old building.

I hear something. Dear God, I hear something in there. I hear—

"Babies, Justin!" Gates exclaimed. "Some babies are still alive!"

"Are you crazy, man? Look!"

Part of the building tottered and fell outward. They had to run to escape the flying debris and fiery embers, dropping the hoses which wriggled uncontrollably on the asphalt of the street in front of the hospital.

"Somebody, help! Grab the hoses," Gates shouted. "We're going inside."

"We? Arnie, you're some kind of nut if you think I'm rushing into that inferno."

Gates grabbed his friend's shoulders.

"They're alive!" he said desperately. "Please believe me."

"But how do you know?"

"I just do. We can't just leave them!"

If it had been anyone but Arnie Gates, Mason would have ended the matter without further discussion.

"God told you something, didn't He?"

Gates nodded and started to run toward the hospital.

"Arnie!"

Gates hesitated for only a second.

"I'm with you, partner!" Mason caught up to him. "Maybe this is my chance to listen to that God you're always talking about."

They dashed toward the front entrance. Once inside, they faced a corridor of flames. Tongues of fire leaped out of the rooms on either side.

Lord, guide us. Show us where to go....

"Down there," Gates said, indicating the stairway at the end of the corridor, "and up those steps."

Mason was wiping tears from his smarting eyes.

"I know," he said simply.

"You—" Gates said, glancing at the other man.

"Yes, I hear them. But, Arnie, they aren't crying. They—"

As they hurried toward the stairs, they glanced into one room and then another.

"Look!" Mason screamed.

Something was moving in the flames, something with a shape so bizarre that the sight of it chilled every inch of their bodies, despite the searing heat around them.

It turned, seemed to notice them, and stumbled toward them.

"Lord, protect us!" Gates said simply.

Whatever it was stood in front of them for only a second or two and then fell, the air torn by its dying agonies.

They made it to the stairway and negotiated the steps two at a time. Just as they reached the top, part of the floor directly in front of them collapsed.

They managed to jump over the resulting hole, just barely making it to the other side. Seconds later a solid column of flame shot up behind them, blocking that avenue of retreat.

At the end of the corridor on the second floor they turned left into a much shorter hallway.

Ahead of them, over a doorway, was a sign: NURSERY.

What they saw momentarily stopped them in their tracks.

Everywhere else, raging flame assaulted them, their skin tingling with the nearness of it.

But down this corridor there were—

No flames!

The walls on either side of the nursery were untouched by the destruction around them.

But that wasn't all.

Light!

"Arnie!"

"Yeah, I see it."

From inside a pure white light shimmered, seeping through the thin break between the frame and the double doors leading into the nursery.

"Let's go!" Gates said.

They entered the nursery.

"My God!" he said, but it was not his usual oath.

Half a dozen babies were lying contentedly in their cribs, oblivious to the chaos around them.

To one side was an intern, sitting on a chair, a white dove perched on a finger of his left hand—but not the only dove in that room. There were scores of others, perched on the edges of the cribs, on a table, on the frame of a mirror hanging from one of the walls. Some fluttered from perch to perch, and one landed on the top of Justin Mason's head.

The intern looked up.

"I came here to slaughter them all, you know," he said calmly. "I was going to use that."

He pointed to a large chain saw on the floor near his feet.

"And then the doves came. Through that window. One after the other."

He got to his feet, tears streaming down his cheeks.

He was at home, asleep, when the vision came to him: a creature of great magnificence, covered with the bright plumage of some exotic tropical bird-reptile.

"I want you to serve me," it said in tones of splendor as it stood before him.

"But I don't know who you are," he replied.

"You will find out in time."

"What do you want me to do?"

"Kill the babies."

"In God's name, what are you saying?"

The creature's countenance began to alter.

"God's name is not involved. You are to be my slave, not His."

What had been beautiful skin, white and pure, became green and ugly, gangrenous sores everywhere on its body but especially the face, the forehead and cheeks riddled with the ugly blemishes.

"I have your soul in here," the creature said.

And with that it cut open its own chest with a giant taloned hand and he was confronted with the sight of his face staring back at him from within!

He turned to run but couldn't.

"You are my slave," the creature screamed at him. "Your sins have wedded you to me forever. There is no forgiveness for your kind."

The creature walked toward him and handed him a photograph of the weapon it wanted him to use.

"Do it!" the voice boomed in his ears. "Do it now!"

And then the vision ended and he awoke. Grasped tightly in his right hand was a photograph of a massive chain saw....

"I got this far, but when I saw the doves, I remembered what I had learned about them in church, what they symbolize, and there was no way I could sacrifice any of these little babies. And I remembered that Satan is the father of lies and that I couldn't believe anything he told me. I dropped the saw and knelt down and confessed my sins."

He looked up at them now, a troubled expression on his face.

"If I could only believe that God has actually forgiven me," he said.

"That forgiveness was already purchased through the shed blood of Christ," Gates told him. "You were cleansed before you ever sinned. You must never forget that."

Then Gates smiled as he added, "Now what we have to do is to get the innocent and helpless out of here."

"Look!" Mason pointed. "Look at the doves!"

The birds, which had been resting on their perches, had begun to stir. Then, as a body, they flew out of the nursery and into the corridor.

"We follow them!" Gates explained. "They're going to help us!"

Each man picked up two of the babies, one in each arm. As soon as the three of them had reached the end of the short hallway, the walls of the nursery ignited, the cribs catching fire.

"But where can we go?" Mason asked, his voice trembling. "The way we came is blocked! We're trapped!"

"Are we?"

Their mouths dropped open at what they saw then....

* * *

"They're goners," the county fire chief told the reporter next to him.

"But heroes, sir, isn't that right?"

"I'm afraid—"

The chief suddenly dropped the cigar on which he had been chomping as he paced back and forth. Mason and Gates were two of his best men, both of them veterans. Why on earth had they done such a suicidal thing?

Three figures appeared from within the inferno, each holding two extraordinarily calm infants who were looking in wide-eyed wonder at the fire trucks and the media vans and the hordes of people who gasped at the sight of this little group emerging unharmed.

But that wasn't all.

Not what would send the observers from that place, talking for many months about what they had seen.

Nor was it even the odd incidence of pure white feathers they found, later, scattered among the ruins of the hospital.

It was the iridescent curtain, shimmering and bright, that surrounded the men and the babies.

And there was something else.

"Listen!" the chief said. "Listen to that!"

The clear, unmistakable sound of trumpets.

* * *

None of the firemen did much talking about what they had seen and heard, afraid that they would be accused of mass delusion. Nor did the intern or anyone else who was there. Television cameras caught shots of the three men and the infants emerging from the flames, but nothing more. With no evidence on tape, the incident was eventually chalked up to the intensity of the moment and a touch of religious hysteria, as the secular media termed it.

Interestingly, the fire chief retired soon thereafter, though still relatively young, and with his wife petitioned the appropriate board of his denomination to let them become missionaries. They were eventually assigned a station in China.

The intern went on to become a pediatric surgeon, while the two firemen resigned and at last report were heading a National Right to Life chapter in their state.

Mass delusion?

Impossible to say. But if anything could be categorized as such, then it would be the stories of scattered survivors who spoke of a giant winged creature with malevolent countenance who stood before the possessed as their Master.

Not a trace could be found of the creature. The mass delusion theory was given further impetus when investigators found the partially charred body of what must have been a teenage boy in front of the shell of what had once been the only church in Valley Falls. The fire may not have killed him, though. Death, they surmised, could easily have come from three very long nails impaled in his forehead, his neck, and the area of his heart.

The cleanup of Valley Falls took a very long time.

New homes and stores were erected after the wreckage was cleared away, and people gradually began taking up residence in Valley Falls again.

Aside from Edith Van Halen, however, the only constant reminder of what had happened there was the small granite monument that was built in the center of the town square.

The young couple stood before the square marker topped with a small cross, reading the inscription:

> *1980*
> *The Year A New Town Was Built*
> *From the Ashes of the Old*
> *With the Hope*
> *That Satan Will Never Again*
> *Be Allowed to Triumph*

"It's amazing we survived, isn't it?" said the young woman. "A handful of people out of an entire town! Not a very high percentage."

They both turned and looked at the new buildings ringing the square, their minds filled with the memories of that conflagration years before, the devastation it left behind. It was the first time they had returned to Valley Falls, but somehow it had seemed right to do so now.

A new church had been built where the old one had stood, with a large cross high over the entrance.

The young woman walked forward and stood at the foot of the steps, looking up at the plain cross. A quick flash of memory crossed her mind, a moment involving an earlier cross on a previous sanctuary at that very spot . . . tears trickling down the intricately detailed face of a man-made Figure . . . and then she shook her head, clearing the memory away, at least for a while, until some night when the dreams would come again.

The young man joined her.

"It's something we'll never forget," he said.

"Never," she agreed.

As they walked away toward their car, she added, "I wonder what ever happened to those six babies?"

"It's strange, isn't it," he said, "that none of the news guys has done a follow-up report. They'd be about six years old by now. What's happened to them? If I were a reporter, I'd think that was a great story!"

"I agree," she said.

"And the older ones sure have some wonderful stories to tell."

She had kept in contact with her old principal, Clement Albertson, who had taken over the ministry of Dr. Lorensen, working with teenagers at retreats and colleges. He had kept in touch with many of the young people who had been at the retreat.

"We've forgotten what I think is the most miraculous group," the young man recalled.

"Which one?" she asked.

"The retarded kids."

When the survivors had finally been gathered together at the county hospital, they had learned about the small band of children who had taken refuge in the basement of the school. Later, when Setterman was participating in a college work-study program at a Christian facility for the mentally handicapped, he had discussed the phenomenon with the director.

"Youngsters who are more than slightly retarded just don't know what sin is, really," he said. "Sin is rejection of the Lord and His commandments in thought and behavior, leading to spiritual blindness and death. But there is no such thing as a significantly retarded child who has ever rejected Him."

"What a beautiful truth!" Lance had exclaimed, savoring the idea.

"They come to Him in innocence and faith. They seem instinctively scared of and repelled by anything smacking of the demonic."

The two of them were quiet for a few minutes.

"All new people here," Jami said finally, turning toward the street behind them where they could see a mother with her baby in a stroller, an elderly couple, a boy on his bicycle.

"It's as though nothing had happened."

"Yeah," she said, her voice hardly above a whisper, biting her lower lips.

"What's on your mind?" he asked.

"I was remembering something I read in Bible class."

"What was that, love?"

"A writer had this observation: 'One great defense against sin lies in being shocked by it.' I—I hope these new people never lose sight of that."

"That reminds me," he said, "aren't you going to do something with that article you mentioned a while back? So that no one does forget the lessons that could be taught by what happened?"

"Someday," she said.

"I'll never forget your last sentence," he said. "Powerful."

If you don't listen to the sounds of our pain, there will come a day when the grave will claim our voices forever....

"Really powerful, honey. Don't just file it away. There are thousands of kids who need to hear that message. Promise me you'll do something soon?"

She nodded and then kissed him tenderly.

"You know," she said, "one thing still puzzles me. Something we've talked about before."

"What's that?" he asked.

"We're alive. So is Paul DeKorte. So are others. But who knows how many died? Some must have been Christians. They resisted Satan. Or think of Dr. Lorensen. He stayed true to Christ until the last second of his life. Yet he and others are gone and we're still here. Why is that?"

"I don't think we'll ever really have an answer this side of Heaven. The closest I come is that the Lord still has a mission of some kind that He wants us to carry out."

He kissed her gently on the forehead and said, "The Lord guided us together for a reason. You provide wisdom that I don't have, and I provide wisdom that you may be missing. That's what He intended between married believers. And I know something else, too."

"What's that?"

"A real mission of mine is to make you happy for the rest of your life, and to see that our children grow up with an abiding love for Christ in this crazy world of ours."

They enjoyed holding each other just then. After lingering for only a bit longer, they got into their car and drove back along the rebuilt main street, past the new homes and sidewalks and vibrant greenery, past the new sign on the outskirts proclaiming the town's rebirth, past a family enjoying a picnic in a little park just off that country road.

If they had hesitated only a few seconds longer, they might have noticed the single white dove that had landed on top of the monument in the town square, its wing feathers dripping blood. Remaining there until they had left, it then took silent flight, following them.

*   *   *

"We lost!" exclaimed one of the uglier of the demonkind.

"And why do you say that?" asked the Master, trying to be tolerant of his brash follower.

"Because the clergyman survived. Because the children survived. Because the babies survived."

"Those are the reasons for your impetuous declaration?"

"Yes, Master, they are."

"My response is that, yes, we lost THEM. But, remember, there have been many others over whom we have had significant victory."

The Master stirred, using his wings to point at the structure in which they were gathered that night, a full moon casting a suitably eerie glow.

"We could make this our next conquest," he interrupted musingly. *"It would be one of our most beautiful headquarters to date."*

"When do we start?" another inquired.

He hesitated.

"I don't know."

"Master, it's not like you to be uncertain."

Their leader's ego prevented him from admitting that the underling was embarrassingly correct. But then if he dodged the matter altogether, he would lose face among them all.

"That's true," he said finally. *"I begin to wonder, though, if this one might prove somewhat deceptive—all glitz on the outside but perhaps some genuine depth that is not immediately apparent when we focus our attention upon the preacher in the pulpit."*

"Should we consider others first?"

"I think that would be prudent, yes. Let's keep this one under study for the moment. We'll reserve judgment. From what I hear, He's doing the same thing. If there's a real opening, we can move in quickly enough."

"Master?" asked the upstart who had spoken first.

"Yes?"

"Where to now?"

He didn't dare confess to them how much the loss of that one minister had depressed him. Deep within his very being, he was furious, vowing to himself that he would one day seek another opportunity to ensnare the man once again.

Seconds passed.

"Master?"

"We must go now," he said with an air of finality. *"I have decided."*

They chattered expectantly.

"There's a certain political party. One of their candidates has been making considerable noise in recent weeks about—" and went on to explain other plans for the coming months and beyond.

Finally he added, "Oh, yes, that article written by the girl who survived our onslaught at Valley Falls—see to it that she never gets it published. It has raw power, I must admit. People might pay too much attention to what she has to say. We can't let that sort of thing get out of hand."

As he finished that remaining pronouncement, a roar of enthusiasm arose from the gathered multitude of repulsive beings, dripping slime and full of the stench of decay as they were. One-by-one, they left, their leader pausing outside as he looked back at the coldly magnificent structure, soaring in its display of architectural genius.

The loathsome creature smiled somewhat wistfully as he thought of so much that could have been done with such a ministry. And then he realized that, though it seemed to have moved back to its original biblical foundation, nothing was certain until Armageddon, nothing at all.

* * *

Epilogue

Gabriel turned away for a moment.

"They fill me with such loathing," he said.

"As all of your comrades in the battle, as Me," the Lord told him.

Gabriel made a gesture toward the glowing wonders around them.

"But they were like the rest of my kind," he said. "To see them change, to see them go from purity to corruption, to shed all that they had here for the damnation that is in store."

"How well I know that."

Gabriel felt somewhat embarrassed.

"Yea, I did not have to remind especially You."

And then there was humankind. A parade of billions through the ages.

"Dear Gabriel, I love them so, despite their failings."

"Else why would You have sacrificed Yourself for them?"

The Lord was silent briefly, then said, "The girl and the one she will marry both puzzle over why some who follow Me perished while others remain alive."

"But they and so many, many others are still seeing through a glass darkly," Gabriel replied.

"Indeed that is so. But how We yearn to reveal what We know."

"Not even the Holy Spirit will take away the fog just yet, Lord?"

"No, Gabriel, not even He will do that."

"Until the fullness of time?"

"Until the fullness of time."

The world they viewed seemed more and more in the grip of the fallen ones.

Gabriel remembered the boy, remembered when the boy's spirit left his body, remembered when Lucifer stood before the gates to torment, remembered the boy screaming, "You promised me power!"

Lucifer had smiled.

"But I did not say for how long," came his sardonic response.

"Now there is only pain. My very spirit is afire."

"Then join the others," Lucifer declared.

And Scott Pennio did join the others, along with Mark Jacobson, his friend in life, his companion in death.

But not the third boy.

"Lord?" the voice interrupted them.

The angel and the Father turned and looked upon the speaker.

"Thank You, Savior," said Wayne Mulrooney. "Thank You for taking my sins upon Yourself."

He looked down across the gulf at Scott and Mark.

"If only it could have been otherwise," he said.

"The cry of the ages," Gabriel told him.

Wayne left them.

"How foolish those who rebel," Gabriel said. "How foolish in their conceits they are. Lucifer and the others continuing madly in their warped maneuverings."

"Yes, quite madly."

"Have they no shame, Lord?"

"That is all they have, and because it is so powerful, so all-encompassing, they delude themselves into trying to drown it out in the flame-scorched cries of their victims."

Gabriel's form slumped a bit.

"Dear Gabriel?" the Lord asked.

"Soon to end, is it not? The burdens shoulder more heavily as we get closer."

"Yes, loyal one."

And the sweetest, purest heavenly language came from Gabriel then, joyous communication with the rest of his kind and with the Trinity, bound together in exultation.

With every year that passes, the link between Satan's mind and the minds of millions of human beings becomes stronger.

—Dr. Billy Graham

*Other Good
Harvest House Reading*

THE ARCHON CONSPIRACY
By *Dave Hunt*

In a story with unusual relevance for our time, bestselling author Dave Hunt describes a confrontation between supernatural powers and humanity that could someday be as real as today's headlines.

Computer genius Ken Inman's lifelong goal to contact highly-evolved intelligences explodes into reality...leaving him face-to-face with the compelling and deadly Archons, also known as "the Nine."

In this fast-paced novel filled with intrigue and suspense, Dave Hunt dramatizes the reality of spiritual warfare and the very real dangers that may be upon us even now.

WHEN THE WORLD WILL BE AS ONE
The Coming New World Order in the New Age
by *Tal Brooke*

Today the pieces are falling into place for a worldwide transformation. In the not-too-distant future a New World Order, unlike anything the world has ever seen, could appear almost overnight. There is an emerging global consciousness that is either an incredible historical coincidence or is, in fact, part of a sophisticated plan whose beginnings can be traced to antiquity. Could this be the global reality predicted 2,000 years ago by a prophet on the Isle of Patmos?

Tal Brooke spent two decades intently exploring the occult. His quest ultimately landed him in the heart of India where for two years he was the top Western disciple of India's miracle-working superguru, Sai Baba. Tal is a graduate of the University of Virginia, and Princeton, and is a frequent speaker at Oxford and Cambridge universities.

ASTROLOGY: Do the Heavens Rule Our Destiny?
by *John Ankerberg*

Forty million Americans today believe in some form of astrology. Its influence is felt throughout government, industry, the sciences, education, the church, and the home.

Well-known occult authorities John Ankerberg and John Weldon examine astrology's major issues and answer most commonly asked questions:

- What exactly *is* astrology?
- Do the heavens really influence life on earth?
- What are the dangers of astrology?
- How much does astrology actually influence Washington?
- What does the Bible say about astrology?

Astrology thoroughly researches astrology's claims, assesses its occult aspects, and emphasizes the personal consequences of its use.

AMERICA: THE SORCERER'S NEW APPRENTICE
by *Dave Hunt* and *T.A. McMahon*

Many respected experts predict that America is at the threshold of a glorious New Age. Other equally notable observers warn that Eastern mysticism, at the heart of the New Age movement, will eventually corrupt Western civilization.

The question is, *Who is right*? Is there really a threat to the American way of life as we know it? Will we be able to distinguish between the true hope of the Gospel and the false hope of the New Age?

Dave Hunt and T.A. McMahon, bestselling authors of *The Seduction of Christianity*, break down the most brilliant arguments of the most-respected New Age leaders. This bold new book is an up-to-date Christian apologetic, presenting overwhelming evidence for the superiority of the Christian faith.

PEACE, PROSPERITY AND THE COMING HOLOCAUST
by *Dave Hunt*

With fresh insight and vision, Dave Hunt dissects the influences that are at work to lull us into a state of euphoria and numb us to the reality of coming destruction. A startling account of the rapidly growing New Age Movement and the part it plays in the imminent return of Jesus Christ.

LIKE LAMBS TO THE SLAUGHTER—
Your Child and the Occult
by *Johanna Michaelsen*

Dungeons and Dragons, Saturday morning cartoons, Star Wars, E.T., yoga, spirit guides, guided imagery and visualization, storybooks on witchcraft and the occult. Are these merely innocent fun-filled activities, games, and toys designed to expand your child's creativity and intelligence—or is there a deliberate, calculated effort to raise a generation of psychics, shamans, mystics, and "channelers"? This book explores basics of the New Age Movement as it relates to children and exposes the deadly effects of the subtle occult practices so prevalent among our youth today.

Dear Reader:

We would appreciate hearing from you regarding this Harvest House nonfiction book. It will enable us to continue to give you the best in Christian publishing.

1. What most influenced you to purchase *Astrology*?
   - [ ] Author
   - [ ] Subject matter
   - [ ] Backcover copy
   - [ ] Recommendations
   - [ ] Cover/Title
   - [ ] _____

2. Where did you purchase this book?
   - [ ] Christian bookstore
   - [ ] General bookstore
   - [ ] Department store
   - [ ] Grocery store
   - [ ] Other

3. Your overall rating of this book:
   - [ ] Excellent [ ] Very good [ ] Good [ ] Fair [ ] Poor

4. How likely would you be to purchase other books by this author?
   - [ ] Very likely
   - [ ] Somewhat likely
   - [ ] Not very likely
   - [ ] Not at all

5. What types of books most interest you?
   (check all that apply)
   - [ ] Women's Books
   - [ ] Marriage Books
   - [ ] Current Issues
   - [ ] Self Help/Psychology
   - [ ] Bible Studies
   - [ ] Fiction
   - [ ] Biographies
   - [ ] Children's Books
   - [ ] Youth Books
   - [ ] Other _____

6. Please check the box next to your age group.
   - [ ] Under 18
   - [ ] 18-24
   - [ ] 25-34
   - [ ] 35-44
   - [ ] 45-54
   - [ ] 55 and over

Mail to: Editorial Director
Harvest House Publishers, Inc.
1075 Arrowsmith
Eugene, OR 97402

Name _____

Address _____

City _____ State _____ Zip _____

Thank you for helping us to help you in future publications!